S0-DBB-211

WITHDRAWN FROM
KENT STATE UNIVERSITY LIBRARIES

SAN SALVADOR

This is a volume in the
Arno Press collection

THE AMERICAN CATHOLIC TRADITION

Advisory Editor
Jay P. Dolan

Editorial Board
Paul Messbarger
Michael Novak

See last pages of this volume
for a complete list of titles.

SAN SALVADOR

MARY AGNES TINCKER

ARNO PRESS
A New York Times Company
New York • 1978

Editorial Supervision: JOSEPH CELLINI

Reprint Edition 1978 by Arno Press Inc.

THE AMERICAN CATHOLIC TRADITION
ISBN for complete set: 0-405-10810-9
See last pages of this volume for titles.
Manufactured in the United States of America

Library of Congress Cataloging in Publication Data

Tincker, Mary Agnes, 1831-1907.
San Salvador.

(The American Catholic tradition)
Reprint of the 1892 ed. published by Houghton, Mifflin, Boston.
I. Title. II. Series.
PZ3.T4918San 1978 [PS3079.T15] 813'.4
ISBN 0-405-10864-8 77-11319

SAN SALVADOR

BY

MARY AGNES TINCKER

AUTHOR OF "SIGNOR MONALDINI'S NIECE," "TWO CORONETS," ETC.

Unless the Lord build the house,
they labor in vain that build it:
unless the Lord keep the city, he
watcheth in vain that keepeth it

BOSTON AND NEW YORK
HOUGHTON, MIFFLIN AND COMPANY
The Riverside Press, Cambridge
1892

Copyright, 1892,
By MARY AGNES TINCKER.

All rights reserved.

The Riverside Press, Cambridge, Mass., U. S. A.
Electrotyped and Printed by H. O. Houghton & Co.

PROLOGUE.

Scene I.

The family in Palazzo Loredan, in the Grand Canal, Venice, had finished their midday breakfast, and coffee was brought in.

There was the Marchesa Loredan, a widow, her widowed only daughter with a little son and his tutor, and Don Claudio Loredan, the Marchesa's second son. Her eldest son was married; and the youngest, Don Enrico, was a monsignore, and coadjutor of an old canon whom he was impatiently waiting to succeed.

The breakfast had not been a cheerful one. Don Claudio, usually the life of the family and its harmonizing element, had been silent and preoccupied; and Madama Loredan's black brows had two deep lines between them, — sure signs of a storm.

She rose as the coffee was bought in.

"Carry a tête-à-tête down to the arbor," she said to the servant; and to her son, "I wish to speak to you, Claudio."

The tutor rose respectfully, making sly but intense signals to his pupil to do the same. But the boy, occupied in counting the cloves of a mandarin orange, did not choose to see them.

A long window of the dining-room opened on a

balcony, and from the balcony a stair descended to the garden. This garden, a square the width of the house, would soon be a mass of bloom; but spring had hardly come as yet. The little arbor in the centre was covered with rosebuds, and the orange-trees were in blossom. There was a table in the arbor, with a chair at each side.

Madama literally swept across the dining-room; for she did not lift a fold of the trailing robe of glossy white linen bordered with black velvet that followed her imperious steps.

Don Claudio was familiar with the several indications of his mother's moods, and he followed in silence, carefully avoiding the glistening wake of her progress. When she had seated herself in the arbor, he took the chair opposite her, half filled a little rose-colored cup with coffee, dropped a single cube of sugar into it, stirred it with a tiny spoon that had the Loredan shield at the end of its slender twisted stem, and gravely set the cup before her.

He had not once raised his eyes to her face.

She watched him with a scrutinizing gaze. He was evidently expecting a reprimand; yet there was neither anger nor confusion in his handsome face. It had not lost its preoccupied and even sorrowful expression. She sipped her coffee in silence, and waited till he had drunk his.

"You were at Ca' Mora last evening and this morning," she said abruptly, when he set his cup down.

"My master is dying!" he responded quietly.

Madama was for a moment disconcerted. The old professor with whom her son had for two years been studying oriental languages was a man of note among the learned. He had exercised a beneficial influence over the mind of Don Claudio; and for a while she had been glad that an enthusiasm for study should counteract the natural downward tendency of a life full of worldly prosperity and its attendant temptations. Only of late had she become aware of any danger in this intimacy.

"Dying!" she echoed. "I did not know that he was ill." She hesitated a moment, then bitterness prevailed.

"Of course his granddaughter has need of consolation," she added with a sneer.

"I have not seen her to-day," Don Claudio said, controlling himself. Then, with a sudden outburst, "I would gladly console her!" he exclaimed, and looked at his mother defiantly.

His defiance of her was like the flash of a wax taper on steel. Madama leaned forward and raised a warning finger.

"You will leave her to be consoled by her equals," she said. "And when her grandfather is dead, you will see her no more. Woe to her if you disobey me!"

The young man shrugged his shoulders to hide a tremor.

"Woe to her!" repeated his mother, marking the tremor.

Don Claudio remained silent.

"Has she succeeded in compromising you?" Madama asked.

The quick blood covered her son's face.

"You might, at least, refrain from slandering her!" he exclaimed. Then his voice became supplicating. "Mamma, all that Tacita Mora lacks is rank. She has a fair portion; and she has been delicately reared and guarded. Her manners are exquisite. And there can be no undesirable connection, for she will be quite alone in the world."

His mother made an impatient gesture, and was about to speak; but he held his hands out to her.

"Mamma, I love her so!" he exclaimed. "You do not know her. She is not one of those girls who give a man opportunities, and are always on the lookout for a lover. We have never spoken a word of love. We have only looked at each other. But I cannot lose her!"

He threw himself on his knees at his mother's side, and burst into tears.

She drew his head to her shoulder, and kissed him.

"You have only looked at each other!" she repeated. "My poor boy! As if that were not enough! Claudio, we all have to go through with it, as with teething. It is a madness. The only safe way is to follow the counsel of those who have had experience. It is only the pang of a day. This kind of passion does not endure; but order does. This is a passing fever of the fancy and the blood. Be patient a little while, and it will cure itself. Do not allow it to compromise your future. You will be glad of having listened to me when your love shall have died out."

"It will never die!" he sobbed.

"It will die!" she said. "And now, listen to me. I have told the Sangredo that you are going to visit them this afternoon. It is a week since Bianca came home from school. You should have gone sooner. Go, and make yourself agreeable. If you do so, I will consent to your going once more to see Professor Mora, and I will myself go to inquire for him."

The young man rose, and stood hesitating and frowning.

"Go, my dear!" his mother urged. "It is only a civility, and commits you to nothing."

He went slowly away, knowing well that further appeal was useless. His mother followed him after a moment.

"My gondola!" she said to a servant who was taking off the tablecloth, and went on to an adjoining boudoir where her daughter sat.

"Boys are such a trial!" she said with an impatient sigh, and dropped into a sofa. "Alfonso has, happily, reached the age of reason. Enrico is under good guardianship, or I should tremble for his future, he is so impatient. It is true, Monsignor Scalchi does live longer than we thought he would; but, as I say to Enrico, can I kill Monsignor Scalchi in order that you may be made a canon at once? Wait. He cannot live long. Enrico declares that he will never die. And now Claudio, with his folly!"

"What will he do?" the daughter asked.

"He will do as I command him!" the Marchesa answered sharply. "I only wish, Isabella, that you would be half as resolute with your son. Peppino may go without his dessert this evening. It may make him remember to rise the next time that the mistress of the house leaves the table."

SCENE II.

In a boarding-house, on the Riva degli Schiavoni, a number of tourists, among them some artists, are seated at their one o'clock dinner.

Says a lady, "They say that the old Greek, or Arabic, or Turkish, or Hindu, or Boston Professor whom we met at the Lido last month — you remember him, Mr. James? — well — where did I begin? I 've lost my nominative case."

2*d Lady*. They say that he is dying, poor old man! My gondolier told me this morning that Professor Mora has visited every part of the globe, and knows a thousand languages. He seemed even to doubt if the professor might not have been to the moon. The gondolier evidently looks upon him with wonderment. And as for the professor's granddaughter, she is one of the marvels of the earth.

1*st Lady*. Mr. James can tell you all about

that. I think he did succeed in getting a sketch of the girl, if not of her grandfather. I don't know where he keeps it, unless it is worn next his heart. It is not among the sketches that he shows to people. In fact, everything about this family in mysterious and uncommon.

A gentleman. What is it, Mr. James? The story promises to be interesting.

Mr. James (sotto voce). Damn the women! (*Aloud.*) This old professor, I am told, came here fifteen years ago, some say, from the East. Shortly after, his widowed daughter with her little girl followed him. I am not aware that they behaved in a mysterious manner, unless it is a mystery that people should be able to live quietly and innocently, and mind their own business; all which the Mora certainly achieved. They were not rich, but to the poor and unfortunate they were angels of mercy.

1*st Lady (striking in).* Everybody did n't think so.

Mr. James. Everybody does n't think that God is good. Of course there were servants' stories and gossips' stories, and those who wished to believe them did believe them.

Gentleman. Will the girl be left alone?

1*st Lady.* Do not cherish any hopes, sir. The mother is dead; but the young lady has an admirer. He is a fine young man with a palace and an ancestry, and the most beautiful eyes in the world. She goes out with him in his gondola by moonlight. It is so romantic!

Mr. James. Did you ever see them out together by moonlight, or at any other hour?

1st Lady. Others have.

Mr. James. What others? Name one!

1st Lady. Really, sir! (*leaves the table*).

Mr. James. The Signorina Mora will not be left alone. There is a respectable woman with her —

2d Lady. A nurse!

Mr. James. — a very respectable woman with her who has been here since her mother died, two years ago. She is an elderly woman of very pleasant appearance and manners. Some one has said that she belongs to some charitable order that nurses the sick.

2d Lady (*in a stage voice*). "Juliet! Where 's the girl? What, Juliet!"

Gentleman. Ahem!

Scene III.

In the church of Saint X. the half of the Chapter on duty that week had just come out of choir, and were taking off their vestments and laying them away, each in his proper drawer in the wall of the sacristy. The sound of alternate singing and praying yet came from the church. A Novena was going on; and Monsignor Scalchi, the old *canonico* for whose place Monsignor Loredan waited so impatiently, officiated.

Some of the clergy hastened away, others lingered, chatting together. One stood watching the gloomy way in which Monsignor Loredan flicked a speck of dust from his broad-brimmed hat.

"Well?" said the young man, aware of the other's gaze, but without looking at him.

"I was wondering how Monsignor Scalchi is," his friend said.

"When he sees me, he coughs," said the coadjutor.

At that moment the person of whom they spoke entered the sacristy, with a priest at either hand. A rustling cope of cloth of gold covered his whole person, his eyes were downcast, his hands folded palm to palm, and he murmured prayers as he came.

The young men stood respectfully aside as he passed, his garments smelling of incense, and went to disrobe at the other end of the sacristy.

"Don't lose courage, Don Enrico!" said one of the group. "He looks feeble. He can scarcely lift his feet from the floor."

"Poh!" exclaimed Don Enrico. "He is as strong as I am. He buys his shoes too long, so that they may drag at the heels and make him seem weak in the legs."

He yawned, saluted with a graceful wave of the hand, and sauntered out into the silent piazza.

"Don Enrico is out of temper about his brother's affairs, as well as his own," one of his friends said when he was out of hearing. "They say that Claudio is in love with Tacita Mora, and is making a fool of himself. If he should offend the Sangredo, Don Enrico will lose the cardinal's patronage. Professor Mora was as blind as a bat. He thought that Tacita was a child, and that Don Claudio was enamored of the Chinese language."

"But the nurse never leaves the girl," some one said.

"Oh! the nurse is dark!" said one of the sacristans.

Yes; they all agreed that the nurse was dark.

One after another they dropped away, till only Monsignor Scalchi was left kneeling at a *prie-dieu*, and an under-sacristan going about his work, filling a silver lamp for the shrine of Saint X., shaving down the lower ends of great yellow wax torches to set in triple-footed iron stands for a funeral, counting out wafers for the altar. There was silence save for a light lapse of water against the steps outside; there was a sleepy yellow sunshine on the marble floor, and a smell of incense in the soft air.

As Monsignor Scalchi rose from his knees, a second under-sacristan entered.

"Here are the books from San Lazzaro, Monsignore," he said. "But the translations from the Turkish are not yet ready. The illness of Professor Mora delayed them. He was to have looked them over."

"Did you learn how the professor is?" asked the prelate, glancing over the books given him.

"I went to ask, Monsignore. Gian says that he

is failing fast. The Marchesa Loredan has been to see him."

"Ah!" exclaimed Monsignor Scalchi, looking up from the volume in his hand.

"Yes; and Gian says that the nurse watches over everything."

"The nurse seems to be a dark one," monsignore remarked.

"Yes," said the sacristan, "the nurse is dark."

Scene IV.

The mistress of Palazzo Sangredo sat in one of her stateliest salons talking with her cousin, the Countess Bembo. At some distance from them, half enveloped in the drapery of a great window, Bianca Sangredo peeped out into the Canal.

"I saw him myself!" said the countess in a vehement whisper. "I saw him go into the house, and I saw him come out. And he was there again this morning, and stopped half an hour. You ought to have an explanation with the marchesa. Everybody knows that the families wish for a marriage between him and Bianca. If Sangredo would stay at home and attend to his duties, Don Claudio would not dare to behave so. But Sangredo never is at home."

"Oh, yes, he is!" said Sangredo's wife languidly. "He is always at home in Paris. But the marchesa declares that Claudio goes to Ca' Mora to study, and that he already speaks Arabic like a sheik. Professor Mora is famous. Papadopoli says that since Mezzofanti no one else has known so many languages."

"Yes," said her cousin sharply. "And the professor's granddaughter will teach him to conjugate *amore* in every one of them."

"Mamma," said Bianca from the window, "Don Claudio's gondola is at the step."

"Come and sit by me, child!" her mother said hastily.

When their visitor entered the salon, the two elder ladies received him with the utmost cordiality. Bianca only bent her head, and did not leave her mother's side; but her childlike dimpling smile was full of kindness. She had a charming snowdrop stillness and modesty.

"I have already seen you to-day, Don Claudio," said the Countess Bembo. "I passed you near the Giudecca; and you did not look at me, though our gondolas almost touched."

"I beg your pardon!" he said seriously. "I had been, or was going, to the house of Professor Mora, and I saw no one. He lies at the point of death. It is a great grief to me."

The ladies began to question and sympathize. After all, things might not be so bad as they had feared.

"He will be a loss to the world, as well as to his friends," Don Claudio said. "His knowledge of languages is something wonderful. Besides that, he is one of the best of men. His mode of teaching caught the attention at once. 'Sometimes,' he once said to me, 'you may see protruding from the earth an ugly end of dry stick. Pull it, and you find a long root attached. Follow the root, and it may lead you to a beautiful plant laden with blossoms. And so a seemingly dry and insignificant fact may prove the key to a treasure of hidden knowledge.' That was his way of teaching. However dry the proposition with which he began a discourse, it was sure to lead to something interesting."

"You must feel very sad!" the young girl said compassionately.

"It is sad," he answered, and let his eyes dwell on her fair, innocent face. Then, the entrance of other visitors creating a little stir, he bent toward her and murmured "Thanks!"

SAN SALVADOR.

CHAPTER I.

It was a still night, and all eastward-looking Venice, above a certain height, was enameled as with ivory by the light of a moon but little past its full. Below, flickering reflections from the water danced on the dark walls. The bending lines of street lamps showed in dull golden blotches in that radiant air. The same golden spots were visible on gun-boat or steamship, and on a gondola moored at the steps of Casa Mora.

Above this waiting gondola a window stood wide open to the night. It seemed to be the only open window in Venice. All the others had their iron shutters closed.

Seen from without, this open window was as dark as the mouth of a cave. But inside, so penetrating an effulgence filled the room, one might have read the titles of the books in cases that lined all the walls.

The wide-open, curtainless window admitted a square of moonlight so splendid as to seem tangible; and in the midst of it, on a pallet, lay the old professor, his face, hair, and beard almost as white as the pillow they rested on. A slender girl knelt at his right hand, her head bowed down. One could see that her thick knot of hair was floss-fine and gold-tinted, and her neck white and smooth. At the opposite side of the couch a young man was seated, bending toward it. In an arm-chair near the foot, with her back to the light, sat a woman. Her cheek resting on her hand, she gazed intently at the dying man.

After a prolonged silence he stirred, and stretched a thin hand to touch the girl's head.

"Go and rest awhile, my Tacita!" he said. "I will recall thee. Go, Elena. I will recall thee."

The two rose at once and went out of the room, hand in hand, closing the door.

"I charge thee to let the girl alone!" Professor Mora exclaimed the moment they were gone.

The young man started.

"This is no time for idle compliments," the other pursued with a certain vehemence. "I know that thou hast taken a fancy to Tacita because she is beautiful and good. She is of a tender nature, and may have some leaning toward thee. I should have been a more jealous guardian of both."

"I know that my mother has been here to-day," Don Claudio said bitterly.

"Thy mother is a worldly woman," the old man replied. "But in this she is right. Marry the girl they have chosen for thee. It is not in thy nature, boy, to be immovable and persistent in rebellion even against manifest injustice. Thy protest would be the passion of a moment. They would wear out thy courage and endurance. But even with their consent, Tacita is not for thee. I forbid it! Dost thou hear, Don Claudio Loredan? I forbid it! "

"You seemed to like me!" Don Claudio exclaimed reproachfully.

The professor moved his hand toward the speaker. "I love thee, Claudio. But that makes no difference. He who would have Tacita must live even as I have, without luxury or splendor, striving to learn what human life means, and following the best law that his soul knows."

The young man sighed. He had no such plan of life.

"It will be a moment's pain," the other went on. "But thy honor and her peace are at stake. I charge thee" — he half rose in his earnestness — "I charge thee to let the girl alone! Remember that one day thou wilt have to lie as I lie here now, all earthly passion burned to ashes, and only the record of thy conscience to support, or cast thee down."

"Be tranquil!" said Don Claudio faintly, and bowed his face into his hands. "I will obey."

The old man sank back upon his pillow with a murmured word of blessing, and looked out at the violet sky. For a while he remained silent. Then he spoke again, as if soliloquizing.

"The unfathomable universe! The baffling

problem! Only the shades of night and of life reveal something of the mystery to us. For eighty years I have studied life from every side. I was hungry to know. And the more I learned of any subject the more clearly I perceived the vastness of my own ignorance. I tried in vain to grasp the plan of it all. I built up theories, fitting into them the facts I knew. Sometimes the mosaic grew to show a pattern; and then, just as I began to rejoice, all became confusion again. I was Tantalus. Again and again the universe held its solution before my soul. Only a line more, and it was mine! Yet it was forever snatched away."

He was silent a little while; then resumed: "In one of those moments of disappointment I recollected a text of the Hebrew Bible taught me in my childhood: *The fear of the Lord is the beginning of wisdom.* When I learned it, two paths of life were opening out before my mind. One was like a hidden rivulet, flowing ever in lowly places, seeking ever the lowest place, refreshing, beneficent. The other was like a mountain path, and a star shone over it. I chose the mountain path. It was often steep and hard, and the star recedes as you climb. But the air on those heights is sometimes an elixir. We had a song at home:—

'Sweet is the path that leads to what we love.'

How many a time I sang it to keep my courage up!

"In that moment of recollection I asked myself if I might not have more surely attained to what I sought by taking the lowlier way, if the supernatural might not have aided material science, as imagination aids in the mathematics. What means the story of the tree of knowledge and the tree of life? Many of those old tales contain a golden lesson. We do not study the past enough; and therefore human life becomes a series of beginnings without visible results. There are a few centuries of progress, something is learned, something gained, a clearer light seems to announce the dawn of some great day, and men begin to extol themselves; and then a shadowy hand sweeps the board clean, and the boasters disappear, they and their achievements. Perhaps out of each fading cycle God gathers up a few from destruction. *Many are called, but few chosen*, said the King. For the others the story of Sisyphus was told."

Again there was a pause; and again he spoke:

"I was tossed hither and thither. I had such failures that life seemed to me a mockery, and such successes that I would fain have lived a thousand years. Of one thing in it all I am glad: I never complained of God in failure, nor glorified myself in success. I give thanks for that!"

He closed his eyes and seemed to pray.

After a moment he spoke again.

"I have known one perfect thing on earth," he said, and clasped his hands. "I have found in life one beauty that grows on the soul forever. One being in touching the earth has consecrated it. There is no flaw in Jesus of Nazareth."

The pause that followed was so long that Don Claudio bent to touch the cold hands.

The dying man roused himself.

"Farewell, my beloved pupil!" he said. "God be with thee! Go in peace! And tell them to come to me."

The young man knelt, and weeping, pressed his lips to the cold hand that could not lift itself.

"Farewell! God be with you!" he echoed in a stifled voice; and rose and went out of the room.

A light shone through the open door of an adjoining chamber, and Tacita and the nurse could be seen each lying on a sofa inside. They started up at the sound of Don Claudio's step.

"He wants you," the young man said, and pressed the hand of each as they passed by him, then went down to his gondola. A moment later they heard the ripple of his passage across the lagoon.

Tacita knelt beside her grandfather and took his hand in hers. He drew her, and she put her face close to his.

"Dost thou remember all, my child?" he whispered.

"I remember all!" she whispered back.

"Thou wilt be strong and faithful?" he asked in the same tone.

"I will be strong and faithful," she answered.

He said no more. His breath fluttered on her cheek, and seemed to stop.

"Elena!" she cried.

After bending for a moment over the bed, the nurse had gone to the window, and stepped out into the balcony. She returned at that frightened call, and knelt by the bed.

In the silence that followed, a gondola slipped under the balcony; and presently there rose from it a singing voice, low toned, but impassioned and distinct. It sang: —

"San Salvador, San Salvador,
We cry to thee!
Danger is in our path,
The enemy, in wrath,
Lurks to delude our souls from finding thee!
We cry to thee! We cry to thee!
San Salvador,
We cry to thee!"

The dying man, half sunk into a lethargy, started awake.

"The mountains!" he exclaimed, looking eagerly out at the dark outline of housetops against the eastern sky. "The mountains and the bells!"

He panted, listened, sighed at the silence, and sank back again.

The singer recommenced more softly; but every word was so distinctly uttered that it seemed to be spoken in the chamber: —

"San Salvador, San Salvador,
We turn to thee!
All mercy as thou art,
Forgive the erring heart
That wandered far, but, weeping, homeward flies.
We turn to thee! We turn to thee!
San Salvador,
We turn to thee."

"The mountains!" murmured the dying man. "The curtain and the Throne!"

Again the voice sang:—

> "San Salvador, San Salvador,
> We live in thee!
> 'T is love that holds the threads of fate;
> Death 's but the opening of a gate,
> The parting of a mist that hides the skies.
> We live in thee! We live in thee!
> San Salvador,
> We live in thee!"

There was one more sigh from the pillow. A whisper came: "We live in Thee!"

"My dear," said the nurse, laying her hand softly on Taçita's bowed head, "Professor Mora is no longer an infirm old man."

CHAPTER II.

PROFESSOR MORA was buried in the cemetery of San Michele, with the rites of the Roman Church, though he had not received the last sacraments. That he had not, was supposed to have been the fault of the nurse. It was known, however, that he had made his Easter Communion; and those who had seen him before the altar at San Giorgio on that occasion spoke of his conduct as very edifying.

Many of them would doubtless have been puzzled, and even scandalized, could they have read his mind. That he was, in soul, prostrate at the feet of his Creator, there could be no doubt. He had often, of late years, spent an hour in some church, kneeling, or sitting in deep thought. He found it easier to recollect himself in the quiet of such a place, surrounded by religious images.

On this last Easter he had questioned: —

"Shall I confess my sins to a priest? Why not? It can do me no harm, and it may do me good. I will declare what I know of my own wrong-doing, addressing God in the hearing of this man. He uses many instruments. Perhaps the forgiveness of God may be spoken to me by the lips of this man. Shall I tell this man that I do not know whether he has any authority, or not? No. I am doing the best that I can; and his claim that he has authority will have no weight with me."

It was the same with his communion.

"Is it true that the Blessed Christ, the Son of God, is mystically concentrated and hidden in the wafer which will be placed upon my tongue, and that he will pervade my being, as the souls of a thousand roses are concentrated in a vial of attar, and scent all the house with their sweetness? I do not know. Nothing that God wills is impossible. If I cry out to him, O my Father, I search, and grope, and cannot find my Saviour! Send him, therefore, to meet my soul in this wafer, that I may live! At this point let me touch him, and receive help, as the sick woman received it from his garment's hem! — he could meet me there, if it were his will, and pour all heaven into my soul through that channel. Does he will it? I do not know. But since it is not impossible, I will bow myself as if he were here. Is there a place where God is not?"

Such was Professor Mora's Easter Communion; and many a formal communicant was less devout.

It is true that he had bent in heathen temples with an almost equal devotion; but it was always to the same God.

"Show me the path by which the instinct of worship in any people, or individual, climbs to what it can best conceive of the Divine," he said, "and there I will find the footsteps of God coming to meet that soul. A sunbeam falls on limpid water and a lily, and they shine like jewels. The same beam, turning, falls unshrinkingly on the muddy pool, that brightens also after its manner, and as well as it can."

To him the Indian praying-wheel, so often denounced as the height of material superstition, might be made to indicate a fuller conception of the infinity of God than was to be found in much of the worship that calls itself intelligent and spiritual. Written over and over on the parchment wound about this wheel is the one brief prayer, "O Jewel in the Lotos, Amen!" Their Divine One was as the light of the morning embodied and seated on a lotos-flower. Their prayer confesses nothing and asks nothing; yet it confesses and asks all. It is a dull longing in the dull, and a lark song in the spiritual. It expresses their despair of being able to tell his greatness, or their need of him. It repeats itself as the flutterings of a bird's wings repeat themselves when it soars. The soul says, "As many times as it is here inscribed, multiplied by as many times as the wheel revolves when I touch it, and yet a million times more, do I praise thee, do I implore thee, do I love thee, O thou Divine Light of the world! Even as the planets whirl ceaselessly wrapped about in the hieroglyphs of obedience to thy laws, so does this wheel, encircled by the aspirations of our worship, speak to thee for us."

He entered one of their temples with respect, and kneeling there, remembered what their Hindu teachers had said to him:

"Owing to the greatness of the Deity, the One Soul is lauded in many ways. The different Gods are the members of the One Soul."

And also: "One cannot attain to the Divine Sun through the word, through the mind, or through the eye. It is only reached by him who says, 'It is! It is!'"

As he meditated then with the door of his soul wide open, it had seemed to him that all the gods and all the worships of men had gathered themselves before him, and mingled, as mists gather into a cloud, and that from turbulent they had grown still, and from dark they had gathered to themselves light, growing more golden in the centre, as though their divers elements were purifying themselves to form some new unity, till the crude and useless all melted away, parting to disclose an infant seated on a lotos-flower, and shining like the morning sun. And the lotos-flower was the figure of a pure woman.

"It is! It is!" he had said then. And that wide essential faith had survived, though for details of dogma he had gone out of the world with the same word with which he had begun his studies: "I do not know!"

A funeral gondola came and took his body away, several gentlemen, Don Claudio among them, accompanying.

Tacita, wrapped in the window curtain, watched them till the gondola disappeared under the Rialto bridge, then threw herself, sobbing, into her companion's arms.

The nurse persuaded her to seek some occupation. "Come and help me make out the list of books that Don Claudio is to have," she said.

Professor Mora had given a large part of his choice library to Don Claudio.

This woman, Elena, had an interesting face. There was something noble in the calm, direct look of her eyes, and in her healthy matronly figure. It would be difficult to describe her manners, except by saying that there was nothing lacking, and nothing superfluous.

One sees occasionally a great lady whose character is equal to her social position, who has that manner without mannerism. A certain transparency of action follows the outlines of the intention. When this woman spoke, she had something to say, not often anything brilliant, or profound, but something which the moment required.

Tacita at once busied herself with the list, and found comfort in it. She needed comforting; for she was of a tenderly loving nature, and her almost cloistered life had confined her interests to that home circle now quite broken up. Her father had died in her infancy. Her mother, not much older than herself, had been her constant companion, friend and confidant. The loss of her had been a crushing one; and the wound still bled.

But she and her grandfather had consoled each other; and while he lived the mother had seemed near. Now he, too, was gone!

And there was yet another pain. Some little tendrils of habit and affection had wound themselves about her grandfather's favorite pupil, and they bled in the breaking. For they were to separate at once. Nor had she any wish to remain in Venice. She well knew that she would not be allowed to see Don Claudio, except at her peril, and that jealous eyes were already fixed upon them.

Yet how slight, how innocent their intercourse had been! She went over it all again in fancy as she took down book after book.

She and Don Claudio had always saluted each other when he came; at first, with a ceremonious bow, later, with a smile. They seldom spoke.

The table, piled with books, at which the professor and his pupil sat, was placed before the lagoon window, where, later, the old man's deathbed had been drawn. Her place was at a little casement window on the *rio* that ran beside the house. They spoke in languages which she did not understand, and she had often dropped her work to listen.

Sometimes, in going, his eyes had looked a wish to linger; but she did not know how he had longed to stay, nor how many glances had strayed from the piles of books to her face. The graceful contours of her form, her delicate whiteness, her modesty, her violet eyes, the golden lights in her hair — he had learned them all by heart.

"Tacita. Yes," he had thought, "that is the right name for her. She stays there in that flickering light and shade as silent as any lily!"

Their world had been the world of a Claude landscape, all floating in a golden haze.

Once they had all gone out into the balcony to watch a steamship from Cairo move up the lagoon that was all radiant and red with the setting sun. Another time a thunder-storm had darkened about them, so that they could scarcely see each other, and Don Claudio, coming to her table, had asked softly, —

"Are you afraid, Tacita?"

Another time he had brought her some roses from his mother's garden.

And now, everything was ended!

"He will come to-morrow for his books," she thought; "and, after that, we shall never see each other again. But we shall be alone together once, and speak a word of the past, and say farewell, like friends."

It was all that she expected, or consciously wished for, a friendly and sympathizing word, a clasp of the hand, the first and the last, and a "God be with you!" It would have sweetened her sorrow and loneliness.

After the visit of the Marchesa Loredan, Tacita's grandfather had talked with her; and the girl had assured him that there was nothing between her and Don Claudio but the calmest good-will. Her naturally quiet disposition had not been disturbed in his regard. But the thought that this was to be their last meeting, and that for the first time they would be alone, could not fail to agitate her somewhat; and when morning came, her expectation became a fluttering.

The books were all sorted, the house all ready for their departure. She and Elena would leave Venice the next morning. She was alone in the room where her grandfather had studied, taught, and died.

There was a sound of oars that came nearer. She listened, but would not look. "What can it mean?" she thought. "There are double oars; and he has but one gondolier."

Gian, the man-servant, entered and announced the Marchesa Loredan and Don Claudio; and at the same instant Elena slipped hastily into the room, that her charge might not be found alone.

Tacita's heart sank heavily. She greeted her visitors with an equal coldness, though Don Claudio's face implored her pardon.

"Your books are all ready, Don Claudio," she said, when she could speak. "Professor Mora said that you were to have those that are marked with a white star. Gian will take them down. Here is the list."

She gave him the paper, and he received it, blushing with shame. He could not utter a word. But the Marchesa's voluble condolences and compliments covered all defects in the conversation.

She was glad that the signorina was going to

travel for a time. Nothing distracted one from sorrow like traveling. Was there anything that the Marchesa could do for her? She would send her maid to the railway-station the next morning with a basket of luncheon for the travelers. If she could help them in any other way, the signorina might speak freely.

Tacita recollected the reply of Diogenes when Alexander asked: "Is there anything that I can do for you?"

"Only stand a little out of my sunshine," said Diogenes.

The Marchesa was most grateful for Professor Mora's gift to her son; and with the signorina's approval, Don Claudio proposed to erect a memorial tablet in St. Michael's to his honored preceptor.

The proposal pleased and touched the desolate girl, and she tearfully thanked Don Claudio.

From her own point of view the Marchesa Loredan had been very kind. Her visit would put a stop to any serious gossip about her son and Tacita; and she had shown a gracious regard and respect for the dead *savant* and his family.

She had a very comfortable sense of having done her duty, and been prudent in her own affairs at the same time. That both Tacita and her grandfather would have regarded such gossip with loathing and contempt, and that they set no very high value on her approval, she did not dream.

"Don Claudio should have been the one to tell me this," Tacita thought.

The books were carried down, the laborious visit came to an end, the orphan was alone again, her sweet, sad hope crushed like a fragile flower.

"Elena, take me away from here!" she exclaimed. "No one has any heart. Take me away!"

"Don't cry, dear! We will go in the morning," her friend said soothingly. "Don Claudio will come to take leave of you at the station. He found a chance to tell me so. He said that he could not get away alone this morning."

"She is cruel, and he is weak," said Tacita. "I like not a weak man."

Elena shook her head. "Ah! my dear, a man is usually weak before a strong-willed woman who loves herself better than she does him."

Don Claudio was, in fact, waiting at the station when they arrived there the next morning.

"I could not let you go without a word," he said in an agitated murmur. "I shall always remember, and regret. Oh! the sweet old days! Tacita, do not you see that my heart is breaking?"

"Dear friend," she answered gently, "we will remember each other with a tender friendship. Your heart will not break. It must not. A loving wife will console you. *Addio!*"

"To God!" There could be no more perfect parting word. They clasped hands for one trembling moment, then bowed their heads, and turned away.

CHAPTER III.

AMONG those who were on the steps of San Michele when the funeral gondola of Professor Mora reached them was a man who seemed to be waiting to assist at his burial. He followed to the chapel, and went away as soon as the service was over.

He was a young man, scarcely more than thirty years of age, a little taller than medium, slender, but athletic, and of a dark complexion. In the light, his dark hair had an auburn tinge, and his dark eyes a violet shade. His fine serious face had a look of high intelligence, and in the church, something even exalted, in its expression. He had brows to which Lavater would have ascribed great powers of observation; and his look was steady and penetrating. It recalled the old story of disguised deities who were recognized by their moveless eyeballs. He was quiet, and his dress was conventional, neither fine nor coarse. Both face and manner expressed refinement. It could be seen that his hands bore the marks of labor. If you had asked what his trade was, he would have said that he was a carpenter. Those who looked at him once with any attention, looked again.

When the funeral was over, this young man crossed the Laguna Morta, and landed at the steps behind San Marco. He went round into the church, looking at every part of it attentively. He did not appear to be either an artist or a worshiper, still less a tourist.

He might have been taken for an artisan who examined intelligently, but without enthusiasm, to see how the work was done. A closer view of his luminous dark eyes revealed a second expression, something mystical and exalted, as though he looked through the object his glance touched, and saw, not only the workman who had wrought it, but his mind and intention.

He made one slow circuit of the church, uttering not a word till he went up stairs and looked at the Judas hanging to a tree, the fresco half hidden in a corner of the gallery.

"*Absit!*" he exclaimed then, shuddering.

As he went out of the church, an old man seated on the step tried to rise, but with difficulty, being lame. The stranger aided him.

"You suffer," he said kindly. "Are you very poor?"

"I do not suffer much," the old man replied in a cheerful tone. "But my joints are stiff. And I am not poor. I have a son who earns good wages, thank God!"

A sweet smile lighted for an instant the stranger's face. "Addio, brother!" he said, and went on, out through the piazzetta, and down the Riva degli Schiavoni.

Near a *rio* along which stretched a garden, several boys were engaged with some object around which they were crouched on the pavement. It proved to be a little green lizard which they had caught on the garden wall. They were trying to harness it to a bunch of leaves. The little thing lay on its back, gasping.

The stranger, with a quick, fiery movement, pushed the boys aside, and released their captive. He took the nearly dead creature in his hand, and carried it to the garden wall, then returned to the boys, who had been surprised into a temporary quiescence.

"Boys," he said, "when some strong, cruel person shall make you suffer for his amusement, remember that lizard. If you should some day be helpless and terrified and parched with thirst, remember it."

He left them speechlessly staring at him, called a gondola, and gave the direction of the railway station. As he passed Ca' Mora, he looked earnestly at the window over the balcony. Elena stepped out and saw him. He raised his hand above his face in salutation, and she replied, raising her hand in the same way.

When he reached the railway landing, two gondoliers were standing on the steps, confronting each other in loud and angry dispute. They gesticulated, and flung profane and furious epithets at each other.

The stranger paused near them, and looked at one of the disputants with a steady gaze that seemed presently to check his volubility. The man grew uneasy, his attention was divided, he faltered in some retort, then turned abruptly away from his still menacing antagonist, and began to fumble with the oars and *felse* of his gondola.

The stranger went into the station and bought his ticket. As he stood waiting, the gondolier he had observed came in and accosted him respectfully, and with some embarrassment.

"I suppose you thought I was behaving badly, signore," he said. "But Piero has got three passengers away from me to-day, and I could n't stand it."

"I have not condemned you, friend," said the stranger mildly. "What does your own judgment say?"

The man's eyes fell. "I need n't have used certain words," he said in a low tone.

"Your judgment decides well," said the stranger. "It has no need of my interference. Addio, Gianbattista Feroli."

"Addio!" the gondolier echoed dreamily, and stood looking after him. "He has a saint's face," he muttered. "But how did he know my name!"

CHAPTER IV.

On leaving Venice, Tacita Mora's ultimate destination was to go to her mother's relatives, after some months spent in travel. Elena was to be her companion and guardian on the journey.

Who her mother's relatives were, and where they were, she did not know. She had once asked her mother, who replied, —

"My child, it is better, for many reasons, that you should not know till you see them. They are quiet, respectable people. You have nothing to disturb your mind about on their account. They know of you. They will keep track of you, and seek you at the proper time.

"But, as I do not wish others, who would be unfriendly, should know of them, it is better that you should remain ignorant for the present. People may ask you questions, and you will thus be spared the trouble of evading, or refusing to answer. Confide in no one. Absolutely, confide in no one, as you value your life! The person who displays curiosity concerning your private affairs is the very last person whom you should trust. Curiosity is a tattler, or an insinuator. Do not talk of your personal affairs outside of your own family. I will give you a sign by which my people are to be recognized. You are never to give that to any one, even to them, nor to intimate that you know such a sign. They will give it to you, anywhere, if there should be need. If no trouble should occur, it will be given you by the side of a rock. To such a person you may trust everything."

This conversation had taken place on their last visit to the Lido, as they walked on the sands, picking up shells, and dropping them again.

Professor Mora had given his granddaughter the same charge, adding, —

"Some one may solicit you artfully, suspecting a secret, and pretending to know it. Beware of the curious. For your life, remain firm and silent! And now, forget it all till the time shall come to remember. Do not let your imagination dwell upon the subject."

It was with this prospect that the orphan set out on her travels.

Never was there a better companion than hers proved to be. The nurse had traveled extensively, and was guardian, friend, and courier in one. She had all the firmness and courage that a man could have, with the more ingratiating ways of a woman. And she was an intelligent guide.

Tacita was to remain under this woman's protection till her friends should claim her. She would then place herself entirely under their guardianship, and remain with them, if contented, five years. If she should desire to leave them before that time should expire, they were to find a retreat for her. Her fortune was invested, and the income regularly paid; but how it was placed she did not ask. She only knew to whom she was to look for money, and to whom she was to appeal in case of accident. These persons were rather numerous, and were scattered over the greater part of Europe. None were of any special distinction, and none were bankers. There was a musician of repute among them, and a public singer.

Elena was also to join friends of her own whom she had not seen for years, when she should have placed her charge in safety. Who and where these friends were, Tacita took good care not to inquire. They were people who lived in a small mountain city, Elena volunteered to tell her. "And perhaps, dear, you might like to go there with me."

"I would go anywhere with you!" Tacita said warmly. "I do not dare to think of a time when I must lose you. I will not anticipate trouble; but when we have to part, you may be sure that I shall insist on an appointment for a meeting not far distant in time."

Traveling was a delight to Tacita. She had all that curiosity to see the world that a child has to whom the world is fairyland. The names of some places were to her like roses, or music, or like rolling thunder. She had read of them in prose and song. When she looked at them, in their possibly unimpressive features, she still found traces of their story, like the furrows left in a face by some tragical experience.

"Oh, the waterfalls!" she exclaimed, as their train rolled through the Alps. "So white above, so green and white below! Where can I have seen a white scarf like that wavering down from a height! Perhaps I passed this way with my mother when first we came to Venice. It is such a fresh wild place!"

She stood to look down at the torrent foaming among gray rocks below; then leaned back on the cushions, and fixed her eyes on the snow-peaks that seemed almost in the zenith.

"I remember so much that my grandfather used to say, though I seemed often to listen carelessly," she said. "He sometimes made such an odd impression on my mind. It might be he would talk half to me and half to himself, as if thinking aloud. He would seem to open the door of a subject, look in curiously, find it unpromising, and come out again. Or he would brighten as if he had found a treasure, and go on talking beautifully. When some astronomer had discovered a new star, he said the Te Deum should be sung in the churches, and he gave an alms and kept a lamp burning all night in honor of it, and we had ices in the evening. And before we separated to go to our rooms, he read the Gloria, and said three times over the sentence, 'We give thee thanks for thy great glory.' Listening to him, I sometimes felt as though people's minds were, for the greater part, like the tossing waves of a stormy sea. He said once of a crowd, 'They do not think; some one has set them swinging. I wonder what sets them all swinging! There is God, of course. But what instrument does he use? The stress of circumstance? Or is the tidal wave that gives the impulse some human mind fully alive?' I think the human mind was his idea. He said that some people were cooled off and crusted over like planets, and others all alive, like suns. He used to speak of reflective men and light-giving men. He was light-giving."

They visited Germany and the North, France, Great Britain, Spain and Algiers; and Tacita was getting very tired, though she did not say so. Elena had acquaintances in all those countries, and appeared to have errands in some. A year passed. It was spring again when they reached Seville from Africa, saw the Holy Week processions, and laid in a store of fans, silver filigree buttons, sashes, and photographs. Already a large number of boxes had been sent "home" from the different countries they had seen.

The evening before setting out from Seville to Madrid, Elena, for the first time, asked Tacita concerning her mother's relatives.

"If you do not know them, nor where they are," she said, "how can you communicate with them?"

"Both my mother and grandfather told me to give myself no uneasiness," Tacita replied. "I thought that it was all settled with you. We are soon to visit your home. After that, they will probably come, or send for me. Are you impatient?"

"Certainly not, my dear! I would most willingly keep you always with me. But you have money, and some dishonest person might attempt to deceive you."

"Oh! I have no fear," said Tacita with a reserve that savored of coldness. She was surprised that the subject had been introduced, and astonished at her companion's persistence. It seemed to have been avoided by mutual consent.

"Tell me how you will know them, and we will seek them together," said Elena.

"I have not to seek them," said Tacita with decided coolness.

"Is there, then, a secret?" asked her companion, with playful mockery.

Tacita looked at her steadily, and grew pale. "I thought that I knew you; and I do not," she said.

Elena resumed her dignity. "If you really object to telling me, then I will not ask," she said. "You had not mentioned the fact that it was a great secret."

"Nor have I said so now," answered the girl with a look of distress. "My mother talked with me of our affairs just before she died, and my grandfather gave me some directions. What they said to me is sacred, and is mine. I do not wish to talk of it."

"You swear that you will not tell me?" said Elena, looking at her keenly.

"I will not swear to anything!" exclaimed Tacita. "And I request you not to mention the subject again."

"We will then dismiss it," said her companion, and rose to leave the room. "I presumed on what I thought was a confidential friendship, and on the fact that your family confided you to me."

Tacita said nothing. Her head drooped. All her past sorrows seemed to return upon her. This woman, heretofore so dignified and so delicate, had appeared to her in a new light. She had sometimes fancied that Elena understood something of her affairs; but, apparently, she did not. That she should show a vulgar and persistent curiosity was shocking.

After a while Elena came into the room, and standing at a window, looked out into the purple twilight starred with lamps. The crowd that in Seville seems never to sleep was flowing and murmuring through the plaza and the streets.

Tacita was weeping silently.

"My dear child!" exclaimed the woman, going to embrace her. "Are we not friends?"

"You made me fear that we were not," said Tacita.

"Dismiss that fear! I will never so offend you again."

CHAPTER V.

ONE morning shortly after their arrival at Madrid, the two went to the great picture-gallery, of all picture-galleries the most delightful.

"When you shall have seen Murillo's Conceptions," Elena said, "you will see the difference between a sweet human nature and a supernatural creature. Raphael has painted good and beautiful women full of religious feeling; Murillo has painted the miraculous woman. The Spaniard had a vision of the Divine."

"You have been in Madrid before?"

"For two years," said Elena quietly.

They entered the large hall. It was early for visitors; but two artists were there copying. One had had the courage to set his easel up before one of Murillo's large Conceptions.

Tacita seated herself before that heavenly vision, and became absorbed in it. It was a revelation to her. The small picture in the Louvre had made but a slight impression on her, weary as she was with sight-seeing. But here was a reflection of heaven itself in the exquisite figure that floated before her supported on a wreath of angels, the white robe falling about her in veiling folds, and the long cerulean scarf full of that same wind that shook the house wherein waited the Apostles and the Marys when the Holy Ghost descended upon them. The two little hands were pressed palm to palm, the long black hair fell down her shoulders, her large black eyes, fixed on some dawning, ineffable glory, were full of a solemn radiance, her delicate face was like a white lily in the sunshine. The figure was at once childlike, angelic, and imposing.

Tacita had not removed her eyes from the picture when Elena came to touch her arm, and whispered: "Do you know that you have not winked for half an hour?"

Tacita roused herself. "I scarcely care to look at anything else now," she said. "I will glance about the room there, and then go home."

She went into the Isabella room, and walked slowly along the wall. Nothing dazzled her after that Murillo. Even Fra Angelico's angels looked insipidly sweet beside its ethereal sublimity. The "Perla" kept her but a moment. Those radiant black eyes of the "Concepcion" seemed to gaze at her from every canvas. She was about leaving the room, when something made her turn back to look again at an unremarkable picture catalogued as "A Madonna and Saints." Of the two catalogues she saw, one ascribed it to Pordenone, the other to Giorgione. She glanced at it without interest, wondering why she had stopped. The Madonna and Child, and the woman who held out to them a basket of red and white roses might just as well not have been painted for any significance they had;

and she was about turning away when she caught sight of a face in the shadowed corner of the canvas behind the kneeling woman.

This was no conventional saint. The man seemed to be dressed in armor, and his hand rested on a sword-hilt or the back of a chair. The shadows swathed him thickly, leaving the face alone distinct. One guessed at a slight and well-knit figure. The face was bronzed, and rather thin, the features as delicate as they could be without weakness. Dark auburn hair fell almost to the shoulders, a slight moustache shaded the lip, a small pointed beard the chin. The brows were prominent, and strong enough to redeem a weak face, even; and beneath them were the eyes that go with such brows, penetrating, steady, far-seeing, and deep-seeing. Those eyes were fixed on the Madonna and Child, not in adoration, but with an earnest attention. He stood erect, and seemed to be studying the characters of those two beings whom the woman before him knelt to worship. Yet, reserved and incisive as the look was, something of sweetness might be discerned in the man's face.

Tacita, half turned to go away, remained gazing at that face, fascinated. What a fine strength and purity! What reserve and what firmness! It was a face that could flash like a storm-cloud. Would anything ever make such a man fear, or be weak, careless, or cruel?

Elena came and stood by her, but said nothing.

"Behold a man," said Tacita, "whom I would follow through the world, and out of the world!"

Her companion did not speak.

"Why was I not in the world when he lived in it!" the girl went on. "Or why is he not here now! Fancy that face smiling approval of you! Elena, do the dead hear us?"

"The living hear us!" replied the woman. "Is the air dead because you cannot see it? Is it powerless because it is sometimes still? It is only the ignoble who go downward, and become as stones."

She spoke calmly and with a sort of authority.

They went out together.

"We are late for our luncheon," Elena said as they got into their carriage. "We must lose no time, if we are to see the king and queen go out to drive. Are you decided to leave Madrid to-morrow?"

"I don't know," Tacita replied absently.

"I shall want to know this evening, dear; so try to make up your mind. I want to send for some of my people to meet us. I hope that you will like my people."

"If they are like you, I shall love them," Tacita said.

"How long will you be content to stay with us?" the woman asked.

"How can I say, Elena? You have told me that your people are quiet, kind, and unpretending. That is pleasant, but only that is not enough for a long time. I want to see persons who know more than I do, who can paint, play on instruments, dance, sing, model, write poetry, speak with eloquence, and govern with strength and justice. I think that my heart would turn to lead if I had to live forever with people who were uncultivated. But if your people are like you, they are not merely simple. You know a great deal more than I do; and you are always *simpatica*."

"By simplicity, I do not mean ignorance," her friend said. "Professor Mora was simple. Some barbarous persons are very involved and obscure."

"Oh! if you speak in that sense" —

They ate their luncheon, stepped into the carriage that was waiting for them, and drove to the Plaza del Oriente. A good many persons were standing about the streets there waiting to see the young king and queen, Alfonso and Cristina, drive out. It was a gathering of leisurely, serious-looking people, with very few among them showing signs of poverty. The sky was limpid above the trees; and in the square opposite the corner at which our travelers waited, a bronze horseman seemed leaping into the blue over their topmost boughs.

Tacita glanced about her, at the people, the palace gate from which the royal cortége would issue, at the bronze horseman in the air; and then, turning a little to the other side, saw a man leaning carelessly against the trunk of a tree — saw him, and nothing else.

She felt as though she had received an electric

shock. There before her was the face of the Giorgione picture, every feature as she had studied it that morning, and the very expression of which she had felt the power. He was gazing at the palace gate, not as though waiting to see, but already seeing. One would have said that the walls were transparent to him, and that he was so absorbed in observing that king and queen whom no one else saw as to be oblivious to all about him.

His dress was some provincial or foreign costume. Black velvet short-clothes were held at the waist by a fringed scarf of black silk. His short jacket of black cloth was like a torero's in shape. He wore a full white shirt, black stockings and sandals, and a scarlet fez on his dark hair in which the sunshine found an auburn tint.

Tacita gazed at him with eyes as intent as his own. The smileless lips, the brow with its second sight, the pointed beard and faintly bronzed skin — they were the same that she had but an hour or two before engraven on her mind in lines as clear and sharp as those of any antique intaglio.

The stranger had not seemed aware of her observation; and the distance at which he stood from her gave no reason for his being so. But presently, when she began to wonder if he would ever stir, he went quietly to a poor woman who, with a child in her arms, leaned against the fence behind him, and took the child from her.

She looked surprised, but yielded in silence. The infant stared at him, but made no resistance.

He had not looked directly at either of them, nor addressed them. He brought the child to the carriage, and held it out, his eyes lowered, not downcast, nor once looking at its occupants.

Both Tacita and Elena silently placed a silver coin in the child's hand.

The man retreated a step, respectful, but not saluting, and carried the child to its mother. She showed in receiving it the same silent surprise with which she had yielded it to him. The stranger returned to his former position under the tree. He had not looked at any one, nor spoken a word; yet he had displayed neither affectation nor rudeness. A winged seed could not have floated past with more simplicity of action, nor yet with more grace.

There was a stir among the people. Two horsemen had issued from the palace gate, and an open carriage followed, behind which were again two other cavaliers. Tacita descended hastily from the carriage. In doing so she glanced at the tree against which the stranger had leaned; but he was no longer to be seen.

The royal carriage passed by, its occupants bowing courteously to the young traveler who courtesied from her post on the sidewalk. The queen was pale and sad-looking, the spirited face of the young king had something in its expression that was almost defiant. The spectators were cold and merely civil. At such a sight one remembers that kings and queens have also hearts that may be wounded, and that they sometimes need and deserve compassion. Few of them, indeed, have willfully grasped the crown; and on many of them it has descended like a crown of thorns.

"The king gives the queen the right hand, though she is queen consort only," Tacita said as they drove away. "In Italy the king regnant must absolutely have the right; and etiquette is quite as imperative in placing the gentleman at the lady's left hand. Consequently, the king and queen of Italy do not drive out together. Gallantry yields to law, but evades a rudeness."

She was scarcely conscious of what she was saying. Her eyes were searching the street and square. "What is his name?" she exclaimed suddenly, without any preface whatever.

"His name is Dylar," answered Elena. "He will make a part of the journey with us."

"He is from your place?" Tacita asked. She could not have told whether she felt a sudden joy or a sudden disenchantment.

"Yes, he is from our place."

"The child was not his?"

"Oh, no!"

"Why did he bring it to us?"

"Probably he saw that they were poor."

"Does he know them?"

"He must know that they are poor, or he would not have asked charity for them."

"He asked nothing," said Tacita.

"Yet you gave."

"It is true; he did ask and seemed sure of receiving. Why does he make a part of the journey with us?"

"He knows the way and the people. He will meet us when we cross the mountains."

"I wonder if they are the mountains that my grandfather remembered!" thought Tacita, and asked no more. Some feeling that was scarcely fear, but rather a sense of coming fate, began to creep over her. She had entered upon a path from which there was no retreat, and something mysterious was stealing about her and closing her in.

"Dylar is here," Elena said as they drove into the gardens of the Ritiro. "Shall we stop and speak to him? I want to tell him when we will leave Madrid. What shall I say?"

"We will leave to-morrow morning," Tacita said, looking eagerly around. Already it seemed to her a wonderful thing to hear this man speak.

He was walking to and fro under the trees, and came to the side of their carriage immediately. He glanced at Tacita, and slowly bowed himself in something of an oriental fashion. One might have hesitated whether to compare his manner to that of a perfectly trained servant come to take orders, or to the confident reserve of a sovereign about to hear if his orders had been obeyed. "The signorina has decided to set out to-morrow morning," Elena said to him. "We shall not stop anywhere."

"I will meet you at the orange-farm," the man answered quietly.

The voice was clear and low, the enunciation perfect.

He looked at Tacita with a reassuring kindness. "Elena knows all that is necessary," he said. "Trust to her, and have no fear."

She felt herself in the presence of a superior. "I have no fear now," she replied; and thought, "How did he know that I was afraid!"

He drew back, and they went on their way, neither speaking of what had occurred.

CHAPTER VI.

TACITA resumed her journey in a dream, and pursued it in a dream. She asked no questions, and observed but little, though at times it seemed to her that the line of their progress was a zigzag. Did they cross the water a second time? Why did they travel so much by night, and sleep by day? She did not care. Her mind became dimly aware of these questions rather than asked them. Had she taken hashish? No matter. All that she wanted was rest. Her very eyelashes and finger-nails were weary. Oh, for the mountains, for a place to call home, and rest!

She received the impression that a part of the country through which they passed was like a burnt-out world, all sand and black rocks, so that the limpid rivulet that met them somewhere was a surprise. She wondered languidly that it was not dried up. Was it a week, or a month, since Dylar had said, "Have no fear"? No matter. She had no fear; but she was, oh, so weary! Fortunately, nothing was required of her but passive endurance of fatigue. She was borne along, and tenderly cared for.

One day she roused herself a little, or something was done to rouse her. They were in an easy old carriage drawn by mules. It had met them at a solitary little station of which she had not seen nor asked the name; and they had been driving through a dry plain, and were now in pine woods.

Elena gave her some little cakes of chocolate and slices of lemon. "We are almost out of provisions," she said; "but in an hour you shall have a good dinner; and then to bed with her, like a sleepy child."

Elena was smiling brightly. Tacita gave a languid smile in return, and leaned back, looking out the window. The pines had ceased, and there was a rice-field at one side, and orange-trees heavily laden with ripe fruit at the other.

The oranges reminded her of Naples, which she had visited when a child. The blue bay and blue sky seemed to sparkle before her, the songs bubbled up, there was the soft splendor of profuse flowers, the fruits, the joy in life, the careless gayety; and, crowning these delights, that ever-present menace smoking up against the sky, telling of boiling rivers from a boiling pit of inextinguishable fire ever ready to overflow, bearing destruction to all that beauty.

"The utmost of earthly delight has ever its throne on the edge of a crater," she thought.

The orange-trees pressed closer, right and left, there were blossoms with the fruit, and the western sun shone through both. The air was fresh and sweet. She saw nothing but glossy foliage and golden balls, and a green turf strown with gold.

"It is Andalusia, or the Hesperides!" she said, waking, and sitting up.

Even as she spoke, the green and gold wall came to an end, and at a little distance a whitewashed stone house was visible.

"Look!" exclaimed Elena; and leaning toward her, pointed upward out of the carriage window.

Behind the house, showing over its roof like a crown on a head, was a curve of olive-trees on a hill-top. Above the trees rose wild rocks in fantastic peaks and precipices, and above the rocks, closely serrated, was a range of Alp-like mountains upholding a mass of snow and ice that glittered rosily in the sunset.

"Is it your home?" asked Tacita eagerly. "How beautiful!"

"Not yet," her friend answered, her eyes, filled with tears of joy, fixed on those shining heights. "But from my home those mountains are visible. To-morrow night I shall sleep under my own blessed roof!"

The door of the house stood open, but no one appeared in it. At some distance were several persons, men and women, gathering oranges. They paused to look at the travelers, but made no movement to approach them.

"We do not need any one," Elena said. "You shall go directly to your chamber; and after supper you shall sleep."

They entered a vestibule from which a stair ascended. The inner doors were closed. They went up to a pleasant chamber that looked toward the mountains and the south. At their left, toward the east, twilight had already come under the shadow of those heights and the pines beneath. But shafts of red gold still shot over their heads from the west, and all the shadows had a tinge of gold. An orange-tree that grew beneath their window lifted a crowded cluster of ripe fruit above the sill, as if offering it to the travelers.

"Thank you!" Tacita said, and detached one from the bunch where they grew so close that each one had a facet on its side.

Elena, who seemed to feel perfectly at home, left her resting and went down stairs for their supper. She had made no mistake in saying that it would be a good supper. An hour later, the shadows had lost their gold, and Tacita was asleep.

How sweet is the deep sleep of weariness that hopes and trusts! It is not alone that every nerve and muscle lets slip a burden, that the heart gives a thankful sigh, and the busy brain grows quiet. The pleasure is more than negative. Such sleep comes as the tide comes in calm weather. Transparent, yet tangible, it steals over the tired senses, its crest a whispered lullaby. Deeper, then, smoothing out the creases of life with a down-like touch. Yet deeper, and a full swell submerges the consciousness, and you lie quiescent at the bottom of an enchanted sea.

CHAPTER VII.

"ARE you prepared for mountain climbing?" Elena asked the next morning when Tacita woke.

"I am prepared for anything! I have had such a refreshing sleep! How long has it been?"

"Nearly twelve hours, my dear. Your ancestors must have come from Ephesus. I thought that I knew how to sleep; but the singleness of purpose with which you lay yourself away is something entirely your own. It is a gift. It arrives at genius. Now, who do you think that I can see coming over a rocky path above the olives?"

"Can it be Dylar?"

"It is Dylar. He will be here in fifteen minutes."

The people of the house paid as little attention to their guests in the morning as they had the evening before. Elena brought the breakfast, if she did not prepare it. Probably they were all out picking oranges. Children were visible at a distance gathering the fruit up from under the trees. The orchard was a good many acres in extent.

When Tacita, prepared for her journey, went down to the door, their driver of the day before stood there with two donkeys girded with chair-shaped saddles, with high backs and foot-rests. Not far away there was another donkey. Beside it stood a man who uncovered his head, and looked with an eager smile at the young traveler when she appeared.

"He is one of my people," Elena said. "I have been talking with him. You should salute him in this way," lifting her hand above her face.

Tacita imitated her with a smiling glance toward the guide, who responded.

Away under the trees talking with the farmers was a third man, who as soon as Tacita appeared, came to meet her.

It was Dylar; but Dylar in a conventional dress such as any gentleman might wear in traveling; and with the dress, he had assumed something of the conventional manner. Had he lost by the change? she asked herself, while he made courteous inquiries, and looked to see if her saddle was firm. No: the face was the same, and could easily make one forget the costume; and there was sincerity in the tone of his inquiries.

"We cross this angle of the mountains, and go back almost in the direction from which you came yesterday," Dylar said. "I am sorry that it was necessary to take you by the longer way. Late in the afternoon we shall reach a house where you and Elena will sleep. It is a solitary place, but more comfortable than it looks at first sight, and it is quite safe. To-morrow you will have but three hours' ride."

They mounted, and took the path that led backward over the heights. They rode singly, Elena with her guide leading. Tacita followed with a man at her bridle, and Dylar came last.

The air grew cooler and finer. It was the air that makes one wish to dance.

Tacita asked herself what it could be in all these faces, — Dylar's, Elena's, the two guides', yes, and in her own mother's and grandfather's, — which made them resemble each other in spite of different features and characters. It was a spiritual family resemblance. Ingenuous was not the word. It was not dignity alone. Strong and gentle did not describe it. It was the expression of a certain harmonious poise and elastic firmness of mind indicating that each one had found his proper place, and was content with it; indicating, too, a mutual complaisance, but a supreme dependence on something higher.

Their way led deeper into the mountains. Now and then, in turnings of the path, Tacita lost sight of her companions. She looked backward once for Dylar. When he appeared, he smiled and waved his hand to her encouragingly.

"He smiled!" she whispered to herself, but did not look back again.

The sky was blue and cloudless, and pulsed with its fullness of light. Somewhere, not far away, there was a waterfall. Its infant thunder and lisping splash pervaded the air. The scene grew more grand and terrible. One moment they would be shut into a narrow space from which exit seemed impossible, dark stone grinding close without a sign of pathway; then the solid walls were cleft as in an instant. In the near deeps lurked a delicate shadow; far below was revealed from time to time a velvety darkness.

Tacita's mind, floating between present contentment, a half-forgotten pain, and a mystical anticipation, confused the scene about her with others far away. Clustered windows, crowded sculptures and balconies, seemed to emboss the cliffs at either hand, or float in misty lines along their surfaces. The sound of the haunting cascade became the dip of oars, or the swash of the lagoon ploughed by a steamboat. She saw their time-stained old Venetian house; and the last scenes she had witnessed there rose before her. A wreath of mist that had risen from some invisible stream and paused among the rocks recalled a narrow bed with a white-haired old man lying on it, peaceful and dead. The hymn sung as he died seemed only that moment to have ceased on the air. Why had it sounded familiar? Perhaps it might have a phrase in common with some song she knew. How did it go? She hummed softly, feeling for the tune, found a bar or two, and sang in a low voice.

To her astonishment, her guide at once took up the strain, and from him Elena and her guide, and then Dylar. They sang: —

"San Salvador, San Salvador,
We live in thee!

'T is love that holds the threads of fate;
Death 's but the opening of a gate,
The parting of a mist that dims the sky.
We live in thee! We live in thee!
San Salvador,
We live in thee!"

Tacita held her breath to listen. Was she indeed riding through mountain paths and morning air, or lying in a dream in some strange land? Dylar's was the voice that had sung beneath their window when her grandfather was dying!

The way grew wilder. The rocks were black and frowning. Sometimes their path was but a narrow shelf along the face of a precipice. Once the guide made her descend, and fastened a rope from iron hook to hook set in the rock for her to hold in passing.

At noon they reached a little plateau, — a few feet of short turf, some tiny vines and spotted lichens, and a blue flower, all of which seemed miracles in that place. Here they dismounted and ate their luncheon.

"What a wonder a flower would be, if there were only one in the world!" Dylar said, seeing Tacita bend over this.

She smiled, and continued to examine it carefully, without touching. It seemed something sacred. Who drew the little lines on its petals, and scattered the gold dust in its heart, and gave it all that seeming of innocent faith and courage? The grass-blades, too, with their fine serrated edges, and sharp points thrust upward, then curving over, as if they were spears changing to pruning-hooks, — what beautiful things they were when there were but few!

Dylar and Elena talked with their guides in a language that she had never heard before, yet which she could almost understand.

It was a clear-sounding and sonorous language, with a good deal of accent, and it almost sang.

"You will soon learn it," Elena said. "It is the flower of all languages, not yet rich, but pure."

They mounted, and pursued their way. After some hours the path began to broaden and descend. They entered a pine wood, and the sun deserted them, showing only on the tops of the highest trees. The way was dim and fragrant, long brown aisles of gloom stretched away at their left. But only a fringe of trees stood between them and the crags at their right.

The path turned with a long curve, and they were at the door of a dark old house, built of rough stones, and set against a cliff. Opposite the door a road went down into the pines, and disappeared. The road by which they had come continued past the door, descended gently, and disappeared around the cliffs.

The house had a sinister, deserted look. The door was off the hinges, and set against an inner wall. The rude shutters of an upper window hung half open. Where the masonry of the house ended and the natural rock began was not apparent. Nature had adopted the rough stones, and set her lichens and grasses in their interstices.

A rivulet fell from the heights into a trough near the door, twisting itself as it fell, and braiding in strands of light. From the trough the water overflowed, and followed the road.

"It is not so bad as it looks," Elena said.

Dylar came to assist Tacita. "I think that you will be able to rest well here, unpromising as it looks," he said. "Do not be anxious. You will be well guarded. And to-morrow your journey will come to an end."

As they entered the house, a man came hastening down the stairs. He saluted Dylar with reverence and Elena with delight. They spoke together in the language the guides had used. The man bowed lowly before Tacita, and smiled a welcome.

The room had no door but that by which they had entered, and no furniture but a rough bench and table. There was a cavernous chimney. The floor was strown all about with twigs and pine needles.

One of the guides brought in some boughs, and kindled a fire on the hearth.

Dylar took leave of Tacita, and pursued his way down the carriage-road leading by the rocks. In parting he said, —

"After to-morrow I will see you, if the King wills."

A stair led directly from the room to a landing. Two doors opened on this landing. One was closed. The other stood wide open into a chamber that was in pleasant contrast with the room below. A wide white bed, a deep sofa, a commode and mirror, a table set with covers for two drawn up before the sofa, and a second table holding roasted fowl, salad, wine, and fruit promised every necessary comfort. The room was rough but clean. A gray muslin curtain was drawn back from one side of the window, and there was a glazed sash in a sliding frame at the other.

"Isn't it cosy!" said Elena, who seemed to bo overflowing with joy at finding herself so near home. "Now, lie down on the sofa, dear, and you shall have some soup as soon as it is hot. We shall fare well. Our supper has been prepared by the housekeeper at the castle, and sent in good order."

"I must not ask what castle?" Tacita said.

"Why, Castle Dylar, of course!" Elena said, and went down stairs for the soup.

There was a sound from below of the door being set on its hinges and barred, and the shutters were closed.

"The guides will sleep below," Elena said.

"Elena," said Tacita, "what did Dylar mean when he said 'if the King wills?' Who is the king?"

"Christ Jesus," replied Elena, bowing her head.

"*Evviva Gesù!*" exclaimed the girl with pleasant surprise. "And is Dylar the master of Castle Dylar?"

"He is sole master!"

"Am I allowed to ask if he has any title of nobility?"

"He is a prince," said Elena.

She asked no more.

Later, when half asleep, she became aware of strange sounds from below, as of a heavy weight falling, and grating hinges.

"Don't be afraid," Elena said. "The men are putting the donkeys in their stable. And our chamber door is strongly barred."

CHAPTER VIII.

THE sun was high when Tacita woke the next morning. The chamber door was open, and an odor of coffee came up the stair. The window sash and curtain had been drawn back, admitting the pine-scented air and a rain of sunshine that fell over everything in large golden drops.

It was late. "But that does not matter," Elena said, coming up with the coffee. "We could not have started sooner. My brother had to come for us; and it takes three hours. There were other things to do besides. And when they were all done, we talked over the incidents of a five years' separation. How glad I was to see him!"

Tears were shining in her eyes. "There is no haste. My brother has to prepare some things. We go by an inner path, not the one Dylar took. We travel in a southwesterly direction across the mountains; and you will reach your chamber long before sunset. I have thought that you would not care to see any strangers to-night. Am I right? Well, now we will go down. But first, I have a word to say to you."

There was something in her face that arrested attention, an excitement that was almost a trembling. "Tacita, do you remember all that your mother and grandfather told you, which you refused to repeat to me?"

Tacita made no reply in words. Already she divined.

The nurse leaned to whisper a word in her ear, and give her a sign.

Tacita looked at her with a mild surprise.

The nurse went to look out the window, and returning, repeated her pantomime and whisper.

"Well?" said Tacita wonderingly.

"Dylar reproved me for having tried you in Seville," the nurse said, and again repeated the whisper and the touch.

"I might have known!" Tacita exclaimed joyously, embracing her. "I did almost know. It is all that was needed to make me perfectly happy! And now, let us start for home. At last I can call it home! 'By the side of a rock,' my mother said."

They went down stairs. There was no one visible, and the door was still barred. Elena led her companion into the niche under the stair, and tapped on the stone wall. Immediately, as though her light touch had pushed it, a part of the wall receded a few inches, was lifted a few inches, and swung slowly backward. It was a door of small stones set in a plank frame, the irregular edges fitting perfectly into the masonry about them. A narrow, dim passage was visible, leading downwards.

They descended, hand in hand, passing by a man

who stood there in the shadow; and the door was closed and barred behind them. It was hung on iron hooks that were round at the top, and square below. When the bars were removed, and the door freed from the wall, a pulley lifted it from the square to the round iron on which it swung.

The incline led to a small cave, scarcely larger than the room above. It was all open to the west, and an abyss separated it from a precipice, leaving only a narrow shelf of rock outside the cave's mouth. Beside this shelf, no other egress was visible.

The place showed signs of having been recently used as a stable. For the rest, it might not have been visited for years. There was an old chest with rusty hinges, an old box full of pine-needles, and some discolored blocks of wood that might have served as seats.

"It is Arone, my brother!" said Elena, when the man came down to them after fastening the door.

He had a sunny face, and he resembled his sister so closely that an introduction was scarcely necessary. His dress set off a fine manly figure. It was a gray cloth tunic reaching to the knees, and girded with a dark blue fringed sash. Long gray stockings and a gray turban-shaped cap with a blue band completed his costume. The band of the cap was closed over the left ear with a small silver hand.

The shelf of rock proved to be their path. Holding by a rope fixed in iron hooks, they followed its curve to a small platform of rock. From this, a bridge of two planks, over which the rope was continued, crossed the chasm to a second shelf. This was more dangerous than the first; for it was wet, and the sheer rock it followed was dripping. Beyond, in a wider path, were their guides of the day before, and the donkeys.

Holding the rope, Tacita passed the wet rock, not daring to look downward, and was received by her companions with a "Brava!"

The worst was over. She sat down to get her breath, and Arone returned to remove the ropes and plank.

"You are going to see, in a little while, why our path is wet," Elena said. "Meantime, look about you. Do you see that window?" pointing to a fissure in the rock above the cave. Ropes extended from this point to another not visible to them, but in the direction of their pathway. "The closed door you saw next to our chamber leads to that room, and those ropes carry signals to a station that is visible to a second station farther on. From there they are repeated to a third, and that third station we see at home. Anything that takes place here can be known there in a few minutes. They must know already that we have passed the bridge. The house is not such a ruin as it appears, nor so far away from everybody. There are several decent rooms above; and it is only five miles round by the road to Castle Dylar. There are always two persons in the house as guard; and they are changed every week. From an upper window, like this, hidden behind a fissure in the rock, all the roads outside are visible. There are tubes leading to the lower room through which the guard can converse, or listen."

Tacita did not reply. She disliked mysteries, having had reason to mistrust them.

"We have no more secrets than we must, dear," her friend said, perceiving the signs of distaste. "All that you have seen is necessary for the protection of good people who have not strength to defend themselves, and would not wish to use force, if they could."

Arone, who had come back to them, looked at the window over the cave, and blew a whistle. Instantly, a bunch of long, colored streamers ran along one of the ropes, and disappeared. While they waited, Elena gave her charge a first lesson in her mother's native language, telling the names of their guides, their animals, the rocks, lichens, and the sky, with its light and sources of light. Then, pausing, she raised her hand, and listened. There was a stir, faint and far away, but coming nearer. It became a rushing sound, and a sound of waters. A huge white feather showed above the wet rock underneath which they had passed, and a foaming torrent leaped over its brink, plunged with a sharp stroke to the shelf, and fell into the abyss. Their whole path from the cave's mouth to within a few feet of where they stood was covered with the wild rush of a mountain torrent.

"That is our beautiful gate," Elena said. "It needs no bolt. Now we will go. From here the way is all plain."

They rode for two hours over a hard mountain path, where nothing but dark rocks, pine-trees, and snow was visible. Then through a gap in the mountains an exquisite picture was seen, lower down, and not so far away but its features could be examined. There was a green hill with sheep and lambs, and a little cottage. Outside the door, under the shadow of an awning, sat a man and woman. The man was carving pieces of wood on a table before him; the woman had some work on her lap which kept her hands in constant motion. A young girl came out of the cottage and brought her mother something which they examined closely together. They were all dressed in gray with bright girdles.

"The man carves little olive-wood boxes and bowls," Elena said. "The woman and her daughter make pillow-lace. The girl is our very best lace-maker. Her work brings a high price when we send it out."

The three continued tranquilly their occupations, unconscious of being observed; and an interposing mountain slope soon hid them from sight.

Tacita began to feel that she had rested but superficially the two past nights. She scarcely cared to look at the changing views where distant snow-peaks and occasional airy distances seemed to intimate that before long they might emerge from their mountain prison.

The path descended gradually; there were glimpses of pine-groves and olives. Suddenly they made a sharp turn, and entered a cave much like that they had started from.

"At last!" exclaimed Elena, and slipped from her saddle.

From the cave they went into a long corridor that led them to an ante-room with a curtained glass door at each of the four sides. There was no window. One of the doors stood open into a charming bed-chamber.

The one large window of this chamber was covered with a curtain of white linen in closely crowded flutings that shone with a reflected sunshine. The color of all the room was a delicate gray, with touches of gilding everywhere. They glimmered in a broad band of arabesques that ran round the walls at middle height; on a bronze vase with its long slender pen-sweep of a handle; on the lance-ends of the curtain-rod; on the railing around three sides of a little table that held a candlestick, bottle, and glass at the bedside. There was a glistening of gold all through the light shadow-tint.

"Welcome! A thousand welcomes to San Salvador!" exclaimed Elena, leading Tacita into the chamber and embracing her with fervor. "May all happiness and peace attend you here; and may the place be to you the gate of heaven!"

"And now, dear, your fatigues are all over," she added. "You are at home!"

"San Salvador!" repeated Tacita, looking about her.

"Do you wish to see and know more now, at once?" the nurse asked smilingly. "There are no more secrets for you."

"Oh, no! Just now I appreciate too well our Italian proverb: 'The bed is a rose.' And that sofa seems to speak." She went to sink on to its soft cushions. "Go to your friends, Elena."

"Presently. You must first be attended to. There is a woman here who will serve you in everything. She speaks French, and her name is Marie. What are your orders?"

"My wish is to rest on this motherly sofa an hour or two, without having to utter a word. Then I would like a little quiet dinner, all alone, after which I will go to bed and sleep as long as nature wills. Those are my wishes. My sole command is that you go to your friends at once, and do not return to me till to-morrow morning. My poor, dear Elena! What a care I have been to you! Now let me see you take some care of yourself. I have all that I want."

The woman, Marie, appeared with a cup of broth on a tray. From her glad excitement, the tray trembled in her hands.

"Oh, welcome home, Elena!" she exclaimed. "Welcome to San Salvador, Tacita Mora! You are a thousand times welcome! May the place be to you the gate of heaven! I am so glad!"

She set the tray before Tacita, but could spare her only a glance as she uttered her hasty and tremulous welcome. Then she ran to embrace

Elena. "Oh, welcome! welcome! You are looking so well. You come laden with good news. Stay with us! We will not let you go again. We will give the moon in exchange for you!"

"Oh, I should miss the moon," Elena said laughingly.

After a little while they went out together, leaving Tacita to rest.

"What, then, is San Salvador?" she wondered, sinking among the sofa-pillows.

Perhaps she might learn by lifting that sunlighted curtain. But she did not wish to lift it. There was pleasure in tasting slowly the unfolding mystery. So far, each revelation had been brighter than the preceding. She slept content, and waked to see on the curtain the deep hue of sunset.

For a little while she lay looking about her, recollecting herself, and examining her surroundings. The floor was of yellow tiles, all the furniture and bed-covers were of pale gray linen as glossy as satin, the wicker chairs were graceful in shape, and the tables gave a restful idea of what tables are meant for, undefeated by sprawling legs and impertinent corner - twiddlings. They were of fine solid wood, dignified and useful, and set squarely on strong legs.

Glancing at the band of arabesques around the walls, Tacita perceived that it had a meaning. It was all letters — but letters run to flower or to animal life. They budded, they ended in tendrils, they were birds and insects, but always letters; and as she studied them, they became letters that made words in all the languages that she knew; and doubtless those which she could not decipher were words of languages unknown to her. And of all those which she could read, every one repeated the same words, over and over, whole, or in fragments, each phrase held up as a honey-dropping flower:

He shall feed his flock like a shepherd; and sorrow and mourning shall flee away.

It was set down in clear text. Then a bird flew with a part of it in his beak. *Like a shepherd, Like a shepherd.* And the word *shepherd* stood alone, all bloomed out with little golden lilies. Dragon-flies and butterflies bore the promise on their wings; and where it bore roses, every rose had a humming-bird or bee sucking its sweetness out. The quick squirrel ran with what seemed a vine hanging from his upturned mouth; and the vine was a promise.

It was the Moorish idea. She had seen among their arabesques the motto of Ibn-l-ahmar: "There is no conqueror but God," so interwoven with ornamentation. But that solemn Moorish reverence and piety did not touch the heart like this consoling tenderness.

Dinner was served on a table set before the window. It was a charming little dinner: a shaving of broiled ham; a miraculous soup; a bit of fish in a shell; a few ribs, crisp and tender, of roasted kid; rice in large white kernels; an exquisite salad of some tender herbs with lemon juice and oil that was like honey; a conserve of orange-blossoms, rich and thick; a tiny flask of red wine from which all acrid taste of seed and stem had been excluded; and lastly, a sip or two of coffee which defied criticism.

Evidently the cook of San Salvador was nothing less than a *cordon-bleu.*

The dinner done a healthy justice to, and praised, Tacita was once more left to herself. But first Marie brought a vase of olive oil and water with a floating flame, and set it in a little glazed niche in the wall that had its own pipe-stem of a chimney; and she drew back the window-curtain. The lower part of it had lost the sun; but a bar of orange light crossed the top.

Tacita waited till the door closed, then looked out eagerly.

There were still mountains in a rugged magnificence of mass and outline; but the color left no room for disappointment. They faced the west with the kindled torch of a snow peak above a tumult of gold and purple and deep-red. There were pines along the lower heights, and olives, and, lower still, fruit-trees. A rock protruding close to either side of the window narrowed the lower view. But only a few rods distant, a wedge of smooth green turf was visible, with a crowd of gayly-dressed children playing on it, tossing grace-hoops, chasing each other, and dancing.

Presently the air was filled with a sweet, tinkling music. The children ceased their play at the sound, and formed themselves in procession, with subsiding kitten-like skips, and passed along the green, and out of sight.

As she watched them, it occurred to Tacita for the first time to think that youth is beautiful. It is a thought that seldom occurs to the young, youth being a gift that is gone as soon as recognized. Her aching languor and weariness taught her the value of that elastic activity, and her sorrow suggested the charm of that unclouded gayety. Yes, it is beautiful, she thought, that evanescent blush of life's morning forever hovering about the sterner facts of human existence.

She sat and looked out till the color faded from the heights, leaving only a spot of gold aloft; and, thinking that she must not go to sleep in her chair, fell sound asleep in it.

It was about midnight when she waked, and with so vivid an awakening that to sleep longer seemed impossible. In place of the languid quiescence of the evening before, there was a consuming impatience to know all without an hour's delay. Close to her was the unsolved mystery of her mother's birth and of her own fate. She could wait no longer.

She lighted her candle, and went softly out into the ante-room. All was still. She tried the door opposite her own. It opened on a broad stair that descended between two blank walls.

Closing the door noiselessly behind her, she went down, candle in hand, and reached a corridor and a second stair. Across the foot of this second stair shone a soft light. It was the same light that shone outside her window above, — a passing moonlight that had gathered to itself all the starbeams in the air and all the frosty reflections of its own crescent splendor from snow-clad heights and icy peaks, and fused them in a lambent silver.

Tacita set her candle on the stair, and went down into a long hall, of which the whole outer side was an arcade, and beyond the arcade was a piazza open to the night, and with a wide space beyond its parapet. As in a dream, she passed the arcade; and before her lay San Salvador, the city of the Holy King!

CHAPTER IX.

San Salvador was built on a plain that might once have been the bed of a lake formed by mountain torrents partially confined. It was an irregular oval, two miles in length from north to south, and a mile and a half wide. As large an exact parallellogram as the space would allow was surrounded by a deep canal, or river, shut in by balustrades on both sides, and having its outlet southward through the mountains. This space was the town, as compactly built as possible.

Across the centre, from east to west, ran a wide avenue that expanded at middle length to a square. Seen from a height this avenue and square looked like a huge cross laid down across the town. Narrow streets, alternating with single blocks of houses, ran north and south, only an open space of a few feet being left all round next the river. The cross-streets did not make a complete separation of the houses, but cut away only the basement and floor above, so that one looked across the town through a succession of arches.

The houses were all of gray stone, three stories high, with a *patio*, a flat roof, and two fronts. There was no sign of an outbuilding, nor was there a blade of grass in the gray stone pavement that covered every inch of ground inside the river. But there were plants on the roofs. At each end of the avenue a bridge as wide crossed the river; and there were four narrow bridges at each of the four sides of the town.

In the southern half of the square was a building called the Assembly, from its use, or the Star-house, from its shape. It had three triangular stories set one over the other in the shape of a six-pointed star, the protruding angles forming vestibules below with their supporting columns, and terraces above. These columns restored the symmetry of the structure, and gave it grace and lightness.

In the northern square was a low bell-tower with a pulpit built against its southern side. The first floor was an open room surrounded by arches.

With the exception of these two structures, nothing could be more monotonous in form and color than the whole town; while nothing could be more varied than its setting.

That part of the plain outside the river, called the Cornice, had a straight edge next the river and an outer edge that showed every wildest caprice. Sometimes it ran into the mountains in bays, in curves and rivers, and sometimes the mountains crowded it to within a few feet of the river. All around rose the mountain wall, lined with hills, gentle, or abrupt; and, inundating all, a flood of verdure was thrown up on every side, like the waves of a sea. The ragged edges of the plain were heavy with wheat, rice and corn; higher up were orchards, vineyards, and terraced gardens, and a smoke of olives curling about everywhere, and groves of trees crowded into sunny hollows, and wedges of pines thrust upward, diminishing till the last tree stood alone beneath a gigantic cornice-rim of rock, snow and ice,—

"Where the olive dare not venture,
And the pine-tree's courage fails."

Around the middle distance of this garden-zone was a wavering path, now visible to the town, now lost, with frequent dropping paths, half stairs, to the plain. This path was called the Ring. Here and there was a glistening watercourse, or cascade; and the whole garden-circle was sparsely dotted with little cottages, some of them scarcely more than huts.

Two great masses of rock detached from the mountains were connected with them by bridges. That at the southwest was covered with a building containing a school for boys, that at the northeast had the hospital.

Directly opposite the eastern end of the avenue was the largest building in the town, called the Arcade. Here was the girls' school, and a hotel for women.

It was here that Tacita Mora stood, in the long wide veranda that followed the whole irregular front of the building, and looked for the first time on the city of her birth. But of all this scene, splendid by daylight, in that midnight hour she saw only a bold mountain outline high against the stars, with an embroidery of shadows beneath, and lower yet, a gray bas-relief that as it approached nearer became houses.

Presently, the waning moon came up over the mountains behind the Arcade, and set a snow-peak glistening opposite, and half unveiled a ghostly sheeted avalanche, and penciled here and there a clearer outline, and showed the embossed surface of the plain cleft smoothly across from beneath the veranda where she stood to something far away that seemed like a white wavering cascade, with a fiery sparkle above it as the moon rose higher.

The desire to know more, to see nearer, to assure herself by actual touch that this was not all a twilight *mirage* became irresistible.

"Be free as in your father's house," Elena had said to her.

There was no sign nor sound of any one abroad. The soft rustle of running waters alone moved the silence.

Tacita found the last stair and went out. In that delicate airy illumination the avenue disclosed itself before her, and the white object far away became stationary. But the sparkle above it had disappeared. She went forward timidly, pausing to listen, turning to retreat, and again advancing, at once resolute and afraid.

A few silvery bird-notes floated through the silence; a white network of cloud, like a bed of anemones, veiled the moon's crescent.

Tacita, gathering courage and excited by the

spirit of adventure, hastened till she reached the Square, paused there but a moment, and then hurried on toward that white object which was her goal. It was a little above the level of the town; it took shape as she drew nearer, and became the façade of a white building with a fragmentary glimmering across it and above; it showed a background of dark rock, and a plateau in front surrounded by a white balustrade. In all the town there was nothing white except this building and the balustrade raised and overlooking every other building. In a Christian community only a church would be so enthroned.

Tacita crossed the bridge, and went to kneel on the steps leading from the level to the inclosed terrace. There was a smooth façade with a great door in receding arches in the centre, above a flight of white steps, five rose windows following the arched line of the roof, and something like a gilded lettering across the middle height.

As the anemone-cloud drew away from the moon, the letters grew distinct, and the text shone out full and clear: —

I AM THE LIGHT OF THE WORLD.

At sight of that shining legend aloft, something stirred in the girl's memory. A thick curtain of years parted, showing a distinct fragment of the past. Once, long ago, she had looked up at that white expanse and seen upon its front the line of shining figures. Her hands held the soft fold of a dress, and a hand rested lightly on her head. In her memory the bright figures were associated with the idea of a great golden lamp, softly luminous, swung by a golden chain down from the skies, and of a face all radiant, and a sweet voice that said: *Of such is the kingdom of heaven.*

"I must have stood on this very spot with my mother while she explained the words to me, and told how he blessed little children."

When the bee has gathered all the honey that it can carry, it flies home.

Tacita's heart was full. She wanted no more that night.

But there was no timidity in her return. The place was walled in as by a host of angels. The fold of her mother's dress seemed yet within her grasp, and the flowing water was a song of peace.

The candle, burnt low, was where she had left it on the stair, and all was silent and deserted on the way up to her chamber.

CHAPTER X.

"You have taken the edge off the surprise I meant for you," Elena said when Tacita told her of her midnight walk. "But there still remains something to please you with its novelty. Go and see the Basilica. The door is open all day. You can go alone, and will enjoy it more so than with company. When you come back I will have your new room all ready for you. It is in front, over the great veranda, a little to the right."

"Shall I meet many people in the street?" Tacita asked.

"You will see very few; and they will all be on some business. We are an industrious community, and there is no one who has not something to do in the morning. It is only toward evening that we walk for pleasure."

"Will any one speak to me?"

"Probably not; but they will bow to you. You have only to bow and smile in return."

"Can I smile to everybody?"

"If the smile wants to come."

"Oh, Elena, that is the best of all!" Tacita exclaimed. "Sometimes I have met strangers whom it seemed impossible to pass without notice. Perhaps the person appeared to be in trouble, or was uncommonly *simpatica ;* or for the moment I happened to feel strongly that we are all 'poor banished children of Eve.' It was an affection that I cannot describe, as though it were heaven to sacrifice your life in order to save or console another. I gave, perhaps, a glance that rested a moment, or a faint — oh, so faint! — hint of a smile; and I was always pained and mortified, the person would look so surprised. It showed me plainly that the earth is indeed accursed when our kindest impulses are so misunderstood."

While speaking, she put on a new dress that Elena had brought her. It was a long robe of thin dark blue wool, bound at the waist by a silken sash, a lighter tint of the same color. The wide straight sleeves fell over the hands, or were turned back, such sleeves as may be gathered up under a brooch at the shoulder. A long scarf of the woolen gauze served to wrap the head and neck, if necessary. There were gloves of fine white kid and russet shoes with silver buckles.

Elena wore the same style of dress in gray.

"Gray is our working color," she explained. "Sometimes it is worn with leathern belts, or sashes of another color. Gray alone, or with black, or white, is mourning. White is our highest gala. The very old wear white always. It gives that look of cleanliness and freshness which age needs. The children are our butterflies. They wear gay colors. We never change the form of our dress. The only variation is in color and material. I think that you will scarcely find anything more graceful, modest, or convenient."

"It 's the prettiest dress I ever had," said Tacita. "And now — and now" —

They went down stairs and stepped out into the veranda, and the full splendor of what she had seen but in shadow burst upon Tacita's view.

There was every shape and shade of verdure, and every shape of barren rock and gleaming snow. There were mists of rose, blue, and gold that were flowers. There was every depth of shadow, from the tender veil as delicate as the shadow of eyelashes on the eye, to the rich dusk lurking beneath some wooded steep or overhanging crag. The houses were of a silvery gray, bright on the roofs with plants and awnings. Wherever there was water, it glittered. The façade of the Basilica was like snow, and its five windows blazed in the morning sun. The wavering path that threaded the gardens was yellow, and shone with some sparkling gravel.

Tacita leaned over the balustrade and looked right and left. At every turn some lovely picture presented itself.

"There is no one in the avenue," Elena said. "But the archways will be cooler."

Tacita chose the deserted avenue, and walked timidly, almost without raising her eyes, till the second bridge was passed, and the Basilica rose before her, standing out from a mass of dark rock that almost touched the tribune.

Nine steps of gray stone led up to the white balustrade. Within, at either side was a square of turf, thick and fine, separated and surrounded by a path of yellow gravel, sparkling with little garnets. Three white steps above led to the double door, now wide open. There were inscriptions on the fronts of the steps. The upper one bore in Latin that most perfect of all acts of thanksgiving, *We give thee thanks for thy great glory.* The vestibule was one third the width of the Basilica, two narrow side doors, unseen from the front, having vestibules of the same size. This was entirely unadorned, except by the two valves of the carved door of cedar and olive-wood shut back against the wall, and the shining folds of a white linen curtain shutting an inner arch of the same size.

Lifting the linen band that drew these folds aside, Tacita was confronted by another curtain, a purple brocade of silk and wool, heavily fringed.

She dropped the linen behind her, and stood cloistered between the two for a moment; then, lifting a purple fold, stood before a screen that seemed woven of sunshine. A gold-colored silk brocade with a bullion fringe that quivered with light closed the inner edge of the arch.

Two contrary impulses held a momentary soft and delightful conflict in her mind: an impatient desire to see what was beyond that veil, and a restraining desire to let imagination sketch one swift picture of what was so delicately guarded.

Then, holding her breath, she slipped past the scintillating fringes and stood in the nave.

Flooded with the morning sunshine, the place was as brilliant as a rainbow. Even the white marble footing of the walls, and the two lines of white marble columns, overhung with lilies instead of acanthus leaves, caught a sunny glow from that illumination. The walls, frescoed with landscapes of every clime, showed all the rich hues of nature. The blue ceiling sparkled with flecks of gold, there were golden texts on the white marble of the lower walls that condensed the whole story of Judaism and Christianity. On the pedestals of the ten lower columns were inscribed the Ten Commandments. The pavement of polished green porphyry reflected softly all this wealth of coloring, and as it approached the tribune was tinted like still waters at sunset. For the Basilica of San Salvador was simply the throne-room of its Divine King; and the throne was in the tribune.

A deep alcove rising to the roof was lined with a purple curtain like that of the portal; and raised against it, nine steps from the pavement, was a throne made of acacia wood covered with plates of wrought gold. From the arch above, where the purple drapery was gathered under the white outspread wings of a dove, suspended by golden chains so fine as to be almost invisible, hung a jeweled diadem that quivered with prismatic hues. The footstool before the throne was a block of alabaster; and on its front was inscribed in golden letters:

Come unto me, all ye that labor and are heavy laden, and I will give you rest.

The white marble steps were in groups of three, each surmounted by a low balustrade of alabaster hung with golden lilies between each snowy post. A broad purple-cushioned step surrounded the lower balustrade. Otherwise there was no seat nor resting-place but the pavement.

Tacita sank on her knees and gazed at that throne that shone full of sunshine, half expecting that the light would presently condense itself into the likeness of a Divine Face. The crown hung just where it might have rested on the brow of an heroic figure enthroned beneath. And was there not a quiver in the jewels as if they moved, catching and splintering the sunrays on diamond points, or drinking them in smooth rubies, or imprisoning their fluttering colors in white veiled opals, or showing in emeralds a promise of the immortal spring of Heaven! And was there not a whisper and a rustling as of a host preceding the advent of some supreme Presence?

She put aside her fancies, and made a heartfelt thanksgiving to him who was truly there, then rose and slowly approached the throne. The work was all beautiful. The fluting of the columns was exquisite, and every milk-white lily that was twined in their capitals was finished with a loving hand. On the fronts of the steps were names of prophets, apostles and saints, highest of all and alone, the name of Abraham surrounded by the words he spoke to his son, Isaac, as they went up the mountain in Moriah: —

My son, God will provide himself a lamb for a burnt-offering.

Lower down were names of beneficent gods and goddesses, all names which the children of men had lovingly and reverently worshiped, each light-bearing god or goddess with a star to his name.

Tacita remembered her grandfather's declaration: "Show me the path by which any human soul has climbed to worship the highest that it could conceive of the Divine, and I will see there the footsteps of God coming down to meet that soul."

Her heart expanded at the thought. It seemed the very spirit of the Good Shepherd gathering all into his fold — all who lifted up their hearts in search of something above their comprehension, but not above their love.

With a deep sigh of utter contentment she turned aside, and walked down one aisle and up the other, looking at the frescoes.

The wall of the three vestibules extended quite across the Basilica with a wide gallery above; and from the golden fringe of the portal to the purple fringe of the apsis, one scene melted into another with such artful gradations that there was no break in the picture; and all ended against the ceiling in mountain, or tree-top, or vine, or in a flock of birds, so that it did not seem an ending.

A glimpse of polar sea with an aurora of the north and icebergs began the panorama; and then came full streams overhung by dark pine-trees that presently showed green mosses and springing delicate flowers under their shadows. The scene softened, and grew yet softer, till a palm-tree was over-brushed by the purple curtain of the apse, and a line of silvery beach, and a glimpse of sea and of a far-away misty sun-steeped island just escaped its folds. There were sunsets shining through forest-reaches, brooks dancing over stones, the curve of a river, the violet outline of a mountain faint against the sky, lambs sunk in a green flowery meadow and half submerged, looking like scattered pearls. There were gray streaks of rain, and a glimpse of a rainbow; there was sunrise over bald crags where an eagle stood black against its opal background. The butterfly fanned its capricious way with widespread wings, the bee and humming-bird dived into the flower, the stag stood listening with head alert, the elephant pulled down the fruit-laden branches, the dragon-fly spread its gauzy wings; but nowhere was there any sign of man, nor of the works of man.

From one aisle to the other Tacita went, wondering more and more of what famous artist this could have been the crowning work. From the portal at both sides the scenes were arctic; but their procession was infinitely varied. The small doors entering from the sides were scarcely visible in rocks and arching trees. A heavy grapevine climbing to hang along the ceiling seemed to hide all but the tiny cove of a pond spotted with lilies, amid which floated a pair of swans.

At the left side, burning the jungle from which

he issued, a tiger stood and stared intently at the Throne.

But in all there was no sign of man, nor of the works of man.

When Tacita reached the Arcade on her return, Elena was waiting for her at the lower entrance, and uttered an interrogative "Well?"

"I have no words! Don't ask me about the Basilica. I met some people coming back. How well they stand and walk. Standing and walking must be taught here. Every one understands it so well. I kissed my fingers to a little girl, and she came and touched my girdle, then brushed her fingers across her lips, and ran away again before I could stop her. Oh, it is all so lovely!"

They went up to a pleasant chamber that looked across the town. "This is your room, dear," Elena said. "The dining-room is just across the corridor. We will have our dinner at our own little table before the school-girls come in; and you can be served in your own room any time you like. It is but a step more to take. And here is the salon, just beside you. It is but little used; for except when a stranger comes, we do not visit in San Salvador. Our houses are for our private life. We meet frequently, may meet almost every evening at the assembly-room in the Star-house; and as it is open every day, and there are a good many nooks and corners there beside the chief rooms, there is always a place for a tête-à-tête, or a little company. But some people will come here to see you.

You will like to make some acquaintances before going to the assembly. I hope that you may feel rested enough to go to-morrow night."

The salon was simply furnished, and had no need of other ornament than the view seen from its windows. There was a single picture on the wall, representing a young woman of a noble figure standing erect, her arms hanging at her sides, and one hand holding a scroll. She wore the costume of San Salvador of a tawny brown with yellow sash and scarf. Under one foot, slightly advanced, lay a Cupid sprawling face downward, the fragments of his bow and arrows scattered about. The face was of a somewhat full oval, olive-tinted, with heavy black hair drawn back from the temples, a delicate rose-color in the cheeks, and sweet red lips. The large dark eyes looked straight out with a lofty and thoughtful expression. The whole figure was instinct with a fine animal life, such life as sustains a strong soul full of feeling and intelligence. All the curves of the face were tender; but they were contradicted by an assumption of reserve almost too severe for beauty. It was the picture of a loving nature that had renounced love.

"That is our Iona," Elena said. "She is the Directress of the girls' school, and she is the women's tribune. All classes have with us their tribune, or advocate. Iona has traveled and studied in both continents. She has advanced so far in astronomy that she teaches it even in the boys' school. Would you like to have her teach you our language? She has offered herself as your teacher."

"If she will take the trouble, I shall feel honored. What a noble-looking creature! Is she a native of San Salvador?"

"Yes; and she has a brother here who has never been outside. Ion is one of the cleverest boys we have. Their parents died when they were very young."

Later, when they had eaten their dinner, and Tacita was alone, there was a tap at the door, and she rose to meet the original of the portrait. Iona had tapped with her ivory tablets, and was pushing them into the folds of her sash as she entered.

There was something electric in the instant during which the two paused and looked at each other without speaking. Then Iona stepped forward, gentle, but unsmiling, laid a hand on Tacita's arm, and, bending, kissed her lightly on the forehead.

"You are welcome to San Salvador!" she said with deliberation, in a melodious, bell-like voice. "I hope that you will be contented here. Does the place please you?"

"I am enchanted!" Tacita said. "I ask myself continually if I have not found the long-lost garden of Eden."

The two contemplated each other with something more than curiosity. Tacita was conscious of a certain restraint and something akin to disappointment while talking with this woman, who was even more beautiful than her portrait. The form, the teeth, the mass of hair were the most superb that she had ever seen; and though the skin was dark, every faintest wave of color was visible through it. While she talked, the color deepened in her cheeks till she glowed like a rose.

The blue dress with its silver clasps might have been too trying to her olive skin but for this lovely blush.

Iona proposed herself courteously as teacher, and Tacita thankfully accepted, offering herself in return for any service she might be able to perform.

"Be quite at ease!" her visitor replied, not unkindly. "You will soon have an opportunity. I have already thought that you might be willing to assist in the Italian classes. You speak the language beautifully. But for some time yet you will have employment enough in seeing the place and becoming acquainted with the people and their customs. Of course Elena has already told you that there need be no restraint on your wanderings. Every one you meet will be a friend, whether he can tell you so or not. The language most useful to you will be French, though there is scarcely a language, living or dead, which some one here does not speak."

Tacita begged to know something of the government of San Salvador.

"We have a few general principles which give form to every detail," Iona said. "For personal disorders in the young, parents and teachers are held responsible; for any social disorder, our rulers are held responsible. Probably, all blame is finally laid on the father and mother, and more especially on the mother. The training of the child is held to be of supreme importance, and there is no more dignified occupation. We say, 'The mother of children is the mother of the state.' No diseased or deformed person is allowed to have children. You will not hear any mother in San Salvador complain of her child as having a bad temper, or evil dispositions. She would be told that the child was what she made it.

"The children stay at home till they are about four years of age. Then their whole day is spent at school, where all their meals are taken. The mothers take their turns, all who have not infants, as matrons of the schools, a week at a time. Their sole duty is to see that the food is good and sufficient, that the little ones have their nap, and that their health is thought of. I suppose you know that we have public kitchens where all the cooking is done. The kitchen for the children is by itself, and so is that for the sick. Here also the ladies serve their week in a year or thereabout, as matrons. They make the bill of fare, and have an eye to the sending out of all but the food for the children and the sick, these having their special matrons.

"We do not lay much stress on the form of a government. The important thing is personal character. A republic may be made the worst of tyrannies; and an absolute monarchy might be beneficent, though the experiment would be a dangerous one. The duty of a government is to obey the laws and compel everybody else to obey them. That is literal. We have no sophistries about it. Of course, Dylar is our chief, and in some sense he is absolute. Yet no one governs less than he. We take care of the individual, and the state takes care of itself. Moreover, the Dylar have always been the first to scrupulously obey our laws and observe our customs. There is a council of elders; Professor Pearlstein is president. No one under sixty years of age is eligible. Each class has a tribune chosen by itself. I hold a sinecure as tribune for the women. I fancy" — looking at her companion with a smile of sudden sweetness — "that you may be our long looked for tribune for the children."

"Surely it should be a mother to hold that office," Tacita said.

"Think a moment!" said Iona, her smiling eyes lingering on the sweet face.

"It is true," said Tacita slowly. "Parents do not always understand their own children."

"They are sometimes cruel to them when they think themselves kind," Iona said with energy. "They sometimes ruin their lives by their partiality. They sometimes tread as with the hoofs of a beast on the feelings of the most sensitive of their flock. How often are children mute! The finer they are, the more isolated are their puzzled and often grieving souls. They sometimes suffer an immense injustice without being able to right themselves, or even to complain; and this injustice may leave them morally lame for life. Children should be shielded from pain even as you shield a young plant from the storm. When the fibres of both are knit, then give them storm as well as sunshine."

"I see that the boys and girls are kept apart both in their education and socially," Tacita remarked. "I have heard that point discussed outside."

"It will never be discussed here," said Iona with decision. "All have equal opportunities; but they do not have them in common. The result justifies the rule. When the boys and girls approach a marriageable age they are allowed a free intercourse and free choice. In questions concerning the honor of the state we have no theorizing; and the state has as much interest in the child as the parent has. It has more. The parent suffers from the sin, or gains by the honor of his child for but a few years; the state may suffer or profit from the same cause for centuries. Besides, a well-organized and orderly government is of more importance to the well-being of every individual than any other individual can be. The love of no individual can console a man in the midst of anarchy, or when he is the victim of a tyrant. You have to thank your parents for human life, if you hold it a boon; and you have to thank your government for making that life secure and free."

"And if you have not security and your reasonable degree of freedom?" asked Tacita.

"Then the greater number of your people are bad, and the few have an opportunity to be heroic."

"My grandfather had no respect for the opinions of majorities," Tacita said. "He said that out of a thousand persons it was quite possible that one might be right and nine hundred and ninety-nine wrong. He said that the history of the world is a history of individuals."

As Iona rose to go, the door opened, and Elena came in followed by Dylar.

Tacita went with some agitation to meet this man, who was still, to her, a mystery. Nor was he less a mystery when she found him simply a dignified and agreeable gentleman, with nothing strange about him but his costume of dark blue cloth, a sort of cashmere of silk and wool, soft and softly tinted. It was made in the Scottish, or oriental fashion, with a tunic to the knee and a silken sash of the same color. He wore long hose of black silk, silver buckles to his shoes, and on his turban-shaped cap, made of the same blue cloth, was a silver band, closed at the left side by a clasp of a strange design. A hand pointing upward with all its fingers was set inside of a triangle that was inclosed in a winged circle.

Seeing Tacita's glance touch this symbol more than once, Dylar explained it. "We have all some badge, according to our occupation," he said. "The hand is manual labor. I am a carpenter, and have served my apprenticeship, though I seldom do any work. The triangle is scientific study, and the winged circle is a messenger. All those who, having their home here, go out on our errands, wear this winged circlet. It is the only badge I really earn; but I wear the three as Director of all."

"I hope that I may be allowed to earn one," Tacita said, trying to settle her mind into a medium position between the strange romance of her first impressions of this man and the not unfamiliar reality of their present meeting. The penetrating eyes were there; but they only glanced at her kindly, and did not dwell. A slight smile, full of friendliness, illumined his face as he spoke to her; but between it and her there floated a shadow-face, having the same outlines and colors, but fixed in a gaze of intense and self-forgetful study.

"I am not clairvoyant," he said presently, his eyes laughing; "but I fancy that your thought has made a flight to Madrid during the last few minutes."

"Could I help it?" she said blushing. "I could not venture to ask; but" —

"You can ask anything!" Dylar said. "If you show no curiosity, I shall think you indifferent. I am told that the resemblance is striking. Of course I cannot judge. The original of that portrait was the founder of San Salvador, and a Dylar, my ancestor. But, my lady, I had already seen something more than a picture resembling you when we met in Madrid. I had seen yourself, not alone in Venice, but years before, in Naples. You spoke to me. Do you remember?"

"Oh! I could not have looked at you and forgotten," she answered with conviction.

"Pardon! You looked and spoke. And you gave me an alms."

He searched in the folds of his sash for a coin, and showed it to her. It was an Italian *baiocco* polished till it looked like gold.

"You went to Naples ten years ago with your mother and grandfather," Dylar said. "You visited the Museum. Two men were seated side by side on the steps as you went up, a young and an old man; and the old man stretched his hand out for alms. Your mother gave him something. The young man did not ask, but you gave him this *baiocco*, and you said, 'My brother, I am sorry that it is not more.'"

For a moment she could not speak. Then she said, —

"I was taught to call the poor brother and sister. I could not know that I was taking a liberty."

"The liberty of heaven!" said Dylar. "Well! I thought that you would come here some day. And you are here!"

He rose, looking down, as if to temper somewhat the joyousness of his exclamation.

"Ask all the questions you choose," he said. "Do in all things as if you were in your father's house. Farewell, till we meet again."

CHAPTER XI.

ALL the social life of San Salvador centred in the Star-house, or assembly rooms, in the Square. This was open at all times to all classes, with certain restrictions. No one should go there in a working dress, nor except by appointment to meet some one, nor when any other convenient rendezvous was available, and no one should enter a room already occupied. It was on no account to be used as a lounging place. The result of these regulations was that all but the library and reading-room were usually deserted by day.

The lower floor was the music and dance room, and was so constructed, the floor being supported entirely from beneath, and detached from the walls, that no jar was communicated to the rooms above. The only vestibule to this room, entered directly from the Square, was that formed by the pillars supporting the protruding angle of the story above. Inside, the corner opposite the door was railed off and raised for an orchestra. The angle at the right was curtained off for a dressing-room, and the third, entered from the outside, contained the stairway. The two upper floors were divided in nearly the same way; a large, hexagonal room with a supporting cluster of columns in the centre, and three small rooms walled or curtained off in the angles, one containing a staircase.

The salon on the second floor was reserved for conversation, the third floor was a library and reading-room, and there was a terrace on the roof.

The structure was solidly built, and, for the greater part, very plainly finished. There was a cluster of columns in the centre of the two upper rooms inclosing a slender fountain jet in a high basin. The lights were all placed around these columns, and from each of them an arch vaulted to a pilaster in each of the six angles of the room. In the upper floor the walls were covered with book-cases, in the lower they were tinted a dark red with a fresco in each side of a Muse or dancer.

The partitioned angles were draped with curtains colored like the walls.

The second floor, the salon *par excellence*, was more brilliant. The walls were lined with small faceted blocks of white glass set in an amber-colored cement, the curtains of the angles were of amber-colored silk, the chairs, divans, sofas, and *amorini* were covered with an amber-colored linen that looked like satin, the floor was of small alternating amber and dark green tiles, the heavy rugs were amber colored. It was a room all light, except the dark green divan that surrounded the cluster of pillars.

These rooms were lighted till ten o'clock every evening but Sunday, and were free to all; but the inevitable law of selection had made it a tacit custom for certain persons to go on certain evenings. To meet a stranger, it was considered proper to give place to those who had been outside.

Elena brought out a beautiful lace dress that Tacita's mother had left behind her on going out into the world. It was of pillow lace woven in stripes, and made over a soft silk in broad stripes of rose and cream-color. Dressed in it, Tacita looked like a blush rose.

They set out for her first assembly at early twilight. Lights in the houses showed them the way, there was a sound of violins in the dewy air, and figures flitting in the dance-room, and outside a number of persons were dancing gayly in the light that shone from the building.

"Our people are much given to dancing," Elena said. "And we have the most beautiful and complex fancy dances in the world."

They went up a winding stair, that started in a lower angle and ended in a terrace, from which a wide arched door opened into the salon, showing the glittering walls, the full light, the tossing fountain in its lightly shadowed seclusion, the silken curtain of the opposite boudoir, and a company almost filling the room.

The music came softened from below, allowing the voices to be heard.

Dylar and Iona met the two as they entered, and Tacita found herself in the midst of the most cultivated and charming company she had ever seen. But for their costume, they would not at first have seemed different from any other gathering of well-bred people who meet with pleasure a welcome guest; but the stranger soon felt in their greeting the difference between mere courtesy and sincere affection. It was a repetition of the heart-warming phrase that told her she was "in her father's house."

The costumes gave an air of romance and unreality to the scene. As Tacita looked about with a pleased wonder, these figures suggested Arcadian groves, Olympian slopes, or some old palace garden shut in by high walls, with fragrant hedges of laurel and myrtle over-showered by roses, with a blush of oleanders against a mossy fountain, the dim stars of a passion-vine hung over a sequestered arbor, and crumbling forms of nymphs, lichen-spotted in the sunshine. These figures would have harmonized with such scenes perfectly.

On the green velvet divan sat several old men and women who wore long white robes of fine wool with silken girdles. All the younger ladies wore the same straight robe, made in various colors, with silken fringed sashes, and fine lace at the neck and wrists. Some wore lace robes like Tacita's. A few had strings of pearls; but no other jewels were visible.

The gentlemen, on the contrary, seemed much more gayly dressed than in any other modern society. Their costumes were all rather dark in color and without ornament; but the silver buckles on their shoes and the silver badge on the turban cap which each one carried in his hand, or under his arm, brightened the effect, and they all wore lace ruffles at the wrists and laced cravats. Dylar wore violet color, and a silver fillet round his cap.

Of the more than a hundred persons present, all but the youngest had been outside, and spoke other languages than their own. Some were natives of San Salvador living outside, and returned but for a time. Tacita found herself charmingly at home with them.

After a while Dylar drew her apart, and they seated themselves in a boudoir.

"You will observe the absence of jewels in our dress," he said. "This is only our ordinary way of meeting; but there is no occasion on which gems are worn here as elsewhere. With us they have a meaning. Diamonds are consecrated to the Basilica. Other stones are used as decorations for some distinguished act or acquirement. The ruby is for an act of heroic courage, the topaz for discovery, the emerald for invention. Pearls are worn only by young girls and by brides at their wedding. When you marry, we will hang pearls on you in a snow-drift."

He bent a little and smiled into her face.

Tacita blushed, but made no reply immediately. A feeling of melancholy settled upon her. Could it be that she would be expected to marry? — and that he would wish to select a husband for her?

"Elena does not marry, and Iona is not yet married," she said after a silence.

"Oh, there is perfect freedom," said Dylar. "But Iona is only twenty-six and Elena scarcely over forty years of age. Both may marry yet. Now there is a gentleman coming in who wishes very much to see you. He has just come from England, and will return in a few days. Shall I call him?"

She consented cordially, and Dylar beckoned the young man to them, and having presented him, retired and left the two together. A moment later she saw him go out with Iona by the way leading upstairs. They were going either to the library or terrace.

How well they looked together, though Iona was almost as tall as Dylar. She wore amber-color that evening, which became her, and her cheeks were crimson, her eyes brilliant. For a little while Tacita had some difficulty in attending to what her new companion was saying, and in making the proper replies. Then something in his manner pleased her, and drew her from her abstraction.

He was simply a well-bred young Englishman in a sort of masquerade, which, however, became him wonderfully. He had hair as golden as her own, and he wore dark blue. While talking with him, Tacita, woman-like, looked at the wide lace ruffle that fell back on his sleeve. It had a ground of fairy lightness, a *vrai reseau* as strong as it was light, with little wide-winged swallows all over it in a fine close *tela*, with a few open stitches in the head and wings. She wondered where she had read of swallows that

> —"hawked the bright flies in the hollows
> Of delicate air."

"You are admiring my ruffles," the young man said with the greatest frankness. "They were made here, and belonged to my father. I have refused a good deal of money for them. Of course you have learned that they make beautiful lace here. I think it the finest lace made in the world, taking it all in all. Look at that dress of yours, now. How firm and clear it is! That's pillow lace, though, and this is point. There's a kind of cobweb ground to some rare Alençon point that is wonderful as work; but you don't dare to touch it. I've seen a fine *jabot* belonging to one of the Bonaparte princes, and worn by him at a royal marriage. You'll sometimes see as good a border of medallions as that had, but not such a centre, lighter than blonde. It was scattered over with bees that had only alighted. Each wing was a little buttonhole-stitched loop with a tiny open star inside. As a *jabot* it could be worn; but as ruffles, you would have to keep your hands clasped together over the top of your head."

The young man proposed after a while that they should go up and see the library, and Tacita somewhat shrinkingly consented.

"If Dylar should be there, I hope he will not believe that I followed him!" she thought.

He was not there. The large room was quiet and deserted. Shaded lamps burned on the green-covered tables, folds of green silk were drawn back from two lofty windows closed only with casements of wire gauze. Globes, stands of maps, movable book-rests, and cases of books of reference were all about. From the stairway and through the open windows the hum of conversation came softened to a hum of bees, the sound of viols from the dance-room was a quivering web of silver, and the feet of the dancers did not make the least tremor in the firmly set walls.

"The library is not a very large one, you see," said Tacita's guide. "It is nearly as much weeded as added to. It is surprising how much literature thought to be original is found out to be only a turn of the kaleidoscope. I won't quote Solomon to you."

"My grandfather," Tacita said, "used to say that one folio would contain all the thoughts of mankind that are worth preserving, and ten all the commentaries worth making on them."

"This is the way they condense here," said her companion. "For necessarily San Salvador must be a city of abridgments. Say that ten authors write on some one subject worthy of attention. The best one is selected and then interleaved with extracts from the others. To this is added a brief notice of the authors quoted. It 's a good deal of work for one person to do; but it saves the time of everybody else who has to read on the subject."

Returning to the Salon they found that Dylar and Iona had come down from the terrace, and some boys were carrying about cups of a pleasant drink that seemed to be milk boiled, sweetened, and delicately spiced.

"Iona must take you up to-morrow night to look at Venus," Dylar said. "It is very beautiful now."

The bells rang ten o'clock, the signal for going home, and they went down stairs. Dylar took leave at the door; but the young Englishman asked permission to accompany Tacita and Elena to their door. The music had ceased in the dance-room, and the lights were half extinguished; but the last couples came out still dancing, humming a tune, and, hand in hand, danced homeward.

"You will like to see our fancy dances," Elena said. "Some of them are very dramatic. There is a good deal of grace and precision in them, but no parade of agility. I know nothing more disgusting than the flesh and muscle exhibition of the ordinary *ballet*. Some of our dances require quite as much command of muscle, but there must be no effect of effort. To see a woman gracefully draped float like a cloud is quite as wonderful as to see her half naked and leaping like a frog. We have a Sun-dance, with the whole solar system; and I assure you the moons have to be as nimble-footed as the *chulos* of a bull-fight. The Zodiac dance is more like a minuet in time. There are twelve groups which keep always the same position with regard to each other; but the whole circle slowly revolves, having two motions, one progressive. It is a science, and requires a good deal of practice. Iona used to be the lost Pleiad, and wandered about veiled, threading the whole maze, but never finding her place. Of course all are in costume; and it is an out-door dance, occupying the whole Square. Her part was like some little thing of Chopin's, plaintive, searching, and unanswered."

When the two had gone up stairs, Elena said: "Do you think that you would ever be willing to marry the young man who came home with us to-night?"

"Oh, no!" Tacita exclaimed. "What should put it into your mind?"

"He wished me to ask you. I thought that it was vain; but I promised to ask. If there is the least chance, he will stay longer. If not, he will go to-morrow. He has long known you by reputation, and he admired you at sight."

"There is not the least chance," Tacita said decidedly, and wondered why she should feel so angry and pained.

CHAPTER XII.

THE next day they went to visit the girls' school.

The Arcade was built around and above a promontory of rock, the stories following it in receding terraces, and the wings following backward at either side, so that the effect from a little distance was that of an irregular pyramid with a truncated top.

There was a narrow vale and a green slope behind one side, where the children played on that first evening of Tacita's in San Salvador; and here they had their gardens cultivated by themselves, their out-door studies and recitation-rooms and play-ground. Thick walls, sewing-rooms, quiet study-rooms, and rooms where the little ones had their midday nap interposed to keep every sound of this army of girls from that part of the building used as a hotel, or home, for single ladies.

Going from her quiet apartment to that full and busy hive was to Tacita like going into another world. In its crowd and bustle and variety it was more like the outside world than anything that she had yet seen.

In one room two or three children were lying in hammocks asleep. Out on the green a group of them seated on a carpet were picking painted letter-blocks out of a heap, and discussing their names. A girl a few years older, sitting near them with her sewing, corrected their mistakes. One lovely girl had a little one on her knee who was reading a pictured story-book aloud. A larger girl sat apart writing a composition, dragging out her thoughts with contortions, like a Pythoness on her tripod. In some rooms were young ladies engaged in study, writing, or recitation. There was a printing-room, with type-setters and proof-readers, where one of the girls gave Tacita a little book of their printing and binding.

Everywhere were texts and proverbs on the walls and doors, white letters on a blue ground; and there was a throne-room where the little gilded chair was filled with flowers for the children's infant king. Underneath was a picture of the three Magi kneeling to the Child Jesus. This was in a little temple on the hillside with a laburnum-tree bending over it full of golden flower-tassels.

"When they have acquired the rudiments of learning," Iona said, "we give them a touch all round, almost as if without meaning it, to find the keynote of their powers. It is done chiefly by lectures. Ladies and gentlemen who have read much, or traveled much, write short essays which they read in school. If no child shows a special interest in the subject, we let it go. Our object is to give talent an opportunity, and also to waste no time and effort where they will meet with no return.

"All the accounts of the town are kept in the

schools, and well kept. It saves a great deal of work. The kitchen accounts, for instance, are immense and complicated; yet they are gleefully and painstakingly smoothed into order by those busy young brains and fingers. Promotion from one class of these accounts to another is taken great pride in. For instance, the girl who is 'in the salt,' as they say, looks with admiring envy on the girl who is in the wheat, the fruit, or the meat. They are also taught to cook a few simple dishes. For that they go to the kitchens. They all dress alike, as you see, and there is no difference made in any way. Even the genius, if we find one, is not taught to set her gift above that of the most homely usefulness."

As the visitors went away, a golden-haired girl of ten or twelve years shyly offered Tacita a white rose half opened, touched the fringes of her sash with timid finger-tips and touched the fingers to her lips.

Her delicate homage was rewarded with a kiss on the forehead. And, "Please tell me your name, dear child!" said Tacita.

The little girl blushed all over her face with a modest delight, as she whispered "Leila!"

"My recollections of school are all pleasant, with the exception of a few sharp lessons given me there," Elena said. "I well remember one I received from Dylar the Eighth, father of our Dylar. I was one day sent on an errand which obliged me to go through the large dining-room where we eat now, and I saw a magnificent peach there on the sideboard. I could not know that it was the first and finest of a rare sort, and that Dylar himself, who was in another part of the house, had left it there in passing, and was coming again to take it out for exhibition. But I did know that we were never to help ourselves to anything to eat without permission, and that I had no right ever to take anything there. The peach tempted me, and I did eat. I was looking about for some place where I might hide the stone, when the Prince returned. He went at once to the sideboard, then turned and looked at me. No words were needed to show my guilt. I stood speechless in an agony of shame.

"The Prince looked at me one awful moment in silence. Then he took me by the hand quite gently, and led me to the room that has the commandments of God on the walls, and pointed to the words, 'Thou shalt not steal.'

"He stood a moment beside me while I trembled, and began to sob, then laid his hand, so gently, on my head, and went away without a word. My dear, it was the most effective sermon I ever heard. You observe there was no sophistry used. It was *stealing*. It was many a long day before I could eat a peach without feeling as if I had swallowed the stone.

"The next time the Prince came, I ran weeping to kiss the fringe of his sash, and he kissed my cheek, and whispered, 'Don't grieve so, little one!

Forget all about it!' From that day to this I loved Dylar above all earthly things. He was forty years old and I was ten; yet he was the one man in the world to me from that day."

While talking they had gone out, and were walking northward in the outside road on their way to see the kitchens. It was a paved street of very irregular width. One side was bounded by the straight line of the river parapet. The other, narrowed to ten feet in width between the Arcade and the bridge, widened sometimes to a rod or two. And everywhere above were gardens, cottages, steep paths and stairs, down-falling streams and trees single, or grouped, or scattered.

In one of the amphitheatres thus formed was a semicircle of small shops, each with a wide awning covering an outside counter. The goods were kept inside, and brought out as called for. A man or woman sat under the awning before each shop. One was knitting, another was making pillow lace; the man was making netting, and having but his right hand, the peg had been fastened to his left wrist, and he threw the cord in position for the knot as rapidly as if the air were fingers to hold it.

The kitchens were set high above the plain on the eastern side of a deep ravine running northward. Long buildings of only one story with attics were surrounded by orchards, gardens, and poultry-yards. There was a laundry, and countless lines of clothes out in the sun. There was a bakery. Beneath these buildings were the wine-caves, and the rooms for pressing the grapes. Farther up, on a rapid stream that came down and disappeared under the pavement, was a little mill.

"It looks small," Elena said; "but all the wool that makes our dresses is woven there. Our silk webs we bring from outside, though we have a small silk farm; but we raise all our own wool. The silk we use for sashes and for hosiery. We send out silk hose, lace, and carved olive-wood.

"And now, my dear, you are to see the folly of individual domestic cooking, and the wisdom of having public kitchens, if they are properly conducted. And at this moment you see coming to meet us one of the chief supports of our system. If we had not a lady of good taste and administrative capacity to matronize our kitchens, they might deteriorate, or fail. If even such a lady were always there, she might sometimes grow weary and careless; but with a short term for each, there is always the sense of novelty and emulation to keep them up to the mark."

It was a very pleasant presentation of a lady who stood in the door to receive them, with a square of white net tied, turban-wise, around her head, and a snowy bib-apron over her cotton dress.

"You do not remember me," she said, smiling at Tacita's intent gaze. "No wonder. You saw so many strangers last night. Besides, my hair was not covered then, and I wore a silk dress."

It was one of the most accomplished ladies whom she had met at the assembly.

They went through the buildings that constituted almost a village. It was the very paradise of a cooking colony, in plenty, order, and cleanliness. There were no silver saucepans tied with rose-colored ribbons; but Marie Antoinette might have gone there and made a cup of chocolate or cooked an omelette, without soiling her fair fingers, or her dainty high-heeled shoes.

The economy, too, was perfect. There were central roasting fires on elevated hearths, with a tunnel-shaped sheet-iron chimney let down over them where a circle of tin kitchens and spits could surround them, losing no heat; and there were lines of charcoal furnaces set in tiles under great sheet-iron hoods.

"We do not waste a bit of coal as large as a walnut, nor a twig of wood that a bird could alight on," the Directress said. "For the food, not the least important part of our establishment is the fragment kitchen."

"Elena, when shall I come and learn to cook something?" Tacita asked as they went away.

Her friend laughed. "You find it fascinating, then! I shall have to make you begin at school. You did not see the preparatory department there. It is a sight, when they are busy for an hour every morning, chopping meat, picking raisins, husking corn, shelling peas, picking over coffee or rice, doing, in short, any preparatory work that the cooks might need. Sometimes they have half an hour of such work in the afternoon. It would, perhaps, interest you more than to see them at their books."

"I have often thought," Tacita said, "that if we could sometimes stop and watch the artisan at his work, we might find it interesting. They know so many things that the idle do not suspect. I especially like builders of houses and monuments. There is so much of poetry and religion in their work."

"The artists who painted the *affrescos* in the Basilica learned cooking first," Elena said. "It is recorded of them that they were very promising cooks, and came near spending their lives in the kitchens. One day a gentleman observed them arranging some fruit and vegetables with a very artistic sense of color, and one of them showed him a butterfly he had painted with vegetable juices and bits of mica. One thing led to another. Paint-boxes and paper were given them, and they took fire. They were sent out to study. The landscape painter had a fame in the world, and died there. The one who painted the insects, flowers, and animals, returned to San Salvador after a few years, and never went away again. He taught here. The schools were then started. Did you see the ant-hill in those frescos? It is in the lower left corner, just above Solomon's text: 'Go to the ant, thou sluggard!' An acanthus leaf half covers it. But there are the little grains of sand perfect, and the ants running with their building materials. In one place two ants are carrying a stick, one at each end of it. It is a little gem. They recorded of this man that it was his delight to search out microscopic beauties that no one else had seen. One said that he could intoxicate himself with a drop of dew. Ah, how many a Psyche of beautiful wings withers away in a dull imprisonment because no Love has sought her out! It does not even know why it suffers, nor what it wants. What an escape little Giotto had! What would have been his after-life if Cimabue had not paused to see what the shepherd boy had drawn with chalk on that rough piece of slate!"

"Only a little before coming here," Tacita said, "I came upon a sentence in a book regarding Giotto and the little church of Santa Maria dell' Arena, of which he was both architect and painter. The writer said: 'Dante lodged with Giotto while the works were in progress.' Dante lodged with Giotto! If I had been there, I would have put rose-petals inside their pillow-cases. I once saw an old picture with a portrait of Giotto in it. He was dark-haired and bright-eyed, and he was dressed all in white and gold, with a hooded mantle. The hood was up over his head, showing only a profile. He looked like a rose, and seemed full of spirit and gladness. I hope that the picture was authentic."

"Yes," said Elena with a sigh, "give them rose-petals, those whom the world showers with laurel. It is well. They also need sympathy. But my thought turns ever backward to the uncrowned, the unpraised! My dear, I have gone among the unknown of many lands, and I have found among them such vision-seeing pathetic eyes in persons whose lives were condemned to the commonplace and the material that I hold him who can express himself at his best to his fellow-man to be happy, even if he has to die for it. True, to the second sight, there is much of beauty in common things. But a person born with an ideal sense of beauty, and a vague longing to be, or to enjoy something excellent, naturally does not look for it in poverty and ignorance. Let us observe our contemporaries, my dear. Perhaps we may discover where we least expect it the motionless eyeballs of some imprisoned and disguised immortal. How happy we, if ours should be the first voice to hail such with an Ave!"

When Tacita was alone, she examined the little book given her at the school. It was only a behavior book for the pupils; but it contained some rules not found elsewhere.

"When you are in the street, do not stop to speak to any one you may meet without an errand which makes it necessary, if it should be before supper, and do not stop at all unless your first movement toward the person should be responded to with an appearance of welcome.

"Do not go to any person's house unless an errand compel you to; go and then, your business done promptly, take leave at once, but without hurrying, even if invited to stay.

"If at the assembly you see two or more persons conversing apart, do not approach them unless called, nor look at them as if expecting a call. It is proper to pass them without saluting. Never approach an alcove which is occupied.

"When kissing the sash of one whom you wish to salute, be sure that your hands are quite clean, and then touch only the fringe, which is easily renewed. To touch the fringe and then carry your fingers to your lips would be better."

A page called "The Five Classes" reminded the reader somewhat in its style of that high-minded and gentlemanly, if rather Turveydropish philosopher, Confucius: —

"1. We begin our studies by acknowledging that our teachers know more than we, and that we have much to learn; and then we have the wisdom of our age, and may be agreeable to the well-instructed.

"2. We acquire the rudiments of a few studies, and begin to think that we may soon know a great deal; and we are still tolerable to the well-instructed.

"3. We progress till we have a superficial knowledge of several subjects; and then we are liable to think ourselves so wise that we become disgusting to the well-instructed.

"4. We go a great deal farther, and if we have good sense, we perceive our own ignorance, and are ashamed of our past presumption; and then we begin to win the respect of the well-instructed.

"5. We progress farther and deeper, studying with modesty and assiduity; and after many years we learn that there is an ocean of wisdom to which all that we could acquire in a thousand years is as a drop of water; and then we are ourselves on the road to be one of the well-instructed."

"It is n't a useless lesson for any one to commit to memory," she thought, closing the book.

CHAPTER XIII.

"It would be a great help to me if I could hear the language spoken in a longer discourse, so as to get the swing of it," Tacita said one day to Iona, after having taken a lesson of her. "In conversation all my attention is occupied in listening to the sound of the words, and thinking of their meaning."

"You can have to-morrow just what you want," her teacher said. "Some of the college boys go up to Professor Pearlstein's cottage with their compositions. He criticises both style and thought. Some of the compositions, if not all, will be in San Salvadorian. They will go up at eight o'clock in the morning. When you see them come across the town, follow them. You can do so freely. My brother Ion is one of the boys; and I sometimes go up to hear them. The cottage is a little above the Arcade, toward the north, and has a red roof. Half way up, the pathway branches. Turn to the right, and you will come to a little boudoir in the rocks from which you can hear perfectly."

The next morning, therefore, Tacita followed the boys as directed, and presently found herself in a charming mossy nook with a roof, and a thick grapevine hanging between her and the little terrace where the professor sat before his cottage door with half a dozen boys in a semicircle before him.

Professor Pearlstein was a striking figure. His handsome face was calm and pallid, his hair and beard were white; and he wore a long robe of white wool with a scarlet sash, and a scarlet skull-cap like a cardinal's. He was carefully dressed, even to the scarlet straps of his russet sandals; and an air of peace and orderliness hung like a perfume about him and his small domain.

Tacita, screened by her vine-leaves, listened for half an hour, eager to catch the thoughts through the veil of this beautiful language which was so sonorous and so musical, and was spoken with little motions of head, throat, and shoulders, like a singing bird.

Then a boy addressed his master in French.

"I considered the ways of a tree," he said, holding his manuscript in hand, but without looking at it. "As soon as the seed wakes, it sends out two shoots. One goes down into the dark earth, seeking to fix itself firmly and find nourishment. The other rises into the light, putting up two little leaves, like praying hands, laid palm to palm. The root searches in that chemical laboratory, which is the earth, and is itself a chemist, and the tree sucks up its ichor, and increases. The tree also searches for food and color in sun and air. The root feels the ever increasing weight which rests upon it, and clings hard to rocks, and strikes deeper when it feels the strain of a storm in its fibres. It does not know what the sun is, except as an unknown power that sends a gentle warmth down into the dark, and calls its juices upward. It does not know that of the particles of air which here and there give it such a delicate touch as seems a miracle, a fathomless and boundless sea exists above where all its gatherings go to build the tree. It does not know what beautiful thing it is building there, all flowers and fruit and rustling music. It crawls and gathers with the worm and the ant, obedient to the law of its being, and draws sweetness out of corruption, and clasps a rock for a friend.

"Master, I could not be content to think that there is no more than this visible tree to reward such labor, and that anything so beautiful as the tree should be meant only to please the eye, gratify the palate, and then return to chaos.

"May there not be yet a third stage of this creature, some indestructible tree of Paradise, all ethereal music, perfume, and sweetness? That beauty would be not in its mere existence, but in the good that it has done; in the shade and refreshment it has given to man; in shelter to nestling birds, and to all the little wild creatures which fly to it for protection; in the music of its playing with the breeze and with the tempest.

"When it drops off the perishable part which was but the instrument of its perfection, the humble instinct in the root understands at last for what and with what it labored.

"I remembered, O my master, that we in the flesh are but the root of our higher selves, our sense feeding our intelligence, which works visibly; while above the body and the studious mind rises some quintessence of intelligence which the spark of life was sent to elaborate out of the universe on which it feeds, a being all pure, all beautiful, which at last gathers itself up into the light of Paradise, dropping off corruption."

"The picture-book of nature has given thee a fair lesson, Provence," said Professor Pearlstein, smiling kindly on the boy; and then, with a few suggestions and verbal corrections, allowed him to resume his seat.

Tacita did not need to be told that the boy who rose next was Iona's brother. He was graceful and proud-looking, with an oval olive face, black eyes and dark hair tossed back in locks that had the look of plumes. He spoke in Italian, which he pronounced exquisitely, with fullness and deliberation.

"I have been haunted by a circle and a whirling and a wheel," he began, looking downward, his head slightly bowed, as if in confusion. "I meant to draw a lesson from the life of water. But when I had followed a drop only half its course, a great machine, all wheels and whirling, caught me up and tore my thoughts to fragments.

"I remembered having read somewhere that men and women are but the separated parts of wheel-shapes, or circles which had been their united form in a more perfect state of being. Then I saw the Hindu walking seven times around the object of his sacred love, as the Mohammedan at the Cordovan *Ceca*, till his footsteps wear a pathway in the stone. I remembered Plutarch's story of the siege of Alesia. When the city had to capitulate, the general came out on his finest charger and dressed in his finest armor, to surrender it. He rode round and round the tribune on which sat Cæsar with his officers, circled round and round them, then dismounted, disarmed himself, and sat down silently at Cæsar's feet. That revolution had some meaning. I remembered the whirling dervish, a clod with a planetary instinct, and the Persian hell peopled with beings which whirl forever in a ceaseless circle, whirling and circling, the right hand of each pressed to his burning heart. That naturally recalls to mind the strange idea that the planets are sentient beings, whirling forever with their hearts on fire, like those accursed ones in the Hall of Eblis.

"The planetary idea is in all this circling and whirling.

"All the old nations have a legend of some great supernatural battle in the past, where rebel and loyal angels, gods and Titans, good and evil spirits fought with each other. Those legends must all be the reflection of a real event. I have wondered if Chaos may not have been the crash and ruin of such a combat, and Creation, as we have read its story, a restoration only, instead of being the original establishment of order. Is not all this whirl the search of scattered fragments for their supplementary parts?

"It might be, then, that there is no absolute evil, but only an evil of wrong associations. There are substances, as chemists know, which are deadly in some combinations and wholesome in others. There is the brute creation, which, perhaps, is but a false humanity unmasked. Look at the trees. Cut down an oak-tree and a pine-tree grows in its place. Why not say, cut down a cruel man and a wolf is born? And from that wolf downward through fierce and gnawing generations, each losing some fang and fire, what wore the shape of man may become mud again. What if the real grandeur of Christ's mission may have been to release all *men of good will* from this primeval expiation. First comes the figure, then the substance. *Let there be Light!* said the Creator. And said Christ, *I am the Light of the world.* Shone upon by the sun, the foul and hateful may produce the exquisite. From mud and dung we have the lily and the rose. From this divine sun shining on *men of good will*, we have the perfect man released from a long captivity. The hell we hear of, the *outer darkness*, of which the King's Majesty spoke, might be this going downward in the scale of being of creatures which had arrived at humanity, but were unworthy of it.

"Here, then, would begin another movement, the Divine way of heaven.

"It is all a whirl! Master, it makes me dizzy!"

Half laughing, the boy pressed his hands to his temples.

"Ion," said the master quietly, "it is well to observe natural phenomena with the hope of drawing some guidance from them in the supernatural. Nature is like our sweet-toned bell in C. The material stroke at the base brings out the keynote, but if you listen higher up where the band of lilies runs, you will hear the dominant whispering. This is our limit. If the universe should propound its riddle to me, I would lay my hand on my mouth and my mouth in the dust."

"I would die guessing, or knowing!" cried the boy. Then, with a quick change of expression, he bowed lowly, and said in a quiet tone: —

"I considered the ways of water. It springs out of the dark earth, is a rivulet, a brook, a river. It labors, and never ceases to be useful till, laden with impurities which are not its own, it falls into the ocean. It has wet the lips of fever, washed the stains of labor, helped to bear malaria from the crowded city, revived the drooping plant, quenched the devouring flame, sung its little song along the roof and eaves, stretched its little film to soften a sunbeam in the hot noon. It rests. No, it rests not. It climbs into the sky only to return, and go over it all again. It was depressing to think that we may come again to go through the same round. But who knows that the drop of water makes the same round a second time? The variety may be infinite. And so, I thought, the soul may come and come, till it learns to sympathize with all. May we not guess who has made many upward-growing circles by saying, he can sympathize with people in circumstances which have never surrounded his apparent life, he can be compassionate where others condemn, he can stand firm where others fail, he is not moved by clamor?"

"Who can say?" said the master, passing his hand across his forehead. "It is wiser not to ask."

"Is it forbidden to speculate?" asked the boy in a low tone.

"It is not forbidden, Ion. But to spend the present in speculating on the unrecallable past and the unknown future is to throw away a treasure. What happens when you try to look at the sun at midday? You see nothing but a palpitating fire that scorches your brain. Turn your eyes to earth again, and do you see it as it is? No: everything is discolored, and over it all are floating livid disks that mimic the sun's shape and slander his color, the only souvenirs of an attempt to strain a power beyond its limits. Do not try to read the poetry and philosophy of a language till you shall have learned its alphabet and grammar."

"Yet I learned German so, and was at the head of my class," said Ion boldly. "I opened a book with Goethe's name on the title-page, and turned the leaves till I saw a poem that was as clearly shaped for music as a bird is. I took the first letter and learned its name and sound, and then the next and the next, till I had a word. I learned that word, and the next in the same way, till I had a verse and a thought. O master, what delight when the dark shadows slid off that thought, and it shone out like a star from under a cloud! When, thought by thought, I had got the whole poem out, every phrase perfect, and each delicate grace with its own curves, then I knew German! I plunged into the sea and learned to swim!"

He laughed with joyous triumph, and lifting his arms, crossed them above his head, bending backward for a moment, as if to draw a full breath from the zenith.

The old man smiled.

"Thou hast an answer ever ready," he said, "and thou art not all wrong, boy. I would not clip thy wings. I like thy life and courage. But I would that thou hadst something also of Holy Fear."

"I like not the name of fear," the boy said, clouding over.

"Yes; if a man fear to do right," said the master. "But there is a noble fear of presumption, and of setting a bad example. You have quoted from our highly-honored Plutarch. Do you remember what he tells of Alexander on the vigil of the battle of Abela? He stood on the height and saw over against him Darius reviewing his troops by torchlight. They marched interminably out of the darkness into the glare and out into darkness. Those moving shadows on the morrow would become to him and to his army showers of arrows and shock of spears, and trampling hoofs, and crushing chariot-wheels, an avalanche of fierce death to bear them down.

"Then Alexander called his soothsayer, and they set up an altar before the king's tent; and there, with the torch-lighted hosts of the foe before them, they sacrificed to Holy Fear.

"When the hour of battle came, did Alexander therefore fail? No! The next day's sun shone on his victory; and ere it set poor Darius was a fugitive, and his conquerer proclaimed Emperor of Asia.

"Ion, thy danger is in rashness and in passion. Guard thyself, boy! To-night, I pray thee, ere thou sleep, go out alone on to the topmost terrace of the college, and there in silence gaze for a little while into the cloudless sky and consider the torch-lights of God's great invisible encampment, cycles and cycles of being, a measureless life of which we know not the figure nor the language. And when, so gazing, the fever of thy soul shall be somewhat cooled, do thou also sacrifice to Holy Fear!"

Ion listened at first with downcast eyes, then looking earnestly at the speaker; and when the exhortation was ended, before taking his seat, he went to kiss respectfully the fringe of the master's sash.

Into the pause that followed there broke a sudden clash of bells all struck together.

The master and pupils glanced at each other and all rose, uncovering their heads.

Tacita recognized the familiar *à morto* of Italy. It signified here that some one was dying.

The clash changed to a melody, and they all sang together the hymn that had been sung that night in Venice: —

"San Salvador, San Salvador,
We cry to thee!"

singing the hymn through.

When it was ended, Tacita, perceiving that the lesson of the boys would not continue longer, hastened down the path before them.

She had scarcely reached the level when Ion overtook her.

"May I speak to you, Tacita Mora?" he asked, cap in hand. "The master gave me permission to follow you."

"Surely!" she answered, blushing. "But tell me first for whom the bells were ringing."

"It must be Leila, one of the school-girls. She was very sick last night. And this morning her brother did not come to the college, so I knew that she must be worse."

"Did not I see you at the assembly?" asked Tacita. "I had but a glimpse; but I think that it was you."

"Yes," said Ion. "It was my first admission. I was sixteen years old the day before. We go there at my age, and the ladies teach us politeness. It is proper and kind for any lady to tell us if we commit a *gaucherie*. They tell us gently in a whisper. Pardon me if I still am awkward. I am but a school-boy. I wanted to kiss the fringe of your sash that night, and did not dare to."

He bent to take her sash end, kissed it lightly, and still held it for a moment as they walked. There was something caressing and fascinating in his voice and manner.

Looking down at the silken fringe, and letting it slip tuft by tuft, he asked suddenly, "Do you love my sister?"

"I admire her," Tacita replied. "I have a sense of subjection in her presence which forbids me to use such a familiar word as love."

"She builds up that barrier in spite of herself!" the brother exclaimed. "She wishes to see if any one will throw it down in order to get nearer to her. She would sometimes be glad if it were down. I know Iona."

"You can approach her nearly," Tacita said. "But who else would push down a barrier that she raises round herself?"

"I want you to," Ion said earnestly. "I want Iona to have some one to whom she can unveil her mind more than she would to me even. Her relations with our people are fixed. Half by her own motion, and half with their help, she has been got on to a pedestal. She is on a pedestal even to Dylar. And there she must remain till some one helps her down. See why I am so anxious about it now."

He took her sash end again, and held it, his fingers trembling as he went on with growing passion.

"Next year some of our young men are going out to take their places in the world. They are all two or three years older than I; but I am a century more impatient than all of them put together. Naturally I should be expected to wait. If I insist, I can go; only I am afraid it would give pain to Iona. But if you love her, you can take my place to her. She is sure to love you. I feel your sweetness all about you in the air. At the assembly a lady quoted something pretty about you:

'Why, a stranger, when he sees her
In the street even, smileth stilly,
Just as you would at a lily.'

Don't let this barrier grow up between you and Iona! Try to get inside of it, and help me."

"I will do what I can, Ion," Tacita said, beginning to feel as if she had found a brother. "May I speak of it to Dylar? I think that she would show her mind more freely to him."

"I leave it all to you, and thank you," the boy said, warmly. "I shall die if I do not go! But don't tell them that I said so. I have such a longing! Last year I climbed that southern mountain we call the Dome. From the top I caught a glimpse between the higher mountains of the outside world. Oh, how it stretched away! Our plain was as the palm of my hand compared with that vast outspread of land. There were small blue spots, so small that if I held two fingers up at arm's length, they were hidden. Yet they were mountains like these. There were trees so distant that they looked a mere green leaf dropped on the ground. I saw where the sun rises over the rim of the round earth, and where it sinks again. How I breathed! This is a dear home, I know. I have seen men and women fall on their knees and thank God, weeping with joy, that they were permitted to return after having been long away. But I cannot love San Salvador as it deserves till I have seen something different."

Tacita took in hers the boy's trembling hand.

"Be comforted!" she said. "I will do all that I can, and you are sure to go. It will not be long to wait. Now, when you go about, look at San Salvador and all that it contains with the thought that you are taking leave of it. On the eve of saying farewell, even a mere acquaintance seems a friend."

They were at the door of the Arcade. Ion took a grateful, graceful leave.

"Addio, O Queen of golden Silence!" he said.

"Poor little Leila is dead!" said Elena, coming in later. "I was with her. It was she who gave you the white rose when we were at the school. You can now give one back."

CHAPTER XIV.

LEILA'S funeral took place the next day, the lovely waxen figure carried on a bier strown with flowers. The family surrounded their dead, a procession of friends preceding and following. The child's home had been in one of the smaller apartments of the cross-streets, reached by stairways under the arches; and as it was the custom for funerals to approach the Basilica by the avenue, they came across to the eastward through alternating light and shadow, and, reaching the outer street, returned by the bridge in front of the Arcade, the bells ringing *à morto* as they passed through the avenue. But it was not the clash of all the bells together. It was a plaintive dropping, a tone or a chord, like dropping tears.

"Will they not enter?" Tacita asked in a whisper of Elena when she saw that not only those preceding the dead spread themselves around the outside of the inclosure of the Basilica, but those who followed were also remaining outside.

"No, my dear. The house of God is no place for corrupting human bodies."

The bier was set down on the uppermost of the first steps; two men with gilded staves drew aside the curtains of the portal, and the lights and the Throne shone out on the mourning and the mourned. A few prayers were said; and then, led by the chimes, they all sang.

Tacita knew enough of the language now to follow the sense of their simple and brief appeal.

> "Thou who didst mourn the friend that silent lay
> In the dark tomb, behold our eyes that weep
> A lifeless form that loved us yesterday.
> Mourning, we lay its silence at thy feet, —
> Thou who didst weep!
>
> "Help of the sorrowful! Help us to say
> Of this dear treasure which we may not keep,
> The Lord hath given, and he takes away,
> And still thy name with fervent blessings greet, —
> Thou who didst weep!
> Thou who didst weep!"

The windows of the Basilica had all been darkened and the lamps doubled; and to those standing opposite the portal the two long rows of columns and the climbing lights and upper glow might have seemed like Jacob's vision of the angelic stairway stretching from earth to heaven, from shadow to light.

The hymn ended, they took up their dead and went on in silence. The road that led to the cemetery led nowhere else. It turned from the plain at the south side of the Basilica, hidden by the elevation of the little rock plateau on which the structure was set, and passing along the side of it, entered a deep and narrow ravine at the back. This ravine was nearly half a mile long and walled with precipitous rocks that shut out everything but the line of sky above and the topmost point of one white snow-peak, serene against the blue.

Entering the ravine was to be reminded infallibly of the "valley of the shadow of death." Here the prayers began. A single voice in the centre of the procession exclaimed: —

"The Lord gave, and the Lord hath taken away," and like waves the response rolled to front and rear and back again,—"Blessed be the name of the Lord!"

The Miserere was repeated in the same way, and the Psalm "The Lord is my Shepherd."

The sun entered the ravine with them. There was only one hour of the day when a direct beam shone in, and that, except when the days were longest, scarcely reached the foot-way. It shone along over their heads now; and as the road near its end made a turn further inward to the mountains, it shone on a great golden legend set high above on an arch springing from cliff to cliff: —

I AM THE RESURRECTION AND THE LIFE!

Some men on the natural bridge that made the archway stood outlined against the sky, looking down at the procession. To them the gray robes and black sashes could have been scarcely distinguishable from the dark rocks; but the form of the little maiden thus taking its last journey, and those of the eight bearers, all in white, would shine out of the shadows.

No perfumed garden flowers grew on that high land where they were working when they heard the bells' *à morto;* but they gathered snowy daisies, scentless and pure, and made a little drift of their petals; and as the dead approached and passed beneath, they dropped them down in a thin shower as fine as any snow-crystals.

The ravine opened beyond the arch to what had been a torrent-bed circling round a cone-shaped mountain almost destitute of verdure. The whole mass of this mountain was a cemetery. Wide stairs and galleries outside led to iron-bound doors at different heights. One of these doors was open. The procession, crossing a bridge over dry stones, went up the graded ascent to what might be called the second story. Here was a full sunshine. The bearers set their burden down in it before the open door. And here, at last, grief was allowed to have its way for a moment. The mourners fell on their knees beside their dead. A choir of men and women broke out singing:—

"Look thy last upon the sun!
Eyes that scarcely had begun
To distinguish near from far,
Star from lamp, or lamp from star;—
Eyes whose bitterest tears were dew
That a swift smile sparkled through.
Lift thy white lids once, before
Darkness seal them evermore!

"Speak, and bid the air rejoice,
Music of a childish voice!
One more word our hearts shall hail
Sweeter than the nightingale!
Smile again, O lips of rose!
Break the pitiless repose

That is builded like a wall
Where in vain we beat and call.

"Nevermore! Ah, nevermore!
Till we touch the heavenly shore,
Voice or smile of hers shall bless
Our heart-bleeding loneliness.
Jesus, King, and Brother mild!
Keep her yet a little child,
That her face we there may see
As we yield it back to thee!"

The parents and the child's brother sobbed as they bent over the unanswering dead, if the peaceful brightness of that flower-like face could be called unresponsive, and they rose only when some of their nearer friends bent over and would have lifted them. Then the bearers took up the bier and passed out of the sun, and disappeared into what from the outside seemed a profound darkness.

It was a long corridor formed precisely like a catacomb, except that the greater part of it was masonry. The roof, floor, and walls were all of unpolished gray stone with white marble tablets set in the walled-up niches. Three iron lamps suspended from the ceiling threw all about a tender golden light. At the farthest end of the corridor something white reflected dimly. There were a few closed niches, but the greater number of them were unoccupied. Outside one of these, opposite the second lamp, a smaller lamp, as yet unlighted, was set in an iron ring fixed in the masonry.

The bier was set down before this niche, which was lined with myrtle sprigs, and had little lace bags filled with spices in the corners. There were two silver rings inside attached to cords, one at the head and one at the foot.

As Tacita entered, she saw the father lift his child and lay her in her fragrant bed, and the mother place a pillow under her head. They crossed her hands on her breast, and slipped one of the silver rings on to a wrist and the other over the slender foot. They had been weeping loudly; but when, their service done, they stood and looked at the peaceful and lovely sleeper, something of her quiet came over them. They gazed fixedly, as if their souls were groping after hers, or as if the wall of her silence and immobility were not altogether impenetrable, and intent, with hushed breathing, they could catch some sense of a light fuller than that of the sun, and of sweet sounds, beautiful scenes and loving companionship in what had seemed a vöid, and of nearness where infinite distances had been straining at their heart-strings.

Tacita laid her bunch of white roses at the child's feet. Then Elena led her down the corridor and pointed to a name inscribed on the marble of a closed niche. It was her father's.

She kissed the marble, and stood thinking; then turned away. "God keep him!" she said. "I cannot find him here."

At the end of the corridor, in the centre of the wall, was an open niche, all white marble, with a gilded cross lying in it, and so many little bags of spices that all the neighborhood was perfumed by them.

This niche was called "The Resurrection;" and at every funeral the mourners brought their tribute of perfumes to it.

Elena drew her companion's attention to the niches around this open tomb. "You see how small they are. They are all young infants. It is the same in all the corridors. The end where the tomb of Christ is, is called the cemetery of the Innocents."

Outside, in the gallery, a choir was softly singing:—

"Thou who didst weep!"

"We will go now," Elena whispered.

As they went, the mourners still stood before their dead, the husband and wife hand in hand. The brother, with his hands clasped before him, gazed steadfastly into his sister's face, that was scarcely whiter than his own.

The little lamp had been lighted, the chains attached to the chain of a bell hung outside the door, and a plate of glass covered the niche.

People came and went quietly. Some had gone home; others were seated on the stone benches outside. Dylar was leaning on the parapet; and when Tacita and Elena came out, he accompanied them down and through the ravine. When they reached the lane behind the church, he asked Tacita if she would like to go up and see his cottage, which was just above the college. She assented gladly, and Elena left them to go up the path together.

The cottage was of the plainest, and contained

but two rooms. The front one had a glass door and two windows overlooking the town. There was a table in the centre of the room with a revolving top surrounded by drawers. A hammock hung at the back, and there were two chairs, a bookcase and a closet. The floor was of green and white tiles, and the roughly plastered walls were washed a dull green.

"You see, I have here everything that I need," Dylar said. "My living rooms are in the college; but I often come here. My writing and planning, especially of our outside affairs, is done here. The business of San Salvador is all portioned out and arranged, and can be done without me. But the outside business requires a good deal of study."

He brought the chairs out, and they sat down, and Dylar pointed out the larger mountains, and named them, told where the torrents were and how they had been or could be deviated, told where the signal-stations were, and how they could know from them all that happened at their outer stations. He showed her her own chamber windows in the Arcade, the heights behind which, scarcely hidden from the town, she had entered San Salvador, and, near the southeastern angle of the opening, a mountain with a double peak, beyond which stood Castle Dylar.

The terrace where they sat was covered with a thin dry turf, and a pine-tree grew at one side and an olive-tree at the other. The olive was so old that its trunk was quite hollowed out, and the side next the rock had long since died and been cut away. The single great outward branch was full of blossoms. From the parapet one could look down and see the river of ripening wheat that flowed quite round the rock on which the college was built.

"This is the only spot in the world that I can properly call home," Dylar said. "It is the only place all mine, and where no stranger comes. If I am wanted, a signal calls me."

"You like to be here!" Tacita said with a certain pensiveness. "You like to be alone!"

"You think so," he said, "because I keep somewhat apart. It is necessary that I should do so in order to avoid complicating intimacies. Then, I have a great deal to think of. Besides, I will confess that when human affection comes too near, and becomes personal, I feel a sense of recoil. Human evil and sorrow I do not shrink from; but human love"—

Tacita moved backward a step, and clouded over.

"Not so!" Dylar exclaimed. "It is precisely because your friendship is as delicate as a mist that I seek you, that I follow you. See that white cloud on the pine-tree yonder! It is like you. The tree-top, the topmost tree-top has caught and tries to hold it. Do you think that it would like to stay?"

"It stays!" she murmured; and a faint rose-hue over her face and neck and hands betrayed the sudden heart-throb. "It stays while it is held."

Dylar looked at her with delight in his eyes.

"I am glad to have here at last the little girl of the *baiocco*," he said. "I never forgot her. When I no longer saw her, she grew up in my mind. I fancied her saying to me across the world: 'Why do you not come? I am no longer a child!'"

Tacita gave him a startled glance, and quickly turned her eyes away. Love the most ardent, the most impetuous, shone in his face.

"Tacita," he said softly, "I am indeed a beggar now! But do not fear. I will wait for your answer; but I could not wait before letting you know surely that my fate is in your hands. And now, shall we go down?"

She turned to descend before him, but stopped, looking back over her shoulder with lowered eyes that did not see his face. "May I have just one little string of olive-blossoms?" she asked.

He gathered and gave it to her over the shoulder her cheek was touching. "Ask me for the tree!" he exclaimed.

"Let it be mine where it stands," she said, hiding a smile, and taking a step forward.

"Ask me for the castle!" he said passionately, following her.

"I will first see the castle," she said, still going, her face turned from him.

"Will you go to-morrow to see it? Elena will accompany us."

"If you ask me, I will go."

They had reached the circle, and some men were

there on their way to the upper gardens. In the town they were alone again, and Dylar sketched their programme for the next day.

"You and Elena will talk it over," he said. "And if you wish any change made, send me word this evening."

They parted at the door, and Tacita went upstairs feeling as though she floated in the air.

CHAPTER XV.

THE sun was not yet in the town. Its beams had scarcely reached the Basilica in their progress down the western mountains when the two ladies mounted their donkeys at the Arcade to go to Castle Dylar. The master of the castle was to meet them on the mountain path above the college.

They found him waiting for them; and as they went up an easy serpentine road, and over bridges binding cliff to cliff, Dylar pointed out hills and streams where the small flocks and herds of San Salvador were kept.

From this path could be seen to the best advantage the rock on which the college was built, and the way the structure followed its outlines and imitated them in pinnacles and terraces of every size and shape. They found the mountains on which the pine-woods bordered, and, close at hand, the height from which the first Dylar had discovered the site of his future city.

San Salvador disappeared; then its gardens were no longer visible; and then the spaces that betrayed the presence of a plain, or valley, were filled in; and they no longer looked backward.

They entered upon a scene like that which had preceded Tacita's first vision of San Salvador, scarcely a month before; and again she began to ask herself if it were not all a dream.

But a word from Dylar was enough to chase the phantom of unreality away. Tacita used every pretext that enabled her to glance at him. He was so picturesque and soldierly, he had such an uncommon figure with his firm profile and auburn-tinted hair; and the dark tunic and turban-cap with its silver band were so graceful.

She and Elena had each a man at the bridle; but Dylar was at her side at every rough place or steep descent. Yet his manner could not be called lover-like. It was rather that of a kind and anxious guardian. She asked herself if he had indeed said but the day before that his fate was in her hands. It seemed impossible. It was he who held her fate. Under his guardianship, how sweet were the dark places, how welcome the giddy cliff edges!

Outwardly quiet, and with a face almost as colorless as an orange flower, Tacita was intoxicated with delight.

Near the end of their journey, they passed across the opening to a deep and dark ravine.

"There," said the prince, pointing, "was found the gold which enabled the first Dylar to buy and cultivate land around the castle, and to found San Salvador. It was a rich mine; and we still find a few grains in it."

A little later they reached a small plateau, and dismounted. Passing a corner of ledge, they came to a long rough stair so shut in as to be in twilight. It descended and disappeared in a turn, and seemed to have been cut in the rock. It ended at a door that opened into a low-roofed cave.

"Courage!" said Dylar with a smile, and gave his hand to Tacita.

He led her through the cave, and up a stone stair lighted by a hanging lamp to a landing that had a narrow barred door at one side. Through this door, masked on its other side by shelves, they entered a large cellar such as one might expect to find under an old castle founded upon rocks.

Here were long vistas of vaults supported on piers of masonry, tracts of thick wall, both long and short, sometimes taking the place of pillars and arches. There were glistening rows of wine-hogsheads diminishing in the darkness; and shelves of jars gave a familiar domestic look to the place.

Dylar pointed out how cunningly the stair from the cave below was hidden. It was set between two walls that ran together like a wedge, a wall starting off diagonally from the point where they met, and pillars and arches so confusing the outlines that the wedge-shape could not be suspected.

From the large cellar they entered a small one surrounded by shelves of bottles.

"I am sorry to welcome you to my house by such a rough way," Dylar said. "But it is, at least, an ascending one."

"You are giving me a charming adventure," Tacita said brightly. "I have entered many a palace and castle by the *portone*, but never before by a cavern and a masked door."

The next stair led to a plainly-furnished study, or office. Dylar hastened to open a door into a noble baronial hall.

"At last, welcome to Castle Dylar!" he exclaimed. "May peace fill every hour you pass within its walls. Command here as if all were your own!"

They entered a drawing-room of which the walls were all a rich dimness of old frescos, and the oaken furniture was upholstered with purple cloth. The tall windows let in a brilliant sunshine through the upper panes; but all the lower ones were covered by shutters. Here the housekeeper came to welcome the ladies and show them to their chambers.

The wide stairway led to a circular gallery hung with tapestries in which was woven the story of Alexander the Great. There was nothing modern. But the two connecting chambers they entered were bright with sunshine, and fresh with green and white draperies. The windows were swathed with a thin gray gauze.

Tacita went eagerly to look out.

"We must not show ourselves," Elena said. "You can look through the gauze."

The first glance, vaulting over a mass of tree-tops and a great half-moon of verdure, saw a plain that extended to a low ripple of pale-blue mountains on the horizon. A few stunted groves were visible on this wide expanse, and a few abrupt hills which seemed to be protruding ledges, the crevices of which had been gradually filled by the dust-bearing winds.

Tacita recollected Ion's description of this scene, which had appeared to him so beautiful that San Salvador, compared with it, had seemed a prison.

"Poor boy!" she thought. "He will find nowhere else such freedom as that which he is so eager to leave."

The near view compensated by its richness for the sterility of the distant. It was a vast fenceless garden radiating two miles, or more, in every direction from the front of the castle, and every foot of it was cultivated to the utmost. There were blocks of yellowing wheat, there was every green of garden, orchard, and vineyard; and through them all the ever-present olive-trees which gave the place its name. They were planted wherever a tree could go. Around the foot of the castle they were clustered so thickly that they hid even from its windows the green turf and gray steps of its semicircular terraces. The large houses of whitewashed stone with flat roofs were scattered about irregularly. By some of them stood groups of palm-trees; or a single tree waved its foliage above the terrace.

The visitors had their dinner in a quaint boudoir, cone-shaped, and frescoed to look like a forest aisle from the pavement to the apex of its ceiling. One could recognize the artist of the Basilica in those interwoven branches, those leaping squirrels, and the bird's-nests with a gaping mouth or downy head visible over the rim.

"I will give you a more fitting service when you come here by way of the Pines," Dylar said. "But on these stolen visits from below we live with closed doors and a single servant."

"He eats," thought Tacita. "Therefore he is human." And she felt no need of puzzling over a major proposition, nor, indeed, of anything but what the painted cone contained.

"It should be a communicable thought which provokes that amused smile," Dylar said when he caught her expression.

Tacita blushed. "I was telling myself that it is a real plate of soup before you, and a real spoon in your hand; and that therefore I need not expect to find myself presently in the Madrid gallery, and see you disappear into a picture-frame."

"Shall I tell you something of that man's history by and by?" asked Dylar. "It may help to lay his ghost."

"Oh, yes!" she exclaimed. "And, oh, yes!"

"When you shall have taken some repose, then," he said, "come with me to the terrace of the tower. There, with the scene of my ancestor's labors before our eyes, I will show you how to distinguish between him and me."

"I cannot sleep, Elena," said Tacita, when they were alone. "Yet a nap is just what I want.

What a shame it is that our rebellious bodies do not know their duty better, and obey orders."

"I fancy," said Elena, "that the body could retort with very good reason when accused of being troublesome, and that it understands and does its business as well as the mind understands and does its own. Why should not body and soul be friendly comrades?"

"My respected friend and body," said Tacita with great politeness, as she leaned back in a deep lounging-chair, "will you please to go to sleep?"

She closed her eyes, and was silent a little while, then opened them, and whispered, "Elena, it won't!"

There was no reply. Elena had gone to sleep in the adjoining chamber.

Tacita sat looking out over the wide landscape. The nearest house visible over the olive-trees had a flame of nasturtium flowers on its lower walls, and a palm-tree lifting its columned trunk to hold a plumy green umbrella over the roof. The foliage waved languidly to and fro in a faint breeze, lifting and falling to meet its own shadow that lifted and fell responsive on the white walls and gray roof. There was something mesmeric in the motion; and the silence and "the strong sunshine settled to its sleep" were like a steadfast will behind the waving hands.

When Tacita woke, Elena was waiting to tell her that Dylar was in the drawing-room, and would show her the castle.

To one acquainted with old countries there was nothing surprising in the massive, half-ruined structure, with its rock foundations, and the impossibility of finding one's way unguided from one part of the interior to the other. The ancient tapestries, the stone floors with their faded rugs from oriental looms, the stone stairways where a carpet would have looked out of place, and was, in fact, spread only as flowers are scattered for some *festa*, — they were not strange to Tacita. But they were most interesting.

A round tower made the centre of the castle; and there was a wing at either side with a labyrinth of chambers. This tower formed a rude porter's lodge on the ground, a fine hall above, a gallery by the sleeping-rooms, and the fourth floor was Dylar's private study. From this room a narrow stair went up through the thickness of the wall to the roof-terrace. There were secret passages, and loop-holes for observation everywhere.

"God knows how many deeds of darkness these hidden chambers may have witnessed!" Dylar said. "If it had not seemed possible that they may be useful in the future, some of them would have been torn down before this. If any large agricultural work were attempted, it might be necessary to lodge the workmen here for a while. When these houses you see were being built, a hundred men dined every day in a hall in the eastern wing."

They had stepped out on to the terrace, where chairs had been placed for them, screened from sight by the parapet, so that as they sat only a green and gold rim of the settlement was visible.

"How beautiful it would be," said Tacita, "if all that plain were wheat and corn and vines and orchards, with the hills crowned with small separate cities, all stone, with not a green leaf, only boxes of pinks outside the windows."

"Just my thought!" Dylar exclaimed, blushing with pleasure. "Who knows but it may be some day? We own some land outside our farms, and have begun by planting it with canes. It is that unbroken green band you see yonder. It is larger than it looks."

They were silent a little while. There was no word that could have added to their happiness. Then the prince began his story.

"Three hundred years ago the name of Dylar was well known in some of the great cities of Europe and the East. The family had occupied high places, and the head of it at that time, whose portrait you have seen, was a brave soldier. He was fortunate in everything, — too fortunate, for he excited envy. He had a beautiful wife and a young son and a daughter.

"His wife died, and with her departed his good fortune. While he mourned for her, forgetful of everything but grief, those who envied him were busy. I need not enter into details. His life is all recorded, and you can read it if you will. It is enough to say that his enemies succeeded in depriving him of place, and in multiplying their own number. They changed the whole face of the earth for him.

"He found himself in that position where a man sees open before him the abyss of human meanness. Trivial minds dropped off their childish graces and showed their childish brutality. Nothing is capable of a greater brutishness than a trifler. Fine sentiments came slipping down like gorgeous robes from dry skeletons. Prudence took the place of magnanimity, its weazened face as cold as stone. Ceremonious courtesy met him where effusive affection had been. In short, he had the experience of a man who has lost place and power with no prospect of regaining them.

"He had no wish to regain them, and would have refused them had they been offered. To astonishment, incredulity, and indignation succeeded a profound disgust. His only wish was to shake off all his former associations, and seek a place where he might forget them.

"He sold his property, and with his two children abandoned a society that was not worthy of him. A nurse and a man-servant only clung to his fortunes, and refused to be separated from him and his children.

"For a time he was a wanderer, thinking many thoughts.

"He had been noble and honorable, but not religious. It is probable that now, when humanity had so failed him, he raised his eyes to inquire of that Deity of whose existence he had formerly made only a respectful acknowledgment. The Madrid picture must have been painted about this time. It expresses his state of mind.

"Doubtless some of the plans which he afterward put in execution were already floating in his imagination when in one of his journeys he came upon this place, for he immediately resolved to purchase it. It is recorded that he exclaimed, 'It was made for me!'

"The place must have looked uninviting at that time to one who had not already plans which would make works of improvement a welcome necessity; for what is now a garden was then a waste almost as barren as that you see beyond; and in place of these houses, which, in a rustic way, are fine, noble structures, were a few miserable huts inhabited by tenants as ignorant, and even vicious, as they were poor.

"Probably Dylar had that feeling from the first which has been ever since one of our principles of action, to take the worst, that which no one else would take, in men and things, and work at their reformation.

"At all events, he set out at once to find the owner of the place, a young man who might be in Paris, or London, or Rome, but most surely, at the gaming-table. Found at last, after a long search, he consented readily to sell, but he did not consent gladly. He could not hesitate, for he was reduced almost to living by his wits; but he suffered.

"Dylar had compassion on him. He saw in

him the victim of an evil education involved in a life from which he was too weak to escape. But it was impossible to approach such a man with the same help which he could give to others. He only begged that if ever the young man, or his children, should wish to live in retirement for a while, they would still look upon the castle of their ancestors as a home to which they would be ever welcome.

"Then he set himself to change the face of his desolate possessions. He gathered a score of outcasts, men and women to whom every door of hope was closed, and brought them to the castle till other shelter could be provided for them. More than one of them had crimes to confess; but they were the crimes of misery and desperation rather than of malice.

"Of a different class of the needy, he added to his own household. There was an elderly lady who gladly took the place of duenna to his daughter; and an old book-worm who was starving in unhonored obscurity became his son's tutor, and later an important agent in the success of his plans.

"Of course, agriculture was their first need; and the tutor was far in advance of his time in this science — so far as to have been considered a visionary. Dylar found him able to realize these visions.

"Before long, the land began to reward them. Huts had been built for the new-comers, and all worked with a will. Dylar had confided something of his plans to these poor people, and had inspired them with an ambition to build here a city of refuge, and to look forward to a time when they might say to the world which had condemned them, Behold! a higher judge has absolved us.

"Whether the thought occurred first to Dylar, or to his son's tutor, we do not know; but they agreed that gold must exist in large quantities in the mountains, and they secretly searched for it. Some grains had been found in a little stream that issued from the mountains where the river now is. To guess how difficult it was to get at the source of this stream you would have to examine the conformation of the mountains about the castle. In fact, they were reduced to the necessity of descending inside by ropes from the castle itself.

"You understand that they succeeded, and found gold in large quantities. You will also understand that they must have confided their secret to others.

"Here was an immense difficulty. Had this discovery been made known to his people, Dylar's community would have been ruined, his plans overset forever.

"He hit upon a device. He made another visit to the outside world, and brought back seven men who might be called desperate criminals. He asked them to work for him five years, separated from the world, with no other companionship than their own, and, the term expired, to go far away taking oath never to divulge what they had seen and done. On his side, he would provide for all their needs, and give them a sum of money which to them would be riches.

"They agreed readily, not doubting but they were wanted to commit some crime. When the term of their service was ended, they were no longer criminals; and among their descendants have been the most faithful guardians of San Salvador.

"These men lived at first in a cave in the ravine. Then they built them huts. Later, wives were found for them, and they made homes for themselves. Long before the five years were ended the plain of San Salvador was discovered, the city planned, and the lower entrance to the castle begun. Outside, land was purchased and cultivated, and the houses which preceded the present ones were built. Many new people had been brought in, and some sent out to study a handicraft or science. Building and agriculture were the chief studies of the people.

"You will see that the story can only be touched here and there.

"Everything succeeded, because all were in sympathy with their leader, and his prosperity was their prosperity. These men and women who had found themselves here, perhaps, for the first time in their lives, treated with respect, had no desire to withdraw the veil so mercifully let down between their human present and their infernal past. They were faithful from self-interest and from a passionate sense of gratitude.

"Now and then a new-comer was hard to assimilate; but indulgence was shown. A mind long embittered may almost outgrow the possibility of peace, not from any deformity of character, but from a profound sense of injustice. A man or woman of middle age who can remember no happy childhood, no aspiration of enthusiastic youth which was not crushed by disappointment and mortification, has amassed a sense of wrong which help comes too late then to cancel.

"Dylar's conviction, which still holds with us, was that a person so unfortunate as to have become an outcast from civilization is most probably the victim of some atrocious wrong in his birth, or in his early training, or that some supreme injustice has been done him later in life. Enlightened by his own experience and by subsequent observation, he perceived a wide and cruel barbarism hidden beneath the fair semblance of what calls itself civilization. Christianity he recognized as the only true civilizer; but Christianity was an individual, not a social fact. There was no Christian society.

"As time passed, some persons of a different character, though all needy, began to be drawn into the Olives, — a mourner who desired to spend the remnant of a blighted life in retirement, or a hopeless invalid, or some student whose life was consecrated to study and starvation. He was astonished to find how many accomplished people in the world were poor.

"He was, therefore, in no want of teachers.

Some remained for a time; some never left him. To the latter only the existence of San Salvador was known.

"In the lifetime of the first Dylar the necessity for preparing for outside colonies was already felt, and his successor began them. He made large investments, and had agents. All young orphans were sent out, and all beyond a certain number in families. Sometimes a whole family will go. Their relatives are their hostages.

"It was the third Dylar, called Basil, who built the Basilica. There had been only a shrine for a throne of acacia-wood. This throne Basil made with his own hands. It was he also who planned and began the cemetery; and he was the first one to be laid in it.

"Basil went out young into the world. He made himself first a carpenter, then studied architecture and mining. He never married. I am descended from his brother.

"Volumes might be filled with beautiful stories that were told of him, and with legends, half true, half false, which the people wove about him. His sudden appearances and disappearances at the castle after he returned to San Salvador were held by some to be miraculous. He lived a hundred years, and was found dead on the summit of the mountain of the cemetery. There is a grassy hollow at the top that is called 'Basil's Rest.'

"It would be worth your while to go there some morning before sunrise, to hear the larks. The story of his finding there, and of the people bringing his body down, is like a song.

"The first and second Dylars called the unfortunates they brought here 'children of Despair.' Basil named those he brought 'children of Hope'!

"I have told you that the first Dylar made friendly offers and promises to the man of whom he bought this castle. His acts were in conformity with his words. He kept a watch over the family, especially after he had discovered gold. He held himself more solemnly bound to them by that discovery. When any one of them was in difficulty, he went to the rescue. But it was long before one of them was admitted to San Salvador. Then a widow came with her young infant. This widow married the fourth Dylar. From the little girl, her daughter, Iona and Ion are descended."

"Oh!" exclaimed Tacita. "Iona!"

"Yes, Iona! In her and her brother alone we recognize now the blood of the original possessors of Castle Dylar. Their presence here satisfies our sense of justice. The girl I speak of married in San Salvador, and she and her husband went out to have the charge of our affairs in France. One of their sons became a messenger, that is. a person who keeps a regular communication between all the children of San Salvador, reports births and deaths, carries verbal messages, and does whatever business may be necessary in his province. It is a messenger who buys and brings all our supplies and carries out all our produce.

"The son of this messenger became himself a messenger. He was Iona's grandfather. He was named Zara for a Greek friend of the family. He was restless and adventurous, like all his race. He went to the East. This was in the time of my grandfather. He married an Arab woman — ran away with her, indeed. But the circumstances of the escapade were such as to render it pardonable.

"He lived but a short time after this marriage, and his widow with her only child, afterward Iona's mother, came to San Salvador. Iona's father was a relative of mine.

"What Iona is I need not tell you; for you know her. She is one of Nature's queens, and of the rarest; and Ion is worthy to be her brother. In both that restless fire of him who, for very impatience, sacrificed his birthright is intensified by this spark from Araby. But they have reason and discipline, and will have opportunity.

"I am telling you too long and dull a story. But having these outlines, you may afterward take pleasure in learning many details of our history. It is full of romantic adventure and Christian heroism.

"Have I wearied you?"

"So far from it," Tacita said, "that I would gladly listen longer. But you also may be weary. Tell me, these details of your history, are they all written?"

"Not all. The simple facts are all written. Our archives are perfect. The rest is left to the memory of the people. We write no books of adventure, and no novels; but we talk them; and our story-tellers are as inexhaustible as Scheherezade. You have not yet listened to one of them, though you may have seen an audience gathered about one in the booths above the Arcade. There is one whom I must soon take you to hear. He is a gardener, and understands more about olives and the making of oil than any other man in San Salvador. His story-telling is picturesque and poetical. He does not change the facts, but he transfigures them. His mind has a golden atmosphere. There is another, a baker, who will tell you stories as lurid as the fires that heat his ovens. One of the elders sometimes tells stories of heroic virtue in our pioneers, or in historical characters of the world. When our messengers come in, they always give a public account, sometimes very prosaic, of their travels."

"Has there never been a traitor in San Salvador?" Tacita asked timidly, fearing to awaken some painful recollection.

"Never!" was the prompt reply. "In the first place, even of persons born here of our most highly-honored citizens, but sent out very young, no one can know that such a place exists till he has returned to it. This is your own case. Those who go out adults are persons who have been tried. Any notable wealth or luxury of living is forbidden, or discouraged, in our people; and having thus nothing which will attract flatterers, they see the world more nearly as it is. Self-interest helps. Besides, with the training our children have, no Judas can come out of San Salvador. We will have no weak mothers here. If a young child show vicious dispositions, it is taken from its mother and carried outside for training. Perhaps it may never return."

"She cannot go with it?" Tacita asked.

"She cannot go. Did she give birth to an immortal creature for her own amusement in seeing it ruining itself and others? I do not speak of any mere infirmity of temper in the child, but of some dishonest propensity which persists."

Tacita bethought her to speak of Ion's affairs, as she had promised; and after discussing the subject awhile, they went down through darkening stairs and passages to where supper awaited them, set out in an illuminated corner of the great hall.

"I had supper here that you might see the castle shadows," Dylar said. "Seen from our little lighted corner, all this space seems to be crowded with dusky shapes. Do you see?"

CHAPTER XVI.

THEY returned to San Salvador the next day. The sun had set when they reached the town, and the streets were full. Elena and Dylar dismounted at the college; but Dylar insisted that Tacita should ride to the Arcade, and he walked there by her side. She made her little progress with a blushing modesty, ashamed of being the only person in town who was not on foot.

At the door of the Arcade Dylar took leave.

"I am sure that you will not go to the assembly this evening," he said, "and I shall not go. Rest yourself well, and to-morrow I will take you to hear one of our story-tellers. To-night I — I want to remember!"

He murmured the words lowly as he lifted her from the saddle, and she answered them with a little half sigh. She also wanted to remember.

Supper was over; and she and Elena had theirs alone in the dining-room, talking quietly over their journey.

"You are happy, child?" Elena asked.

"I never dreamed of being so happy!" Tacita answered. And they looked into each other's eyes, and understood.

Going to the salon, they found Iona waiting there.

"I suppose that you are not going to the assembly to-night," she said. "But I hope that you are not too tired to tell me how you like the Olives."

"The little glimpse I was allowed was charming. I never saw such verdure. The foliage, the fruit, were in billows, in drifts, in heaps. And how I longed to go to one of those great white houses, and sit on the roof under the palm-shadows. I said to the prince, 'Why have we no palms in San Salvador?' and he is going to have some. I thought of the Basilica as a proper site; but he doubted a little. It is not decided. He said, we worship Christ as King, and shrink from holding the impious insult of his martyrdom forever before his eyes. And the palm is for the martyr. But the palms will grow somewhere, and will be my special garden; and the first person who dies in the effort to serve or save San Salvador shall be carried to his grave with a waving of palm branches, and a song of hosannas, and a palm-leaf shall be entombed with him, and one cut in the marble that bears his name. For that, I would almost wish to die a martyr."

"For that?" said Iona coldly. "The martyr, I fancy, is not thinking of the crown when he throws his life into the breach."

"I was thinking of the people's love," said Tacita, faltering, her eyes cast down to hide the tears that started. She was so happy that she could not bear a check. Her heart had unclosed itself without a thought, a fear, and it shrank at the little icy breath of Iona's answer.

"But why do not you ask me how I like your castle?" she said, recovering herself quickly.

"My castle?"

"Yes; the prince told me the story."

"It is very true that the original owner would never have sold his castle if he had known that there was a mine of gold within a stone's throw of it," Iona said. "But neither did the purchaser know. All was done in honor; and the Dylar have spent time, thought, and money, in compensating my family. I do not hold that I have a shadow of a claim; yet if I should to-day ask Dylar for a house and an independent competence outside, I should have it."

Tacita had already felt more than once that, however welcome her presence might be to every one else in San Salvador, Iona regarded it with a feeling that could scarcely be called by any warmer name than indifference. To-night her manner was more than usually stately, though she talked as much as ever, was, in fact, rather more voluble than her wont. But her talk was like an intrenchment behind which her real self was withdrawn.

Presently she began to question Tacita concerning her first journey to San Salvador, and especially that part of it made in the company of Dylar. Where had she first met him? Had she seen much of him? Were they long in Madrid together?

Surprised, Tacita answered with what frankness she could, and tried not to feel offended. She said nothing of the hymn under their balcony in Venice, nor of the picture in the Madrid gallery. The details of the rest were meagre enough. She had not realized how little there was to tell when the story was divested of those glances, tones, and movements which in her imagination filled out the gracious and perfect memory. Those few facts had been to her like the pale and scattered stars of a constellation which to the mind's eye vivify all the blue air between. She tried to think that in the freedom and confidence of this life such questions were not intrusive, and that Iona, from her position, had a peculiar interest, and even right, in knowing all that concerned Castle Dylar and its master. But in spite of her self-exhortation a troubled thought would come. Could it be possible that Iona would set herself against her friendship with Dylar? Did she suspect anything more than an ordinary friendship between them?

Their conversation grew dry, and Iona rose to retire, with a leave-taking which could have been kinder, but not more elaborately polite. Looking out, Tacita saw her go toward the assembly-rooms, and was glad to remember that Dylar would not be there. It was twilight, and at the highest point of the college she saw his light shine out like a beacon.

Seeing that light made her forget everything else.

"Perhaps he will look for my light," she thought, and drew her curtain quickly, and lighted a lamp. "I wonder if he will look!" Blushing, she passed slowly between the curtain and the light, then covered her face with her hands, ashamed of herself as if she had committed a sin. "I hope that he did n't see me!" she whispered.

Soon after she extinguished her lamp, and sat down by the open window. At that hour of early evening San Salvador was as gay and crowded as it was silent and deserted in the morning. There was a sound of violins from the Star-house; and underneath her window two girls were dancing, trying to keep time to the music that was smothered by the sound of their steps. There was a murmur of talk from some of the near housetops, and the voice of a child singing itself to sleep. Leaning out the window, she could see a little farther up the road an open lighted booth where two men sat playing chess with a group of men and women watching the game. An old man wearing a scarlet fez sat close beside the players, intent on the game. The light on their faces made them look golden, and the fez was like a ruby.

"How beautiful it is! And how happy I am!" murmured Tacita.

CHAPTER XVII.

THE next evening Dylar came for Tacita and her friend to go with him and hear a recitation of one of their story-tellers.

The place was a nook of the ravine leading to the kitchens, and was so completely shut in by high rocks as to be quite secluded.

An irregular circle capable of admitting fifty persons had a shoal alcove at one side, and all around it low benches on which were laid thick straw mats stuffed with moss. In the alcove was a chair; and an olive-oil lamp of four flames was set in a niche of the rock above. These flames threw a strong, rich light on a score or two of men and women in the circle, their faces shining out like medallions; but they touched the man who sat in the chair only in some fugitive line on his hair, or cheek, as he moved. His form was scarcely defined. He sat there, a shadow, with his face bowed into his hands, splashes of black and of gold all about him. He seemed to be waiting, and Dylar spoke.

"Here is one who waits to hear for the first time how Basil of the Dylar lived and died."

At that voice the story-teller lifted his face, rose, and having bowed lowly, resumed his seat.

"How did Basil of the Dylar live and die!" he

exclaimed. "Ask of the poor and the sorrowing how he lived. Ask of the men and women who stood at bay, facing a stupid and dastardly world. Ask, and they will answer you: 'He was a dove and a lion, — a dove to our hidden sorrow, a lion in our defense.' Ask of the heart bowed down with a sense of guilt so heavy it fain would hide in the night, and follow it round the world; fly from the light, and hide in the night forever around the world. They will say, 'Has the Christ come back? Can a mercy so overflowing be found in a human soul?' Ask of the children who clung to him when he stood white in the gloaming. He was white, his hair and beard; his face and his robe, they were white.

"The children coming from school cried out when they saw, and ran to him. They ran, they flew, they clung around him like bees or butterflies, joyous. They held the folds of his robe. They pressed to hold his hand, and kissed it finger by finger.

"He lifted and tossed the smallest. 'Reach up to heaven,' he said, 'and pull me down a blessing. Stretch your innocent hands and gather it like a star-blossom.' And then would the little one, all wide-eyed, reach up and wait till he said, 'It is done!'

"'How did the King come down?' they asked him. 'How was God made man?' He answered them: 'The sweetness of the Godhead dropped like honey from a flower. The brightness of the Godhead fell like a star-beam from a star.'

"And he would say to them: 'Ask of your angels how God looks. How does he smile and speak? For your angels, said the King's Majesty, ever behold his face. Mine has followed me out into a century's shadows, walked with me out through a century's falling leaves. But ask your angels to-night to whisper close to your pillow, or come in a dream and tell you what are his hair and eyes, his voice and his smile. Ask one time and ten times. Ask ten times and a thousand. Ask again till they answer, "His face I behold no longer; for you are no longer a child."'

"And then their mothers would hear them at night whispering on their pillows.

"How did he die, our prince? How at last did we lose him?

"There was a thought that hovered, dove-like, over the people, that Basil would stay till his coming, stay till the coming of Christ. It hovered, coming and going, but never alighted in speech. Quieter grown, but hale, he lived to a hundred years, lived in the midst of his people, going no more abroad. He sat in the sun, or the shadow, judged, and counseled, and pardoned, peacemaking, scattering blessings.

"But when, of the hundred years, the last few sands were sifting, he girded him for a journey, and climbed the southern hills. After a week, returning, 'I bring you a message,' he said, 'from our ancient Mother, the Earth.'

"He showed them a grain of gold as it comes up

out of the mine, set in the gray and white of a rock with clay in the crevices pressed. Pure and sparkling it lay in its crude and worthless bed.

"Said Basil, 'What pay you for bread? Is it dust? And for raiment, a crumbling stone? For house and land, and a gift of love, do you offer dust alone? A careless kiss is easy to give, and a careless word to say. Will you fling your dust in the face of God? You have gold in your hearts, my children. Cast your follies away like dust, and break your pride like a stone. Dig for your gold, my children, says Earth, your Mother. Deep in your hearts it lies hidden.'

"That gold that he brought is set at the foot of the throne, and the words that he spoke there engraven: —

"'Dig for your gold, my children, says Earth, your Mother. Deep in your hearts it lies hidden.'

"He went to every house. Not a threshold but felt his footsteps. Children passed by him in line for a touch of his hand, and old men knelt for his blessing.

"He went to the house of the King, and walked with his head bent lowly, walked to and fro in the rough new building, saying never a word. But, standing without, he cried: 'My heart for a step at the door! and my soul for a lamp at the footstool!'

"He entered the dark ravine, he and the sun together. He was led by the hand by a sunbeam over the stony way. He went to the place he had set for the dead, where as yet no dead were sleeping. What he did, what he said thenceforth, no creature knoweth.

"Basil, our prince, and the sun went to the ravine together. The sun went in and came out; but Basil, our father, lingered. Twilight settled and deepened; but Basil, the White Father, came not. The stars came out in the night; the people gathered and waited. They whispered there in the dark, and dared not search, nor question. They whispered and waited and wept: 'We shall nevermore behold him! He has bidden us all farewell, and gone from our sight forever!'

"But at the dawn they said: Awake! Let us find him! Nor food nor drink shall be ours till we know where his foot has faltered. Homes we have none till Basil, our father, is found!

"The light was faint in the east; they could see but their own pale faces. They entered, a crowd, the ravine; they covered its stones like a torrent! Praying and weeping they went, but softly, not to disturb him.

"They reached the Mountain of Sleep that he had chosen to rest in. Only one hall was finished, one bed made smooth for slumber. Basil, the prince, was not there.

"But a lark sprang up outside, springing and soaring upward. They followed his song and his flight; for he seemed heaven's messenger to them.

"They climbed the rough, steep rock; they wept no more, but they panted. Wide and bright were their eyes with a solemn and high premonition. They climbed to a verdant spot like an oasis in the granite.

"There, like a fountain of song, jetting and singing upward, climbing from song to song, the larks were bursting and soaring out of the thick fine grass all over-floated with blossoms.

"And, lo! a beam of the sun shot over the eastern mountains, touched the grass where he lay, and seemed to say, Behold him! And beam after beam shot over, seeming to say, We have found him! while the larks sang pæans of joy.

"The people gathered around, and silently knelt in a circle; knelt, and folded their hands, but wept not, spoke not, prayed not. Silent they gazed and listened, as though on the threshold of heaven.

"There he lay, all white, in the hollow top of the mountain, straight and peaceful and fair, his hands crossed on his bosom. All white, save an azure glimmer seen 'twixt the snowy eyelids, he lay in the deep soft grass with the lark-choir singing about him, — singing as if they saw the dawn of the Resurrection.

"As they looked, his silvery whiteness grew bright in the sun of the morning. Would he melt like frost, and exhale! Would he rise like a cloud on the sunbeams!

"Thus stayed they an hour, the living as mute as the dead.

"Then one, not turning his eyes, spoke lowly: 'He moves not, neither to rise and speak, as we knew him; nor moves he to float away and be lost in the air of the morning. Passive he lies, our prince, in a sweet obedience to death. Passive and humble he lies, obeying the law of our Maker. Is it not then that he waits for his people to bear him downward where he has hollowed his bed, to his resting-place in the shadows?'

"Then said another lowly, his eyes still fixed on the dead: 'Send we messengers down to bring what is meet to bear him. And bring the children to walk closest of all beside him. For their angels see the face of the Heavenly Father.'

"Then he looked in their faces, and said: 'We are fainting with thirst and hunger. For a night and a day we have fasted and grieved and searched. Let the strong among us bring bread and meat and a litter. I, who am strong, will go.'

"So they went down, half a hundred, and brought a litter well woven, hung on staves of ash wood strong and long and polished. They brought up meat and drink; and the children, wondering, followed, knowing not what death is, not being let to know. They gathered about him softly, seated themselves in the grasses, decked their heads with the flowers. And in the folded hands and on the pulseless bosom of Basil they warily slipped sweet blossoms of white and blue.

"For the elders whispered them: 'Hush! he is sleeping! Hush! he is weary!'

"Then the people sat in a circle, and ate and drank in silence, prayerful, as if they ate the Holy Bread of the altar. Ending, they rose and gave thanks; and tender and reverent, laid their dead on the litter, and took the staves on their shoulders.

"The children, wondering, ran, lifting questioning eyes, puzzled, but no wise grieving, and clung to the edge of the litter. They were close to his head and his feet, they pressed inside of the bearers, making a flowery wreath all fluttering round his whiteness. And where a fold of his garment wavered over the border, a dozen dimpled hands proudly bore it along.

"So they went down the mountain, weeping, but not with sorrow. For they felt a stir within them, a trembling, an unfolding, a lifting sense in the temples, a glimmering sense of kindred to clouds where the sun is calling the rainbow out of the rain.

"There was a woman among them, a singer of songs. Basil had named her the Lark of San Salvador. As they went down, she made a song and sang it; and to this day the song is sung by all the scattered children of San Salvador. Later times have added penitence and supplication to the one stanza that she sang to them that day. Our hymn suits the dark hours of life: hers was all victory and exultation. She sang: —

'San Salvador, San Salvador,
We live in thee!'

"While she sang, they laid him in the bed that he had chosen. And when Dylar, the heir, came home to them, 'You have done well!' he said.

"Behold! Thus lived and died Prince Basil, the White Father of San Salvador!"

CHAPTER XVIII.

ABOUT a week after, one day when their lesson was ended, Iona said: "I have seen Dylar to-day, and he proposed that I should make a visit with you. Professor Pearlstein, whose class of boys you will recollect, would have come to see you, but he is quite lame. He sprained his ankle some time ago, and cannot yet walk much. He knew Professor Mora well. They were boys together. Would you like to go up?"

Tacita assented eagerly, and they set out.

"You are going to see an admirable person," Iona said as they went along. "He is very useful to the community. He sets the boys thinking, and guides their thoughts, but not so severely as to check their expression. He especially urges them to study what he calls the Scriptures of nature. He keeps the records of the town, and in the most perfect way, knowing how to select what is worth recording. He will make no comment. His idea is that most histories have too much of the historian in them."

"My grandfather had the same opinion," Tacita said. "He held that the province of an historian is to collect as many authentic facts as possible, and present them, leaving the reader to draw his own conclusions. He did not thank the historian for telling him that a man was good or was wicked from his own conclusion, giving no proof. He preferred to decide for himself from the given facts whether to admire or condemn the man."

They reached the path leading upward; and there Iona stopped. She was very pale.

"Would you mind going up alone?" she asked. "I do not feel quite well."

Tacita anxiously offered assistance.

Iona turned away somewhat abruptly. "I need nothing, thank you. Go in peace, since you are willing. I am sure that you would have much more pleasure in a tête-à-tête conversation with Professor Pearlstein. Present my salutations."

Tacita, feeling herself decidedly rejected, looked after her a moment. Iona was evidently neither weak nor faint. She walked rapidly, and, instead of going homeward, had followed the outer road northward.

The Professor was seated in his little terrace with a table beside him. He was weaving a basket. Silvery white roots in assorted bunches were piled on the table, and strips of basket-wood lay on the ground in coils. His robe was of gray cloth with a white girdle and hood, and he wore a little scarlet skull-cap. Tacita saw now, better than before, how handsome he was. The face was strong and placid, the hands fine in shape, the hair gleamed like frost.

She stood on the edge of the terrace before he

saw her, and was in some trepidation lest she had not taken pains enough to make him aware of her approach.

When he looked up suddenly, secretly aware of some other human presence, his face lighted with a smile of perfect welcome, and with a faint, delicate blush.

He brought out a pretty chair of woven roots with leathern cushions.

"The terrace is my salon," he said. "And I have the pleasure of asking you to be the first to sit in a chair of my own making. Are not the roots pretty? See the little green stripe running through the silver. It is second sight, already dreaming of leaves. Till I began basket-making, I had not known the beautiful colors and textures of woods. It is a pleasant employment for my hands. It enables me to think while working. Is the chair right for you? I am grateful to you for coming up. Shall we continue to speak in Italian? It must come more readily to you; and I am always pleased to speak the beautiful language. It is not more musical than San Salvadorian; but it is richer. Our language grows slowly. It is limited, like the experience of our people. Every new word, moreover, is challenged, and tried by a jury of scholars. We adopt a good many imitative words, especially from the Italian. You will hear *fruscio*, *ciocie*, *rimbomba*, and the like."

They spoke of Professor Mora, and Tacita answered a good many questions concerning him.

Professor Pearlstein, in return, recalled their early days together; and she found it delightful to hear of her grandfather as a boy, leaping from such a rock, picking grapes in vintage time in the road below, studying in the college yonder, and sliding down from terrace to terrace on a rope. It was charming, too, to hear of her mother as a little girl, quaint and serious, with golden hair and a pearly skin, and of her father as master of the orchards, with eyes like an eagle, and a ready, musical laugh. He died from a fall in trying to jump from one tree to another. "Who would have thought," he said, "that it is only three feet from time to eternity!"

"I am glad," Professor Pearlstein said, "that my old friend was able to live his own life to the last. It is not so hard for a student such as he. In such cases people can understand that they do not understand, and they let the student alone. In going out into the world, the most of us feel the pressure of a thousand petty restraints. I reckon that I lost five years of my life in wondering what people would think of things which they had no right to notice at all."

"It is like a person trying to run in a sack," Tacita said, "or like rowing against the tide a gondola all clogged and covered with weeds."

The old man brought a little table and placed on it a dainty refreshment for his visitor, setting it out with a pleased, hospitable care: a slice of bread, a conserve of orange-flowers, and a tiny glass of wine; partaking also with her at her request.

"I always expected some great discovery from Professor Mora," he said, folding his arms and looking far away to the western mountains. "At first I thought that it would be in physics. But I soon found that he looked through, rather than at, natural objects and phenomena. Visible nature was to him the screen which hid the object of his search. I recollect walking home with him one day in Paris after we had listened to a lecture on electricity from a famous scientist. 'What does electricity mean?' your grandfather exclaimed. He held that the greatest obstacle to the discovery of truth is the insincerity of man.

"I liked the same studies that interested him, though my proficiency in them was small; and when I saw the way he went, I hoped that he would set the seal of his guess, at least, on some grand eclectic plan of creation toward which my lighter fancy spun blindly its filmy threads. That terrible 'I do not know' of his was crushing! But later I learned to be thankful for one man who searched far into psychical and theological problems, yet spared the race a new theory."

Tacita listened with pleasure to his dreamy talk. And she told him of the recitation she had heard the week before.

"That flowery nook, with its larks, is to-day what it was when Basil laid him down there to die," he said. "The mountain is excavated in halls that concentrate like the spokes of a wheel, with a column left solid in the centre. The hollow called Basil's Rest may be called the upper hub. The lower one is in the centre of the earth. There 's a narrow stair goes up on the outside."

When Tacita went down, she saw Iona coming toward her, seemingly quite restored to health. Her cheeks were crimson, her eyes sparkling.

"I feel better," she said. "Let us go to the Star-terrace for a view of the sunset."

They went, and she pointed out effects of shadow in the western mountains and of colors in the eastern.

"I have sometimes an impulse to go out into the world again," she said then, abruptly. "When I was there, it was during my silence. I was there to study, not to talk. When we first go out, especially the young, we are held to a period of silence as to decisions, opinions, wishes, and plans. Obeying, we save ourselves trouble and avoid a good deal of foolishness. The story of Sisyphus is impressed on us as that of one whose first years are spent in a foolish effort and his last years in repenting of it.

"The only opinion we express from the first and at all ages is that touching our faith. A child may reprove a blasphemer, or assert its devotion to Christ in the hearing of one who expresses doubt. One subject after another is freed for us, as we learn what the world means by it. Of course, for a person of vivacious temper and strong feelings to remain silent, or to say always, 'I do not know,' gives full employment to the will and the nerves. I used sometimes to feel as though I should burst.

"Now, if I should go, it would be to speak when occasion calls, and to act in accordance with my speech. I could call a falsehood a falsehood, and a wrong a wrong."

"You would have to speak often," Tacita said dryly.

"Should I not!"

Iona began walking to and fro. "I have had visions of what might be done," she said, her manner warming as she proceeded. "The time is past when San Salvador can be long hidden, when it should hold itself only a refuge for a few, and a nursery for a few. I think that the time is come when it should prepare, prudently, yet with energy, to practice a Christian aggressiveness. We have our little circles in every part of the world. They are silent and true, and they are not poor. We have no weak hearts. The children of San Salvador are baptized with fire. The tests of our virtue and fidelity are severe. Our people have never occupied public office, because we hold officials responsible; and by the world they are not so held.

"We have capital. It might be spent in acquiring territory. Concentrated, we should be a power in the world. It is possible. I have the whole plan in my mind. I have studied over it for years. I have settled where our outposts should be, and how they might be strengthened.

I would deprive no ruler of his realm; but he should call himself viceroy, and sit on the footstool of an inviolate throne. I would mock at no faith of person, or society; but I would show the whole truth of which each belief is a fragment, and I would surround worship with such a splendor as should satisfy any lover of pageantry; and I would attack all organized wickedness.

"In the early days of our faith Christians did not fear persecution; for above the head of threatening king, or pontiff, they saw the face of an approving God. Only the spirit of Christ himself, simple and literal, can reawaken that faith. The first Dylar said that when he abolished preaching, and set the words of the King in letters of gold before the people.

"Tell me what to do!" said Tacita, leaning to kiss Iona's hand as she passed her by.

Iona paused. "See what I have thought," she said in a softened voice. "San Salvador is in danger, and the danger increases every day. How long, with explorers and mountain-climbers everywhere, can we hope to escape? Already, more than once, we have escaped but by a hair's-breadth. We hide by a miracle. Once discovered, what rights have we? A vulgar, if not malignant, curiosity follows you everywhere in the world. Every kind of science and astuteness would be employed to invade and subdue us. Every sophistical argument on the subject of sovereign rights, and even of human rights, would be quoted against us. Fancy a man educated in the tricks of diplomacy and the falsehoods of official life coming here and claiming the right to investigate and command, and bringing his subordinates to enforce submission!

"Our people are sent out into the world with every precaution. All are placed above want; but no one is made rich enough to win the world's blinding flatteries. Depending solely on their intrinsic worth for respect, they are seldom deceived. But, known as we are, even if force did not invade, what flatteries! What imitations of our ways without the spirit! Our realities made theatrical by their paraphrases — it might be worse than war. Ordinary society can see no difference between its own fire of straw and stubble and that primal fire which, now and then, bursts through some human soul.

"I have thought, then, to acquire all the land possible about the Olives, planting the plain and peopling the hills. A mile or two distant there is a group of hills much like those on which Rome was built. Our people could come, not as one people, but as if they were strangers to each other. Those who would, might even come at first as laborers. We all know how to labor. For wealth, if we had workmen and engines, the mountains would be an immense storehouse. There are beautiful marbles, and there must be more gold. Then what refuges we could have, not hidden and crowded, but open!"

"Did you think to go out into the world in order to stir up the people to this movement?" Tacita asked, when she paused.

Iona had stopped with her eyes fixed southward, as if she saw through the mountain-wall that measureless garden, and the city of her imagination shining in the setting sun.

She turned quickly, seeming startled to be reminded that she was not alone.

"Yes," she said, almost sharply. "And my brother has told me that Dylar thought I might wish to go. He spoke to you and you spoke to the prince. Ion will go."

"Ion feared to grieve you," Tacita said, surprised at this sudden address.

"Dylar also had spoken to me of it," Iona continued, her brows lowering. "He thought that I might like to go awhile with Ion. Why did he think so? I have never spoken of these plans to him. I waited for other conditions to arrange themselves. Why should the idea of my going out occur to him?"

"I do not know," said Tacita, more and more astonished at the tone in which she was addressed. "He said nothing of it to me. Perhaps he has some important mission for you."

"Why should he intrust a mission to me instead of Elena, or of going himself?" demanded Iona. "Can you think of any reason?"

"I do not know," Tacita repeated, and her eyelids drooped.

There was a moment of silence, and it seemed to have thundered. Iona gazed with scrutinizing and flashing eyes into the downcast face before her, and seemed struggling to control herself. A shiver passed over her, and then she spoke calmly.

"I have not told you all my mind. The country I have planned must have a dynasty, not a luxurious one secluded from the people, but one as simple and law-abiding as that which rules us here. But who will succeed Dylar? While I planned, that became the difficult question to answer. He has no child, and seemed vowed to celibacy. I thought of Ion. He alone, outside the prince's blood, might be said to have a certain prestige, though he has no claim. Ion has force, and, when he shall have been tried in the alembic, will have a fine character. He has courage, magnetism, and enthusiasm. It seemed certain that Dylar would never marry; and I approved of his apparent resolution and imitated it. It seemed fitting that the two highest in San Salvador should give an example of exceptional lives devoted to its cause. I had, moreover, a sort of contempt for that maternity which we share with the beasts, reptiles, and insects. I almost believed that common people only should have children and superior people mould and educate them. In that frame of mind I had that foolish portrait painted.

"Later, I saw my mistake.

"I have called the portrait foolish, and it is so in one sense, in the sense that most people would give it, but not in the sense which still to me is true. For I do set my foot on trivial love and mere fondness for love's sake alone."

She was walking to and fro again, her brows lowering. Tacita sat mute and pale, the vision of a terrible struggle rising before her mind.

"How perfectly logical an utter mistake may be!" Iona exclaimed with a sort of fierceness. "I reasoned with myself. I made it quite plain to my mind that the people of San Salvador needed an example of lofty and laborious lives which set aside for duty's sake all the joys of domestic life. I said, 'This people was elevated for a century to a higher plane of feeling by such an example.' It is a proverb here that the face of Prince Basil shone a hundred years after he died.

"I was half right. What kept the Israelites up to that pitch of enthusiasm which preserved them great so long? Not the goodness of the mass, which seemed as base as any, but the divine fire of the few. What made the great republic of the west something that for a time was equal to its own boast? The greatness and disinterested earnestness of the few. The nation which has no heroic leader is a prey to the first strong arm or cunning voice which seeks its subjugation. My plan would have been perfect if another leader had been growing up, as in the time of Basil, one of unquestioned right and character. But as I studied longer, I saw the flaw. Ion has been known here as a wayward boy, though noble. Besides, there has always been a real Dylar.

"Gradually the question readjusted itself in my mind without my own volition.

"Dylar and Iona married would unite the actual right and a shadowy one of sentiment, and the need of a leader would consecrate the marriage as still something ideal. Our son could not be a common one. I would pour all my soul into him. I would make him enthusiastic, courageous, wise, and eloquent. He should go down and work beside the daily laborer, as I have seen Dylar do, till only labor should seem worthy of a crown. He should be full of fire, like the old gods. That dead moon-like calm that people call Olympian is not Olympian. They were creatures of fire. They trembled with strong life like flames.

"It all flashed upon me. I saw what should be. But how could I inspire Dylar with my thought! A woman has limits in such circumstances. Nature imposes them. I could only wait till my plan of empire was perfect, then set it before him in all its splendor. What could he say but 'Let us work together for this new Eden! Let the future viceroy be our son!' There could be no other conclusion. It seemed sure, and on the point of realization. I waited only for his return to lay the whole before him. And then — and then" —

She choked, and, tearing the lace scarf from her neck, cast it away.

Tacita was deathly pale.

"Iona," she said gently, "may it not be that you expect too much of mankind in the mass?

Can you hope that any nation will long keep its ideal state? How many such a bubble has burst! Human life is not a crystallization, but a crucible. Your kingdom of Christ extended and prosperous, would it not become a kingdom of the world, as in the past? It is the old story of the manna, food from heaven to-day, and to-morrow corruption. Your saint in power would become, as in the past, a sinner, and your trusting people, also as in the past, a populace first of children, then of slaves, and lastly, of rebels. Forgive me, dear Iona! Your vision is as noble as yourself; but all are not like you. Are not you afraid to be so confident? Your plan opens such a field to ambition!"

"I was not ambitious for myself," said Iona, writhing, rather than turning herself away. "And I believe that rulers may be educated to see how much grander and happier they would be if the love of their subjects should exceed their fear. I thought of the future of our people submerged in a deluge with no counteracting influence. Perhaps something suggested" — she turned again to Tacita, and spoke breathlessly — "When Dylar first saw that portrait, he did not seem pleased. I asked myself why he should look so dark if he approved of my renouncing love. It was my way of silently telling him that I would take no lower stand than his. I thought that he would be pleased. He had never said, but had always seemed to intimate, that he would not marry. Once, on going out on a long and dangerous journey, he said to me: 'If I should never return, educate Ion to take my place.' He trusted me. He always confided his affairs to me. I never feared to have him go out. Nothing could seduce him. I felt sure that he would return even as he went. To me he was not utterly gone. I told myself that our spirits communed." She paused a moment, then added bitterly: "I thought that they did!"

"I am no queen nor sibyl," said Tacita faintly. "I cannot judge of these questions; and I could never hope to be able to stir a man up to great enterprises. I am only fitted to be a tender, and in some small things, a helpful companion."

"You think that I could not be a tender companion!" exclaimed Iona jealously. "I have put a rein upon myself. I will not make my smiles and caresses so cheap as to give them to everybody."

"I know that you are capable of great devotion, Iona," Tacita said tremulously, her eyes filling with tears. "Yet the hearts of humbler women may not be cheaply given, though they may be more accessible. They may be in something like the Basilica, — I speak with reverence! — no one rejected who wishes to enter in kindness, but one alone enthroned above all the rest, one to whom all who enter must pay respect. And perhaps the very kindness felt for all may be an outshining from that enthroned one, a reflection of the happiness he gives."

"It is well in its way," Iona said, trying to

speak more gently. "But such love is not good for Dylar when our existence hangs upon a thread. It is no time for him to think of repose and tender companionship. It would weaken him. He needs one who, instead of weeping if danger should threaten, would send him forth even to death, if need were, sure that such a death is the higher safety for him, and for her love the higher possession. Yet" — she made a haughty gesture and turned her darkening face away — "it is not that I love him: it is for San Salvador."

"Teach me to be useful, to be strong, Iona!" said Tacita earnestly. "I would give my life to the same cause."

"Would you give up a fancy for it?" asked Iona, looking sharply into her eyes. "It is so easy to offer a world that is not wanted, and refuse a grain of sand that is asked for."

"I would give all that I have the right to give," Tacita replied, and felt herself shrivel before this imperious woman, who stood before her with the sunset golden on her head and the shadow of a mountain on her bosom, with her brow made for a tiara, her lips to command, and her eyes to scathe with their anger.

"Dylar has asked you to be his wife?" Iona said, low and quickly.

There was something blade-like in the outcome of this sentence; but it brought help in seeming to call the conduct of Dylar in question.

Tacita folded her hands, raised her head with

a dignified gesture, and looked the speaker steadily in the face without replying.

"Ah!" Iona turned away with a fierce gesture, then returned. "It is not a son of yours who will save San Salvador!" she exclaimed.

"Perhaps God will save it, Iona," said Tacita gently, and rising, went toward the stair.

She had descended but a few steps when Iona followed her. "I hope that I have not been too rude," she said. "Pardon me if I have offended you! The subject is to me of such supreme importance that I forget all lesser considerations in it."

Her voice, though conventionally modulated, had something in it which told her heart was beating violently.

"I am not offended," murmured Tacita. "I respect and appreciate your position, your authority, your rights."

At the lower landing they found Dylar. He looked anxiously at Tacita. "I have been waiting for you to come down," he said. "And Elena has gone to order our supper to be brought here. We are going to have the sun-dance in the Square. Do you wish to go home first?"

She shook her head, and tried to smile. She could not speak.

"I will leave you both in better company," Iona said courteously, declining to stay; and bowing, left them.

For a time, to Tacita, it had seemed as if San

Salvador had opened its walls to admit a salt wave from the outer world; but the gap closed again while Dylar attended to her with a careful solicitude sufficiently reassuring as to his regard for her, but with no suggestion of fondness. He was a kind friend; and the cheerfulness and decision of his manner gave her strength.

"He is not one," she thought, "to need the strength of a woman's will to keep him in the path of duty. And she — I am glad that Iona does not love him. It would break my heart, if she did."

CHAPTER XIX.

IONA went away with a stately step, but with a brain on fire. It was only when near the Arcade that she quickened her steps; and when inside the door, she ran upstairs.

Having found Elena, "I am going out to the Olives for a few days," she said, "and I want to start at once for the Pines. Will you have Isadore called to go with me? I will meet him at the water-gate."

She waited for no reply, but hastened to her own room. In a few minutes she came out dressed in the gray costume of labor.

"Everything is ready," Elena said, meeting her, and expressed neither surprise nor curiosity.

The sun had set, and it was night when Iona met the men who had been sent up to attend her. But she would suffer them to go no farther than the water-gate.

"I know the road well," she said, "and am in no danger. When at daylight you see the signal that I am at the Pines, you will turn the gate again. It will be sooner done if you stay here."

They obeyed unwillingly, and she went over the wild mountain road alone, guiding her donkey with a careful hand, and conscious only of a dull discomfort. It was midnight when she reached the Pines.

"Don't be alarmed!" she said cheerfully to the guardian. "I am sorry to disturb you; but I wish to go to the Olives. Go to bed now, and be ready at six in the morning to accompany me."

The man said no more. They questioned Iona as little as they did Dylar.

They were in the lower room. Iona went to the chamber above; but when she heard the upper door close, she came down again, unbarred the outside door, and went out into the Pines. Space was what she wanted, — space and solitude.

It was a sultry night, and the still air under the pines was heavily perfumed, not only with their branches, but with the oppressive sweetness of little flowering vines that ran about through the moss underneath them. A mist that was mingled of moisture and fragrance hung in the tree-tops, and above them, dimming the stars. It was stupefying.

Iona felt her way, step by step, over the slippery ground, and leaned against one of the great pine-boles, scarcely knowing where she was. There was left in her mind only a vague sense of ruin and a vague impulse to escape. She stood there and stared into the darkness till she was faint and weary, then sank down where she stood and sat on the ground. There was an absolute stillness all about her. The only motion perceptible was in the narrow strip of sky between the tree-tops and the rock, where one dim hieroglyph of stars slowly gave place to another. Once from some bird's-nest not far away came a small complaining note. Perhaps a wing, or beak, or claw, of some little sleeper had disturbed its downy neighbor. Then all was still again. But the little plaintive bird-note touched the listener's memory as well as her ear. The atmosphere of her mind was as heavy as that around her body, and the suggestion was dim. She had almost let it slip when it came of itself, a Turkish proverb: "The nest of the blind bird God builds."

It was the first whisper of Divine help that had risen in her soul. Perhaps then it was an angel's wing that had disturbed the bird in its sleep.

Iona glanced upward and saw the pale mists beginning to quicken with the coming day. "God help me!" she murmured listlessly, and rising, went into the house and to her chamber.

The early training of San Salvador was expressly calculated to give the child a few indelible impressions. One of these was to do no desperate nor extraordinary act without first taking counsel from some disinterested person, or taking a certain time "to see if the King would interpose." In absenting herself for a while from San Salvador, Iona had obeyed the sudden command of necessity. But that step taken, her instinct was to do all as silently and calmly as possible.

"I will not mention Tacita Mora's name, and I will work," she thought. It was the one step in advance which she could see.

Shortly after sunrise she started for the Olives. Reaching the turn of the road where the green began, she descended from her donkey to walk to the castle, and the man went on to make the necessary gossip concerning her arrival. For some reason the first step on the greensward under those gray-green branches awakened her sleeping passion. Was it grief that the peacefulness of the scene knocked in vain at her heart for entrance? She would willingly have thrown herself down in those quiet shadows and wept. The strong check she drew on the impulse brought up its contrary, and she laughed lightly.

There was no one in the great circular ground-room of the tower, nor on the grand stairs where a man might ride up and down on horseback; but reaching the top, she was met by the housekeeper.

"Take my arm," the woman said. "You must be very tired. I saw you from the window," and she gave no intimation of surprise nor curiosity.

"I am tired and hungry and sleepy," Iona said smilingly, availing herself of the offered support. "I find that I have not had exercise enough, and am too quickly fatigued. That is so easy with what I have to do. But I have come out here to work. If you will bring me a cup of chocolate, I will then try to sleep. I reached the Pines very late last night."

She went to the chamber that was called hers, drank the chocolate that was brought her, and, overcome by fatigue, fell asleep.

"Prince Dylar has sent you the keys," the housekeeper said to her when she woke. "He said that you forgot them. The messenger is waiting to know if there is any word to take back."

"None except to thank the prince for taking so much trouble," Iona said.

If she were more irritated or soothed by Dylar's evident anxiety it would not have been easy to say. The sending of the keys, too, besides giving an opportunity to learn if she were well, was a reminder of his confidence in her and of her importance to San Salvador. They were the keys of his private apartment, the treasure-vault, and of the door leading to the ravine where a stream of water still brought an occasional grain of gold.

She opened the case with a little key of her own, and looked eagerly to see if there were any written word, snatching out the slip of paper that she found.

She read: "I think that the late rains may have washed out a few grains of gold. I did not go when I was last at the castle. Will you look? DYLAR."

Just as if nothing had happened! Iona put her hand to her forehead and for a moment wondered if anything had happened.

"I must work hard!" she thought. "'When nature is in revolt, put her into the treadmill;'" and she went out to see what there was to do, going from house to house, greeting the people and welcomed by them. They supposed that she had just arrived from some distant city, but asked no questions, knowing that she was one of Dylar's messengers.

There was a field of wheat ripened, and Iona put on a broad-brimmed hat and thick gloves, and taking a sickle, went out to it across the vineyards. "I am to do it all," she said laughingly. "Let no one come near me."

Had any one in San Salvador seen her speaking to those people, he would have thought that he had never seen her so gay; and had he seen her when, leaving all behind, she went out alone, he would have wondered at the gloomy passion of her face.

She put her sickle into the grain, and bent to her work like any habitual laborer. In fact, she had done the same work before in play. Handful by handful, the golden glistening stalks fell in a straight ridge across the field; and as the movement grew mechanical, her thoughts took, as it were, a sickle, and began to reap in another field. With a savage strength it cut through the years of her life, all its golden promise and fulfillment, all its holy aspirations, all its towering visionary building which had been, indeed, but a dream of empire and of love. It cut through the humbler growth of sweetness blooming like the little blue flowers she severed from their roots and cast aside to wither, or trampled under her feet. As she wrought thus, sternly, with a double blade, the mental harvest even more real to her mind than this one that the June sun shone upon, her breath kept time with a sharp hiss to the hiss of the sickle, and her heart bled.

With no cessation from her labor except to wipe the perspiration from her face, she reaped till sunset. Then, after standing a little while in doubt what next to do, she bent again, and reaped till the stars came out. Their lambent shining through the falling dew lighted her back to the castle. The windows were all open in the houses as she passed them, and some of the people were seated at supper in their great basement rooms, as large as churches, with their rows of arches, instead of walls, supporting the ceiling.

"Let no one touch my work," Iona called gayly in at one of the windows, "unless you should wish to bring in what I have reaped. I have put a cornice around the field. I would have reaped all night if there were a moon. Good-night. Peace be with you."

They echoed her salutation; and she hung her sickle on the outer wall, and took her way to the castle.

"Don't tell me that you have had your supper!" the housekeeper said; "for I have taken such pleasure in preparing one for you."

"I shall eat it, for I have earned it," Iona replied, taking off her coarse gloves and straightening out her cramped fingers.

But what she ate she knew not, nor what good fairy suggested to her questions and answers and remarks that were to her as dry as husks, yet which served as a screen to her misery. She seemed to have a secondary mind which worked mechanically.

There are certain proverbial sayings which have an air of such owl-like wisdom and are such a saving of mental work to those who repeat them that they seem immortal. One of these is that no person is fit to command who cannot obey. If it were said that no person is fit to command an inferior who cannot obey a superior, a reasonable idea would be conveyed.

Setting aside such cases as the apprenticeship of Apollo to a swineherd, and the voluntary self-humiliation of an ascetic who seeks to win heaven by effacing himself on earth, there is no more murderous injustice than the enforced subjection of a lofty nature to a lower one. It is not a question of pride, nor of fitness; it is a question of individual existence.

Iona had been like a queen in San Salvador; and she had been a wise and gentle sovereign. She had assumed no authority, and fully acknowledged that she had none. She was always consulted, and she had made no mistakes. Her whole strength had been expended to make herself worthy of this preëminence, and she had succeeded. Her powers had risen with the need of them, and she stood upright, sustained by this pressure from all sides.

The pressure removed, for to her mind it was almost removed and would be totally so, she collapsed and fell into confusion. With Tacita the wife of Dylar, she took for granted that her reign in San Salvador was at an end. For it was her power in the community, she persistently told herself, not her power over the heart of Dylar, which she lamented. "It is not love! I do not love him!" she had repeated a hundred times.

To her mind, Tacita, however sweet and lovely, was a girl of limited capacity, but also one who could assume a dignified and even haughty reserve when her relations with Dylar were called into question. As his wife, she might object to any other female authority in the place; and Iona well knew that the fair-haired girl, with her charming grace and caressing manners, would win a greater affection from the people than she herself would be able to win by the devotion of a life.

She went to her chamber with the hope of sleeping; but sleep was impossible. She rose, took her lamp, and went downstairs, meeting the housekeeper on the way.

"I am going out through the cellar," she said. "Give me a long roll of wax taper, and the key of the cellar door. I will take care of all."

She tied the great roll of taper to her girdle, took a little wallet and a lamp, and went down to the cellar. But instead of descending the second stair, she went along under the damp arches, past the rows of moist hogsheads, to a little stair that went up to a walled-up door. The stairs had been utilized as shelves, and rows of jars and little bottles of olives were set along them.

Iona cleared them all away from the four lower steps, and with a deft hand took out two or three screws from the boards; then, turning back the three lower stairs like a door, disclosed a steep stair underneath through a square opening. The stair ended in a corridor from which was heard the sound of waters, growing clearer as the passage led into a cave that had a high opening at one side, like a round window, almost lost in a long, close passage that looked as if broken in the rock by an earthquake, louder again when a door was unlocked and opened into a roofless passage of which one side diminished in height and showed a fringe of little plants and mosses, and the other soared, a precipice. Here was a little hollow through which flowed a brook coming through crevices northward to disappear southward into crevices. Where it issued from the rock in a fall of a few feet were two troughs, side by side, turning on a hinge, so that the water might be made to pass through either. Both were lined with nets that could be raised and drained.

Iona set her lamp on the rock, changed the troughs, and carefully raised the net in the one through which the water had been passing, and with a little wire spade turned over the débris left there. Where a yellow glimmer showed, she picked it out and put it into the wallet hanging at her side.

The night was so still that the flame of the lamp scarcely wavered; but she swung her coil of lighted taper to and fro, and round in a circle, to catch any glimmer of the precious metal hidden there.

There was neither tree nor shrub in sight. Grotesque peaks and cliffs rose on every side, shutting her in. Scintillating overhead was the Milky Way, a white torrent of stars from the heights of heaven flowing between the black rock-rims that it seemed almost to touch.

The gold came in glimmer after glimmer, some almost too small to gather out of the slippery débris, others half as large as the flame of the lamp, and brightly glowing.

Iona's spirit revived a little. The place, the time, and the occupation took her out of the track of her habitual life. She recollected her first visit to this place, when she and Dylar were children. They came with his father. The prince had brought her after her father's death, hoping to distract her; and while she and the boy picked out the shining grains, he sat on a lichened rock beside them, and told how men had spent their lives in searching for and compounding the philosopher's stone in order to make at will this bright king of metals which they were gathering from the sand.

He told how kings and queens had lavished patronage and treasure on such seekers after hidden knowledge, and the names by which the magic stone was called: *The daughter of the great secret; The sun and his father; The moon and her mother.* He told them the legend that St. John, the

Evangelist, could make gold; and young Dylar paused in his search to learn the verses of an old hymn to the saint that the alchemists applied to themselves: —

> "Inexhaustum fert thesaurum
> Qui de virgis facit aurum,
> Gemmas de lapidibus."

He described to them the *dry way* and the *humid way*, the *white powder*, that changed metals to fine silver, the *red elixir*, which made gold and healed all sorts of wounds, the *white elixir*, *white daughter of the philosophers*, which made silver and prolonged life indefinitely. He told them the prediction of a German philosopher that in the nineteenth century gold would be produced by galvanism, and become so common that kitchen utensils would be made of it. "But that," the prince added, "will surely be a gift of wrath, and will come like a thunderbolt. Men will play with fire, and it will turn upon them. They will laugh in the face of God when they snatch his lightnings out of his hand, and he will reduce them to ashes. But to him who kneels and waits, into his hand will God put the lightning, and it shall be as dew to his palm when he smites with it."

As he had talked, sometimes to them, and then as if to himself, to her imagination all the space about and above had become filled with watching faces. There were pale brows over eyes grown dim and hollow with fruitless study; there were clustering locks that wore the shadow of a crown;

there were dreamy faces whose eyes were filled with visions of the golden streets of the New Jerusalem; there were the hungry cheeks and devouring eyes of poverty; there was avarice with human features; and over the shoulders of these, and peering through their floating hair or widespread beard, were impish eyes and glimpses of impish mirth; all which, with sudden explosion, were wrapped one moment in flame, and the next, fell in a mass of gold like a mountain, writhing one instant, then fixed. And in the place where they had been remained unscathed one face still gazing in a dream at the golden streets of the New Jerusalem.

The childish vision rose and fell; but it left a scene almost as unreal.

There showed no more sparkling points in the trough, and Iona changed it for the other, glancing into the second as she withdrew it. At the bottom of the net was a spark like a star. It was a little ball of gold that the water had brought while she was searching. She smiled at sight of it, scarcely knowing why it pleased her; and instead of putting it into the wallet, found a dew-softened flake of lichen to wrap it in, and hid it in her bosom.

"I will ask Dylar if I may give it to Ion when he goes out," she thought; and the image of Ion warmed her heart. "Dear boy!" she murmured.

The dew, the darkness, and the silence soothed her as she walked homeward. Seen from a distance she might have seemed a glow-worm creeping along the face of the rock. Her lamp grew dim, and she lighted her taper again by its expiring flame, and went on uncoiling it as it rapidly consumed in the faint breeze of her motion.

Weary, and in some way comforted, she reached the castle and her chamber, and was soon asleep.

But anguish woke with her, the stronger for its repose. The novelty of the change was gone, and a consuming fever of impatience to return to San Salvador took possession of her. But she had come for a week, and she stayed a week, passing such days and nights as made her cheeks thin and her eyes hollow.

The morning she had set for her return she was scarcely able to rise; but at noon she reached the Pines, and while everybody in San Salvador was at supper, she quietly entered the Arcade, and sent for Elena to come to her room.

"Give these to Dylar with your own hand," she said, consigning to her care the wallet and the case of keys. "And please send me some supper here. I am going up the hills this evening, and may stay all day to-morrow. Whoever comes with my food can set the basket on the terrace, if I am not in sight."

Elena looked at that worn face, and could not restrain an expostulation.

"Iona, dear, you look too tired to go up there alone to-night," she said. "Wait till morning, and no one shall come near you, nor even know that you are here."

"I should suffocate here!" Iona exclaimed impatiently.

Elena urged her no farther. "At least, make me a sign in the morning that you are well," she said. "Tie a white cloth to the terrace post."

"Yes, yes! Don't fear!"

She went out. It was twilight, and the windows were beginning to be lighted. In the Square she saw Ion going toward the college. She drew the silver whistle from her sash and blew his name.

The boy stopped, then came running back.

"I am going up the hills to stay to-night," his sister said, holding him in her arms. "Don't tell any one, unless Dylar should ask you. And see! I have a gift for you. It is a little ball of pure gold. Say nothing of it even to Dylar till I tell you. Keep it as a memento of San Salvador when you are far away. And now, good-night, my treasure, my better than gold!"

She kissed him tenderly.

"O Iona, why do you go up there to-night?" the boy cried. "What is the matter?"

She freed herself from him gently, but decidedly. "Don't oppose me, Ion. Do as I bid you, and say good-night now."

He urged no more, but went away dejectedly.

The cottage to which Iona went was a tiny one with a plot of herbs in front of it and a huge fig-tree. It contained but one room, across which was slung a wide hammock. She opened the door, prepared her hammock and got into it, dressed as she was. There was a floating wick in a vase of oil and water that gave just light enough to faintly define the objects in the room and show a small fragment of paper on the floor. As she lay, glancing restlessly about, her eyes returned again and again to this paper, and finally with a sense of annoyance. She was naturally orderly and neat to a fault even; and now it seemed as if all her characteristics had become either numbed or fantastic. That scrap of paper grew to be of such importance to her that she could not rest while it lay there; and having risen to pick it up, it was still of so much importance to her that she could not set fire to it in the little night-lamp without looking to see what it was. It was a fragment of an old pamphlet in which had been an article on mediæval customs. The few lines remaining referred to a custom in the isle of Guernsey.

It related that if a sale of property were being made by heirs, one heir objecting, this non-consenting one could stop the sale by crying out: "*A l'aide, mon prince! On me fait tort!*"

She read, then burned the paper. It was an interesting fact. She thought it over, going to lie in her hammock again; and thinking of it, dropped asleep.

There were a few hours of repose. Then she waked and could sleep no more. The little lamp had burned out, and the dark dewy night looked in at her open window. She rose and went out.

The fig-tree before her door grew a single straight

trunk to a height of four feet, or a little more, then divided into two great branches, hollowed out and widespreading. Iona leaned into this hollow, hanging with all her weight, and looked over the town.

"*A l'aide, mon prince! On me fait tort!*" she murmured, recollecting the words that she had slept repeating. And she stretched her hands out toward Dylar's dwelling-place.

"They think that she alone has power to charm you!" she went on. "Blind that they are! And are you also blind? They see me preside with dignity, and they think that I am nothing but stately. Cannot you understand that I am as full of laughter as a brook? I have come up here alone many a time and talked with the birds, the plants, and the wind. I came to give vent to the life that was bubbling in me. If I had but shown it! If I had but shown it! The greatest force I ever put upon myself was to be cool and calm with you. It was honor made me. I thought you were resolved to lead the angelic life, and I would not by a smile, or a glance, or a wile make it harder for you. How could I imagine that you would surrender yourself unsought to a lesser woman! Oh, I could have charmed you! Cannot I call you now? Shall I submit without a struggle?"

Iona knew in herself a compelling power of will, without defining it. It had sometimes seemed to her that when roused by some vivid interest, her will had flung out an invisible lasso that bound whomsoever she would; not so much, indeed, here in San Salvador as out in the world, where minds were less firmly anchored. Yet even here, finding one in a receptive mood, she had more than once made him swerve as she had wished.

Could she not in this hour of supreme upheaval send her soul out — all her soul — through the space that divided her from Dylar, make it grow around him like a still moonrise, find him where he lay thinking, or dreaming, perhaps, of that fair-haired Tacita, reach into, shine into, his heart and blot that image out, gather all his will into the grasp of her strong life, and so melt and bend him that he should turn to her as a flower to the light? Dylar had a strong will. She had seen him as oak and iron. But, if she should slip in at unawares!

Iona caught herself leaning over, straining over the inverted arch of the fig-tree, her arms extended toward the college, the fingers cold and electric, the very locks of her loose hair seeming to be turned that way, her whole person having a strange feeling as if a strong current of some sparkling, benumbing essence were flowing from her toward the spot where Prince Dylar lay helpless and unconscious.

She started back. "God forbid!" she cried. "*A l'aide, mon prince!*" The last words came as of themselves; and her prince was still Dylar.

"Yet it would be for his good and the good of San Salvador," she said, and began to weep.

And then again, half frightened at her own passion, her mood changed. After all, was she certain that her fears were well-grounded? What proof had she? Nothing strong except Tacita's silence; and might she not have mistaken the significance of that? Her nature seemed to divide itself in two, one weak, wretched, dying, the other seeking to comfort, reassure, and save this despairing creature from destruction. Her imagination began to hold up pictures to divert the weeping child of earth.

She fancied Dylar in the first enthusiasm of knowing all her plans. He would adore her. But there should be no silly dalliance. For, "I do not love him in that way," she still persisted. When she should crown herself with the white betrothal roses that must be gathered by her own hand, it would be with the thought of authority wearing the crown of pure justice. When she should assume the rose-colored robe and veil of a bride, it would be to her a figure of that charity all over the world which it would be the aim of her life to promote. Both she and Dylar would be stronger for this companionship; and she would be, not only his inspirer, but his soothing and comforting friend also. Every lion in his path should become his beehive. When he was weary of empire she would charm him with many a folly. For sometimes he would be depressed, perhaps, even out of temper. It was delicious to think of him so — as quite a common man — for a little while. It would be the dear little flaw in her gem.

All should come as she had planned. Their colonies should condense in the plain and on the hills outside, little by little, stealing in as silent as mists, not seeming one, but as strangers to each other. Here at San Salvador should be their stronghold, as now, and their inmost sanctuary. But they would live outside, on a hill, or going from place to place. When all was well ordered without, they would come back for a while, and she would lead Dylar to some height, to the summit of the North Peak, where there should be a mirador, and pointing to their colonies embossing the whole circle even to the horizon, she would say: "Behold the marriage-portion I brought you!" She would tell him of a time when, their earthly lives ended, they might be borne, like Serapeon, over mountain top and plain, while their son —

Their son!

Her fancy descended from its cold mountain height to a green hollow in the hills, and a cooing of doves, and a veil of heliotrope shutting them in. She hung over the face of the child. His cradle should be formed like a lotos-flower, and there he should sit enthroned like Horus, the young Day. As her fancy dwelt on him, he grew, — a youth with inspiration shining in his eyes, a man, with command on his brow. He should bring in a golden age. Peace and brotherly love prevailing should make men look upon their past lives as the lives of wolves. He should wear white while young, and purple when he began to take the reins of government. The white should have a violet border.

Here the dreamer's fancy seemed to stumble as if caught in the train of a white robe with a violet border that brought some disenchanting reminiscence in its folds.

It was the robe that Tacita had worn the last time they met at the assembly, and she had looked like a Psyche in it.

As that figure floated, smiling, into her dream, Iona's empire crumbled, her lover became a mocking delusion, her shining babe faded to a snow-drop broken from its stem, her enthusiastic youth shrank like dry leaves, her purple-robed prince fell with a crash at her feet.

"A—a—a—i!"

It was almost like the growl and spring of the tiger. But the rein was drawn as involuntarily as a falling person seeks to maintain his equilibrium.

"*A l'aide, mon Roi!*" she cried, and stretched her hands out, not toward Dylar, but toward the Basilica, showing faint and ghost-like against the western mountains. "*A l'aide, mon Dieu!*" and lifted her face to heaven.

To a strong, high soul, despair is impossible. However dark the overhanging cloud, it never believes that there is no help. It has felt its own wings in the sunshine, and it knows that somewhere there must be a way for them to lift it out of the storm.

But where?

"My father told me to do without love, if I could," thought Iona, and sank down, and sat leaning against the tree. The time-blurred image of that father rose before her mind, and the scenes following his death. Of her life with him, except that it was happy, she could recollect nothing definite. With the egotism and ignorance of youth she had taken a father's loving presence for granted, as she had taken sunshine and air. He had died at Castle Dylar, and she was with him. His illness was brief, she had scarcely known that he was ill. For one day only she had not seen him.

She seemed again to stand, a child, in the middle of the great salon, looking at a closed door. The prince held her hand and murmured words of consolation. Her playmate, young Dylar, stood at a distance wistfully gazing at them. She did not understand for what she needed to be consoled; but an undefined dread oppressed her.

"What is in that room?" asked the child with a gloomy imperiousness. "They close the door, and tell me not to open it."

"Only a mortal body from which the soul has fled," said the prince. "Your real father has gone to see the King, to see your dear mother; and both, unseen, will watch over you and your little brother. Do not you want to go home and see poor little Ion? He is alone."

"I want to see my father's body," said the child.

"Iona, he sleeps!"

"Wake him, then!" she cried. "Or, no. I will be quiet and let him sleep. I will sit by him till he wakes."

Dylar looked distressed. "Dear child, no one ever wakes from that sleep, it is so full of peace and rest. His heart does not beat. His hands are as cool as dew."

"Wake him!" she cried, beginning to sob; and, snatching her hand away, ran to beat on the door, and call "Father! Father!" with an awful pause of silence between one call and the other. "If he were warm he would speak. Give him wine! I can make his heart beat. Let me in! I will go to him!"

"Nothing can make the body warm when the soul has gone out of it," said Dylar, following her to the door. "It is like a candle that is not lighted."

"If I kiss him, he will light," persisted the child. "He always does."

"His light is in the court of the King," said Dylar. "You must not, cannot call it back."

The child stood silent a moment, a statue of rebellious grief, trying to understand the cold science of death, now for the first time presented to her. Then, with something more of self control, she asked: —

"Can I make the King give back his soul, in any way? no matter if it is not by being good. Could I by being wicked? I am not afraid."

"By being bad you would only separate yourself still more from your father. My child, he was not torn away. He went submissively, obediently. He bade me love you as my own child, and

I will. The King took him gently by the hand. Wait a little while, and he will come for you."

The child's head drooped. She leaned against the door, putting her arms up to it in a vain and empty embrace. "I want to go in!" she said faintly.

The prince opened the door and led her in.

A white-veiled shape lay stretched out on a narrow bed. The prince folded back a cloth, and the child's dilating eyes, startled and awe-stricken, looked for the first time on death.

"Is it a statue?" she whispered.

"It is his own body in its long sleep."

"I have always seen him breathe," she whispered, looking up at her guardian with frightened eyes. "His breast went up and down — so!" she panted. "I felt it when he held me in his arms. I did not know that it could stop."

Sobs broke out. She threw herself on to the cold breast and clung to it. "He spoke; and I thought that it was a little thing," she cried, in a storm of tears. "Sometimes I did not listen. I thought that I could always hear him speak. Sometimes he told me to do a thing, and I said no. I did not think that he would ever be 'no' to me. He is all 'No!' Speak one word, father! It is Iona. Why can he not speak? This is his hair, his face, his own self, — all but the cold!"

"He cannot hear you," said the prince.

The child rose and looked wildly about. "I would climb over all these mountains, barefoot and alone in the dark, to hear him say one word!"

And then, in that day of revelations, there was yet another which startled her for a moment out of her own grief. For Prince Dylar, raising his arms and his face upward, exclaimed with passion: "O Heavenly Father, do we not expiate the sin, whatever it was!" and for the first time she saw a man weep.

How vividly it all rose before her! How like was that child to herself!

"How glad I am that I put my arms around him and tried to comfort him!" she thought.

"My heart has been broken once before, and it healed," she said, and returned to the present, where her mind swung idly to and fro, like a pendulum, counting mechanically the minutes.

The dawn began. It was not like the tingling white fire, alive to its faintest wave, of dawns that she had seen. It was still and solemn.

"*A l'aide, mon Roi, mon Dieu!*" Iona murmured drearily; and speaking, remembered the invitation: *Come unto me, all ye that labor and are heavy laden, and I will give you rest.*

What did it mean? She understood duty and obedience toward God; but an ardent worship of the whole being, a clinging of the spirit through the sense, she did not understand. It had seemed to her material and unworthy. She forgot that the sense also is the work of God. The spirit should rise above the sense, leaving it behind, despising it, she had thought; but to lift the sense also, to bathe it in that fire that burns not, to lead it by the hand, like a poor lame sister, into the healing Presence, that she knew not. Her worship dispersed itself in air.

"I will go to him!" she said. "But where? He is everywhere; therefore he is here."

She knelt, folded her hands, and said, "Help me, O Lord! for I am in bitter need," and said it wearily. The universal affirmation of his presence had for effect only universal negation. She did not find him.

The dawn grew. She rose from her knees, weary and faint. "How are we to know when God helps us? Perhaps when some path shall be opened for me out of this labyrinth. Is this all that religion can give me? — the patience of exhaustion, or the apathy of resignation? Is this rest? No matter! I will obey. I will ask help every day, and try to do my duty. What is meant by loving God? I cannot love all out-doors. If Christ were here as he was once upon the earth, he would not make me wait one hour with my heart all lead. If he were here! Oh, I would walk all barefoot and alone in the dark over the mountains, over the world, to hear him speak one word!"

The sun rose, and its golden veil was let down slowly over the western mountains, creeping toward the Basilica. When it touched, she could see from where she stood in her door the sparkling of the crown-jewels. They seemed to rejoice.

"I will go to his house to ask help," said Iona. "Why should he have a house among us, if not to give audience there to his children! But now I must sleep."

She went to tie her handkerchief on the little balustrade of her terrace for a sign to Elena, and returning, closed the door, leaving the window ajar. Getting into her hammock then, she swung herself to sleep.

It was late in the afternoon when she waked, and the sun was shining into the room in a long, bright bar through the window. In the midst of that light was the shadow of a head. As she looked at the shadow-head it turned aside in a listening attitude.

Iona rose and opened the door, and Ion sprang up joyfully. He had brought her breakfast and left it outside the door, and come again with her dinner, both waiting untasted.

"I peeped in and saw that you were asleep," he said. "Are you not hungry?"

She ate something, not more from faintness than to please him.

"I was so tired. I worked hard at the Olives, and did not sleep till late. And now, dear boy, go down. I have something to do, and something for you to do. To-night, after the people are out of the street, I am going to the Basilica. I wish to go alone. When the portal is closed, get the key of the south side door, and leave it in the lock. Thank you for coming up! You are always good to Iona!"

She kissed him smilingly, and let him go.

CHAPTER XX.

In a great mental upheaval, to be able to decide, even on a point of secondary importance, is helpful. It is like a plank to the shipwrecked.

Such to her was Iona's resolution to go to the Basilica and watch all night. Christ had said "Come!" and she would go as near to him as she knew how. The sense of blind obedience was restful. She looked across the town, and a certain peacefulness seemed to hover over the white building beyond the river. She thought herself like that river, flowing in silent shadow now after a wild rush from height to depth, and through dark and stormy ways.

There was no assembly that evening, and the avenue and square were unlighted. But the roof-terraces were populous, and a murmur of voices and of music came from them. They called to each other across the narrow streets; and when some one sang to mandolin or guitar in one terrace, the near ones hushed themselves to listen. It seemed to Iona like something that she had heard of long before, it was so far away, and had so lost its spirit and color.

There are times when to hear laughter gives one a feeling of terror such as might be felt if it came from a train of cars about to roll down a precipice. When Dante came up from the Inferno, careless laughter must have affected him so.

As Iona entered the Basilica, locking the door behind her, the sweet, true word of an English writer recurred to her: "Solitude is the ante-chamber to the presence of God."

She knelt before the Throne a moment; then, seating herself on the cushioned step, waited for some plan of life to suggest itself to her as possible and tolerable.

"It must be outside the mountains," she began, then checked herself. "It shall be where God wills."

But, oh, the torment of it! The utter collapse of all spirit and elasticity!

The shadows of the portal came up to fall before the light of the tribune, and the light went down to meet the shadows. Darker slanting shadows of columns crossed the dim side aisles. There were panels of deep, rich color between, growing brighter toward the tribune. On the balustrades were thirty-three lamps, one for each year of the King's life. They climbed in a narrowing flame-shape with the Throne and the tiara. In the jewels a sleeping rainbow stirred.

Iona rose and wandered about the church. What more could she say, or do? Was she to go out as blind and unconsoled as she had entered? The silence was terrible. It occurred to her that having had no conscious and pressing need of God, she had gone on fancying herself in communion with him when there had been no living communion.

"Do we, indeed, know that God whom we profess to believe in?" she asked herself. "Have I not as 'ignorantly worshiped' him as did the Athenians of St. Paul's time? Oh, if I find him not to-night, I shall die!"

Passing up a side aisle, she paused before the picture of a tiger there, which stood in a strong light, and stared at the Throne. She lifted her hand to pat his head, and whispered, half smiling, "Have you found the secret, brother?" Then she went on and knelt again before the tribune, questioning: —

"Who, then, have I come here to seek, and what? A glorious and triumphant Deity? Something more, indeed! I seek one who knows sorrow, poverty, and betrayal. Where is he? Where is the compassion, the power, the voice of him? I must find him, meet him! Where is he?"

She set herself to call up some image of him as human creatures had seen him face to face in their need. She recalled other vigils of knight, crusader, mourner, and sinner. Above all was the supreme vigil of Mary Magdalen. Ah, what a night of anguish! Ah, what a rapturous morn! To hear him speak her name as he uttered that "Mary!" on the first Easter morning would be better than a thousand princes of her blood ruling through ten thousand years, would be better than to have Dylar look at her with love's delight.

She evoked that scene out of the past, — the chill, dewy garden, the lonely sepulchre, the dull hour before dawn. The present faded from her view. Gleam of gold and sparkle of jewel, she set them aside. Blotting out the glow of lamps and the glimmer of marble, it came. She was in the garden with Mary Magdalen. The stone was rolled away, she heard the woman's bitter outcry: *They have taken my Lord away, and I know not where they have laid him!*

Darkness, sorrow, and desolation reigned. Even the Magdalen, weeping bitterly, departed. She was alone before an empty sepulchre.

Said faith: "He is here even as he was there, the same. He is invisibly here in this place, even as he was there. If he be God, he is here. Hush, my soul! He is here! He is here!"

A Presence grew in the place, felt by her whole being, a sense of life, gentle and potent. Seen by her soul, Christ stood there looking at her, and waiting to hear what she might say.

She stretched her hands out to him with a wild burst of tears. "What shall I do?" she sobbed.

And, oh, wonder of wonders! A voice "still and small," — the voice that was heard by Elijah, — a voice more distinct to her soul and her senses than her own sobbing question had been, answered her!

The angel of truth guides the pen with which I write these words!

The voice came not from the shadows where she had evoked his image by the mystical incantation of faith. It spoke at her right side, each word let fall like a pearl, so that she turned her head to listen.

Were they words of compassion, or counsel? Did they propose a plan, or commend her obedience?

No. They only repeated the Divine invitation: *Come unto me, all ye that labor, and are heavy laden, and I will give you rest.*

But as they fell softly on her ear, the darkness that had enveloped her parted, and slipped down like a tent, and a flood of light entered and illumined her soul. Her hands were still outstretched; but they were clasped in ecstasy: her tears still flowed; but they were tears of rapture.

"Oh, why did I not think of it!" she exclaimed; and in that first inflowing of heaven did not remember that she *had* thought, and *had* come, and that the words were but a reminder that she had done her part, and there remained only that he should fulfill his promise.

She was in heaven!

There was no thought of explanation, no study of phenomena. She knew at last what sort of miracle Christ came on earth to perform, and what his kingdom is.

How was her life to proceed? It mattered not. Whatever might happen, all was well, was more than well, was best! Should she go, or stay in San Salvador? No matter. She was blest either way.

"And this heaven," she thought, "lies just outside the door of every human heart!

"*Behold, I stand at the door and knock.*"

How simple is a spiritual miracle, after all! It is but the substitution of harmony for discord, the finding the keynote of the universe.

Not the least marvelous part of her change was that she recognized this state as her true one; as one who has long been cramped and bowed down breathes deep with relief, the pressure removed, and knows that he was made to stand upright.

No earthly storm clears so. Even when the sun bursts forth, he shows a rack of flying mists. But Iona no longer thought of a shadow, even as past. Trouble had no longer any existence, even as fugitive. *In the twinkling of an eye*, says Saint Paul.

It was early dawn when she issued from the Basilica. Some one was pacing one of the paths in the green above, but came running down as soon as she appeared.

"Why, Ion! What brings you here?" his sister exclaimed.

"I could not sleep," the boy said, trembling. "Oh, Iona, what is the matter with you? What has happened? Let us both go away from here!"

She put her arms around him. "Dear Ion," she said, "the brightest, the sweetest, the most glorious thing has happened! Some time I will tell you, but not now. Your hair is wet with dew, and your cheeks with tears, my dearest. Do not fear. All is well! All is well! Do not I look happy?"

"Your face shines!" said Ion, his own growing brighter. "I was afraid."

"You are to fear no longer. You must go to rest, and then wake happy. But first let us kiss the panels of the portal; for they have been to me the gate of heaven."

They went, hand in hand, knelt on the upper step, and kissed the panels of the door, then walked in silence across the town. In the dawn, the face of Iona could be seen radiant with a light that was not of the sky. It was the outshining of an illuminated soul.

"Brother," she said, pausing at the door of the Arcade, "what the King said is not a figure of speech, but literal truth. When he commands, or invites, do not stop to question. To him there are no impossibilities. Do not forget him, nor disobey when life is bright; but he is a star, best seen in the dark. If you should ever be in great anguish, set your soul searching for Christ, and do not leave off till you find him. He is near! He is always within call!"

She went upstairs, planning. First sleep. Then this duty, then that, quite as usual. And every duty, even those heretofore most nearly irksome, had a new face, smiling and peaceful. Every little weed and brier of life put forth its blossom.

Reaching Tacita's door, she stopped; and hearing a movement within, she whispered: —

"Tacita Mora! O Tacita!"

Tacita was awake. Her heart had been sorely troubled by Iona's talk the week before; and her sudden absence had increased the pain. She opened the door, wondering at that whisper, and shrank on seeing who was there. "What do you wish for?" she asked, fearing some new and more violent scene.

"To restore you the peace I have disturbed," said Iona. "To ask your forgiveness. All the wild things I said that day were a dark delusive cloud which has been driven away by sun and wind. I was wrong, and you right. It is the Holy Saviour himself who will save the refuge they have named for him. I hope, dear, that you and Dylar will marry, and be happy; but it would be presuming in me to ask of your intentions. Peace!"

She went swiftly away before Tacita, astonished, could answer a word.

To be in heaven while yet upon earth, what is it? It is to have a sense of security which extends to the bounds of conception, — and beyond, a sense which no peril can disturb. It is to be steeped in a silent contentment which no words can express. It is to call the bird your sister, and the sun your brother. It is to study how you may serve those whom you have hated. It is to say farewell to those who are dearest to you, and know that they are not lost. It is to see the sorrows of earth as motes in a sunbeam, yet be full of compassion for the suffering. It is to know for what purpose you were created.

CHAPTER XXI.

EARLY in the autumn Iona was to go out into the world, having instructed Tacita thoroughly and lovingly in all her work, and seen with what a modest dignity the girl she had thought almost childish could preside in her place.

She was in haste to go, but solely from a conviction that she was needed elsewhere.

"Wherever I am not absolutely needed, I am lost," she said. "My life here is, and has been for a long time, that of a Sybarite. I am terrified when I think of a longer waste."

"Stay till after the vintage," they all urged her.

"I will stay on one condition," she said to Dylar. "And that is that I may plan, and help to prepare a house for you and your bride. Once outside, I may not be able to come back and see you married; and it would be cruel if I could have no part."

"But, Iona, Tacita has not promised to marry me," Dylar said, smiling. "However, do as you please. May I ask what your plan is?"

She pointed to the college. As we have said, the building was large and irregular, crowning a mass of rock that broke roughly toward the town, and fell sheer on the mountain side, the narrow space spanned by a bridge from the college gate to the Ring. A small part of the structure toward the town was detached, a point of rock rising sharply between it and the main building. The only mode of communication between the two was by means of a stair at either side to a mirador built on the top of this point of rock, and a narrow gallery hung over the steepest fall of the rock. This semi-detached portion, containing but four rooms, was Dylar's private apartment.

"With two large rooms in addition," Iona said, "that would make you a charming apartment. There is yet space enough on the rock if we fill up that narrow interstice with masonry solid from the plain. The two rooms will be large, one a few steps higher than the other. They will be very stately, with the steps and curtain quite across one end. Where the stone breaks to right and left, a stair can start, double at the top, and meeting over an arch midway, to separate again below. There will be space also for a small terrace outside the door. It can be made something ideal. You use but two of the four rooms now. The little museum in the other two can be removed to the college. There is plenty of room. This work should be begun at once, masonry takes so long to dry well. But as your living-rooms would be the old ones, you need not put off your marriage till it is quite dry. There is no time to be lost."

"No one plans like you," Dylar said. "It will be charming. Do as you please. I will see if I can find a bride for your pretty house."

He took his way to the library, where he had seen Tacita enter. She was there alone, lighting up a shadowed corner with her fair face and golden hair.

It was a very studious face at that moment. Her arms stretched out at either side of a large volume, she read attentively. Other books were piled at right and left. Now and then she put her hand to her forehead, then made a note on a long strip of paper, writing with a serious carefulness.

She was preparing a lecture on history for the youngest class of girls in that study.

"It must be to the great complex subject what a globe with the great circles only is to the whole geography of the earth. It must be as though, on that globe with its few lines, you should draw at one point a little black circumflex, and say: 'Here is found the asp of the Nile. The monarchs wore it in jewels on their diadem. One laid it alive on her breast, and died. And here, where this black line goes past, and never stops, but always returns, the Wise Men of the East found the Infant Christ. And here grow roses, oh, such roses! in full fields, to make the precious attar of. And here grows the pink coral, like that coral rose Iona wears. No; the lesson must not be dry, nor yet too rich. It must make them wish for more. Only a few sparse sweetnesses. O land of France, what noblest, fairest deed for children to hear was ever done on your soil since you were France?"

So the young student was thinking, deep buried in her study, when she heard a voice say:—

"O Minerva, may I come in? Is there a gorgon on your shield of folios?"

She looked up with a glad welcome. "Not for you. You are come in good time, perhaps, to check my wild ambition. Do you know, prince, that I aspire to become an historian?"

"Then I come indeed in good time," he said. "For it is a history which I wish you to write."

She looked inquiringly; but he did not meet her glance.

"Will you come out to the terrace?" he said, indicating the one near them toward the college.

And as they went, he said reproachfully: "You hide yourself from me. I find you always surrounded. You seem to like me less and less every day."

Tacita's lips parted. "Shall I tell him that I like him more and more?" she thought. "No. Yet he must be satisfied."

"I do not know what reply to make," she said, somewhat breathlessly.

"Do you know what to think?" he asked.

"Oh, yes!"

"Would it pain me to know?"

"Oh, no!"

He smiled, even laughed a little; she had said, in fact, so much more than she was aware.

"Look at the college," he said. "Iona has a plan of a house there for me." He explained it.

"She will remain till vintage time to see it well started. Will you go there and live with me, Tacita, when it is done?"

"Yes!" she said quietly, her eyes on the college.

"Will you go next Easter?" he asked, after a pause.

"Yes!" she said again.

"God's blessing on you!" he exclaimed fervently.

They stood a moment longer in silence.

Then: "Shall I go back to my writing?" asked Tacita, looking at Dylar with an expression of entire contentment and confidence. And when he answered her smile, and bowed assent, she left him there, to build up his house with one swift flash of fancy, to bring his bride home rose-veiled, to draw from her reluctant lips all that they now refused to tell, to tear himself away presently with only a few gentle words, and not even a pressure of the hand.

"You have made me very happy, my Tacita!" he said. "I leave you now only because I must!"

In San Salvador engagements were very brief, as they could well be between persons who had known each other from childhood; and whatever friendly intimacy there might have been between them before, it ceased in a great measure during that time. It might be said that courtship was almost unknown; and between the betrothal and marriage the couple did not meet alone. Tacita's promise, therefore, remained a secret between herself and Dylar.

And so the summer passed with no apparent change in their relations.

Autumn was always a stirring time in San Salvador. The whole town was given up to the labors and pleasures of harvesting. Every one had some task. Even the children were made useful. The vintage, as in all grape-growing countries in times of peace, was a season of gayety, and all its picturesque work, except the grape-gathering, was done in that part of the outside road, or cornice, between the Arcade and the kitchens. A crowd of children were seated here in groups on straw mats, with awnings over them. Boys and men brought huge baskets of grapes supported on poles over their shoulders. In the centre of each group of six or seven was a large wooden tray heaped high with the fruit which they picked from the stems into basins in their laps. Women, girls and boys went about and gathered from these full basins into pails for the wine presses. Dressed in the stained cotton tunics of former vintages, their hands dyed a deep rose-color, the children chattered like magpies. Even little lisping things, under the guidance of their elders, were allowed to take a part in the business, or fancy that they did. Some of the boys had taken a little two-years-old cupid and rubbed grape-skins on his hands, face, legs and feet, till they were of a bright Tyrian purple, and set a wreath of vine tendrils on his sunny hair; and he went about from group to group vaguely smiling, not in the least understanding the mirth which his appearance excited.

The boys capered about like goats when free from their burdens. One of them ran to the Arcade, turning summersaults, walking on his hands, running backward, went up the stairs, like a cat, and appeared in the veranda, cap in hand.

Tacita was seated there by a little table, making notes of the harvest as reports were brought her. The boy delivered his message like a gentleman, bowed himself out, and became a monkey again.

Not far from the noisy grape-pickers, under another awning, were women sorting nuts and olives. They suspended their work as Iona came down the street and paused to speak to them. All looked up into her face with an earnest and reverential gaze. They had not ceased to wonder at the change in her, nor had they learned to define it; for while, in her gentleness and simplicity of manner she was more like one of them, they were yet conscious of a superiority which they had never before recognized in her. It was as though a frost-lily should in a single night be changed to a true lily, fragrant and still.

She spoke a few words to them, and then went up to the veranda to Tacita.

"Stay with me a little while!" said Tacita eagerly, bringing her a chair. "I think of you all the time, and cannot keep the tears out of my eyes."

Iona embraced her. "The same hand leads us both, dear. Do not grieve. For me, I am in haste to go. You have yourself made me more eager with your munificent gift."

For Tacita, with Dylar's approval, had given all her little fortune to Iona to be disposed of "not in doing charity," she said, "but in doing justice."

And Iona had replied: "Yes, justice! For though charity may move us to act, that which we do of good is but a just restitution."

"My heart is in anguish for the world's poor," she said now. "And not for the beggar alone. I think of those who can indeed escape physical starvation by constant labor, but whose souls starve in that weary round that leaves them no leisure to look about the fair world in which they exist like ants half buried in sand. I think of homeless men and women, oh! and children, eating the bread of bitterness at the tables of the coarse and insolent; of artistic souls cramped by some need that any one of a thousand persons known to them could supply, could understand without being told, if they had a spark of true human sympathy in their hearts, but which they behold with the insensibility of stones. Your fortune, my Tacita, will be a heaven's dew to such. For your largess will be given only to the silent, who ask not. I do not know the world as well as many of our people do; but those who have had most experience say that the almost universal motto acted on, if not confessed, is the saying of Cain: 'Am I my brother's keeper?' Now, I wish to have as my motto that I am my brother's keeper whenever and wherever one has need of me. I will have nothing to do with agents nor organizations. I will see the suffering face to face. Wherever I see the eyes of the Crucified looking at me through a human face, there will I offer help. The King shall send me to meet them."

"There are those," said Tacita, "who will affect anguish in order to move you. They rob the real sufferer, and they create distrust and hardness in the charitable."

"I shall sometimes be deceived," Iona said. "Who is not? Sovereigns are deceived by their courtiers, husbands by their wives and wives by their husbands, and friends deceive each other, and children deceive their parents. I go with no romantic trustfulness, I assure you."

The hour for her departure hastened to come.

On the last evening she went to the assembly, passed through all the rooms, saying a few words, but none of farewell. Then she went to the Basilica.

The rapture of her vigil had subsided; but the seal of it remained stamped on her soul, never again to be overwhelmed in darkness. Doubt and fear were gone forever, and she went on cheerful and assured, if not always sensibly joyous.

It had seemed to her that on this last visit she should have a good deal to say; but no words came. What she was doing and to do spoke for her. She walked about, looking at the temple from different points, to impress its features on her memory, and sat an hour before the throne in quiet contemplation.

What her leave-taking was of that sacred place, we say not.

Early the next morning she was seen walking along the mountain-path with Ion at her side. At the last visible point of the path she turned, stretched her arms out toward the town, then went her way.

Ion came back an hour later, his eyes swollen with weeping. "I shall see her in the spring, in the spring, in the spring," he kept repeating, to comfort himself. And when Tacita came to meet him with both her hands held out, "O Lady Tacita, I shall go out to her in the spring, in the spring!" he said.

CHAPTER XXII.

THE short southern winter drew to a close. Everything that could fade had faded. The vines stretched a network of dry twigs, the olive trees were ashen, the pines were black. The gray of crags and houses looked bleak under the white dazzle of the mountain-wreath, and the dazzling blue of the sky. Sometimes both were swathed in heavy clouds, and the town was almost set afloat in floods of rain.

It was the time for in-door work, and closer domestic life.

The last days of this season were given up to penitential exercises similar in intention to the Holy Week of the Catholic church, though different in form, — having, in fact, only form enough, and that of the simplest, to suggest the spirit. Like all the instruction given in San Salvador, its object was less to act upon the passive soul than to set the soul itself in action.

The admonition to these devotions was brief: "At this time, while Nature sits in desolation, mourning over her decay and trembling before the winter winds, let us invite those veiled angels of the Lord, sorrow and fear, to enter our hearts and dwell awhile with us. Let us read and ponder in silence the life and death of the Divine Martyr. Let us remember that while we have rejoiced in peace, plenty, honor and justice, thousands and tens of thousands of our kind in the outer world have suffered starvation of body and mind, have been hunted like wild beasts, and branded on the forehead by demons disguised as men; and let us remember that that same Divine Martyr, our King and our Lord, said of these same children of sorrow and despair: *Inasmuch as ye have done it unto them*—whether good or evil—*ye have done it unto me.*"

The exercises began on Saturday night, and continued eight days, ending on the second Monday morning. There was a visit at night to the cemetery by all but the children, the sick, and the very aged. On Saturday the children would visit the Basilica to commemorate the blessing of the children by Christ, and, strewing the place with freshly budded myrtle twigs, would ask his blessing before the Throne. Mothers would take their infants there and hold them up, but would not speak. "For their angels shall speak for them," they said.

Sunday was kept as Easter, and was a day of roses; and on Monday morning the whole town, all dressed in white, would go to the Basilica in procession, tossing their Easter lilies into the tribune as they passed, till the sweet drift would heap and cover the steps and upper balustrades, leaving only the Throne, gold-shining above a pyramid of perfumed snow.

For up through the dark soil and out of the prevailing grayness, already a wealth of unseen buds were pushing their way out to the broadening sunshine, to burst into bloom before the week should be over. The gardens had their sheltered rose-trees and lily-beds, and every house its cherished plants, watched anxiously, and coaxed forward, or retarded, as the time required.

The first Sunday was called the Day of Silence; for no one issued from his house after having entered it on returning from the cemetery, and each head of a family became its priest on that day, reading and expounding to his household the story of the passion of Christ, the Divine Martyr.

On Monday morning, after the procession of lilies, Dylar and Tacita would be publicly betrothed; and a week later their marriage would take place.

"I do not know, Tacita," he said to her, "if our form of marriage will satisfy you. It has nothing of that ceremonial which you are accustomed to see, though we hold marriage to be a sacrament."

It was Saturday morning of their Holy Week, and the two were walking apart under the northern mountains. They had already assumed the mourning dress of gray and black worn by all during that week, and the long gray wool cloaks with fur collars worn in the winter were not yet discarded. But their faces were bright, Tacita's having a red rose in each cheek.

"Elena has told me something," she said. "And how could I be otherwise than satisfied? For so my father and mother were married, and so — you will be!"

"Our position in regard to a priesthood, if ever to be regretted, is still unavoidable. Our foundation was a beginning the world anew, all depending on one man, with the help of God. No authority whatever was to enter from outside; but all was to conform as nearly as possible to the word of Christ; and as if to atone for any omission, he was elected King. Our people were of every clime and every belief; yet they were all won, by love, — not by force, nor argument, nor fear, — to accept Christ, and to live more in accordance with his commands than any other community in the world is known to do. When any of them go out into the world they choose the form of Christian worship which suits them best; and some, returning, have wished to see a priesthood introduced here. But that question brought in the first note of discord heard in our councils since the foundation. Some wanted one form, and some another. The subject then was forbidden, and we returned to the plan of our founder: to live apart, a separate and voiceless nation, waiting till God shall see fit to break down our boundaries. On Easter Sunday we lay our bread and wine on the footstool, opening the gates, and with prayer and song ask him to bless it, our invisible High Priest. Then each one, preparing himself as his conscience shall dictate, goes humbly up the steps his foot can touch at no other time, and takes of the sacramental bread, touches it to the wine set in a wide golden vase beside it, and comes down and eats it, kneeling. The little square of snowy bread looks as if a drop of blood had fallen on it where it met the wine. I think that many a heart is full of holy peace that day."

"Well they might be," said Tacita. "But of the marriage, tell me. What have we to do? I am half afraid."

"First, then," said Dylar, "On Saturday you lead the girls to the Basilica for the Blessing, as Iona used to do, Ion leading the boys. On Sunday you do only as the others. On Monday morning a company of matrons go for you and take you to the Basilica for the lilies. All are in white and all wear veils of white, you like the rest. But you alone have a lily on your breast. All come out. You, surrounded still by your guard of matrons, remain in the court just outside the portal, at the right, and I, with the Council, at the left. All the others are below, outside the green. Professor Pearlstein, as president of the council, then asks in a loud voice if any one can show reason why I should not demand your hand in marriage. He waits a moment, then says: 'Speak now, or forever after hold your peace.' No sound is heard. I forbid the wind to breathe, the birds to sing!"

"And then?" said Tacita, smiling, as he stopped and flashed the words out fierily.

His eyes softened on her blushing face, and they stood opposite each other under the lacelike branches of an almond-tree where minute points thick upon all the boughs betrayed the imminent blossom-drift.

"And then," said Dylar, "I shall come forward into the path where the lamps of the sanctuary shine out through the portal, and I shall say: 'If Tacita Mora consents willingly to promise herself to me this day as my betrothed wife, in the presence of God and of these my people, let her come forth alone and lay her hand in mine."

He pronounced the words with seriousness and emphasis. His tones thrilled her heart.

"And then?" she said, almost in a whisper.

He smiled faintly, but with an infinite tenderness. "And then, my Lady, if even at so late a moment you doubt, or fear, you need not answer."

"How could I doubt, or fear!" she exclaimed, and turned homeward.

They walked almost in silence, side by side, till they reached the Arcade, where they were to separate till they should meet in the scene which he had just been describing. And there they said farewell with but a moment's lingering.

That evening all retired as soon as sundown; but they rose again at midnight and assembled in the avenue and square, from whence, in companies of a hundred, each with its leader, they started for the cemetery.

As they went, they recited the prayers for the dead by companies, the Amen rolling from end to end of the line.

Entering the ravine was like entering a cavern. But for the sparse lamps set along the way they could not have kept the path. They went in silence here, only the sound of their multitudinous steps echoing, till a faint light began to shine into the darkness before them from where, just out of sight, every letter had been outlined with fire of that legend over the arch: —

I AM THE RESURRECTION AND THE LIFE.

Then from the midst of the long procession rose a single voice reciting the psalm: *The Lord is my Shepherd.*

No one, having once heard it, could mistake the voice of Dylar for any other. It was of a metallic purity, and gave worth to every word it uttered.

Yea, though I walk through the valley of the shadow of death, I will fear no evil, for thou art with me, thy rod and thy staff they comfort me.

As they listened they felt not the stones under their feet. Solemn and buoyant, into their souls there entered something of that spirit which has made and will make men and women march singing to martyrdom.

They passed under the arch, and in at the lower door of the cemetery. All the doors from top to bottom were open, and the lamps shed a dim radiance through the long, hushed corridors of the dead; but their flames caught a tremor as the breathing multitude went by, two by two.

They ascended inside, by ways that seemed a labyrinth, to the upper tier just under the grassy hollow of Basil's Rest. Issuing there, they descended by the outer stairs, filling all the galleries on the eastern side of the mountain. The waning moon, rising over the eastern mountains, saw a great pyramid of pallid faces all turned her way, a dim and silent throng that did not move, — as though the dead had come forth to look at the rising of some portentous star, long prophesied, or to watch if the coming dawn should bring in the Day of Judgment.

Presently a murmur was heard. All were reciting in a whisper the prayers for the dead, each striving to realize that they would one day, perhaps not far distant, be said for himself.

This multitudinous whisper, the chill of the upper air, the solemn desolation of the terrestrial scene and the live scintillating sky with that gleaming crescent unnaturally large between the eastern mountain-tops, all made Tacita's hair rise upon her head. Into what morning-country did it mount, like mists from the earth at sunrise, this cloud of supplicating sighs from out their earth-bound souls? Were these shadowy forms about her, indistinguishable from the rock save for their pallid faces, were they living men and women? or would they not, at the first hint of dawn, reënter, mute and slow, those cavernous doors, and lie down again in the narrow beds which they had quitted, for what dread expiation! — for what hope long deferred!

Not much of earthly vanity can cling to such a vigil. The ordinary human life, slipped off so like a garment, would be assumed again, freed for a time, at least, from dust and stain.

When, at length, a faint aurora showed in the

east, a choir of men's voices sang an invocation to the Holy Ghost as the Illuminator.

That song dispelled all fear, and life grew sweet again: — life to be helpful, joyful, and patient in; life in which to search out the harmony and worth of life; — life to grow old in and wait after work well done; — life to feel life slip away, and to catch dim glimpses and feel blind intuitions, in the midst of creeping shadows, of a sure soul-rise in some other sphere!

As they went down, Tacita heard a whisper from Elena close to her cheek: "'Dig for your gold, my children, says Earth, your Mother. Deep in your hearts it lies hidden.'"

CHAPTER XXIII.

THE week of commemoration passed by. On Saturday the children went in procession for the King's blessing, the Basilica all theirs that day. No one else might enter save Tacita and Ion as leaders, and the mothers with their infants. Going, they left the place fragrant with their strown myrtle-twigs.

Easter came and went with its blush of roses everywhere, its rose petals mingled with the children's myrtle on the pavement, roses between the lamps, and roses in the girdles of the people. The bread and wine, on silver trays borne by Dylar and the elders, was set at the foot of the Throne, and after prayer, and music sweet as any heard on earth, the people made their communion as the sun went down, having fasted all day since sunrise.

When it was over, Ion walked to the Arcade with Tacita.

"If only Iona were here!" she said. "And now we are to lose you also. Truly, our joy is not without a cloud."

"What joy is cloudless longer than a hour?" the boy exclaimed. "For me, it is now hard to go. Only the thought that my sister is there attracts me. You were right, Lady! At the point of leaving San Salvador, each little stone of it becomes precious to me."

"Do not forget that love, dear Ion!" said Tacita. "And remember, too, that you have left behind you something tenderer than stones."

"Dylar will bring you to England," he said. "I imagine myself running to meet you; and that comforts me. I cried so when Iona went. I was like a baby. She made me almost laugh describing our next meeting. She would appear to me in a London street. She would be dressed in those fashions we laugh so at. I must not speak to her. If I should speak, she would call a policeman. I told her that I would run and kiss her in the street if I had to go to prison for it. How glad I shall be!"

He wiped his eyes.

The next morning all the people, all in white, a white wreath round the city, went with their lilies to the King, till they were piled, a fragrant drift, up to the very gold, and the lamps shone through them like stars through drifted snow.

All came as Dylar had said, and Tacita was betrothed to him before God and his people, the lights shining on them through the open portals which they reëntered then, but only with a few chosen ones, to repeat their vows before the Throne.

The people waiting outside strowed the way with flowers; and Dylar led his betrothed to her own door, and left her there. There was music in the afternoon, and at twilight the sun-dance in the Square.

At last the bride-elect was alone in her chamber, all the lights of the town extinguished. The shadows were soothing after the excitement of the day, and she was glad to be alone. She had refused to take a candle, and had even blown out the little watch-light. Yet sleep was impossible, though she felt the languor of fatigue. A tender melancholy oppressed her heart. Never had she so loved Dylar as at that moment. To be able to dream over his looks and words had been almost more pleasant than to be with him; for, gentle as he was, there was something in his impressive quiet and almost constant seriousness which made her sometimes fear lest she should seem to trifle. But now she longed for his presence.

"If I could see him but a moment!"

She watched a glow-worm coming up her balcony, its clear light showing the color and grain of the stone, itself unseen.

How lovely had been her betrothal! She went over it again in fancy, catching her breath again as when, her guard of matrons parting to disclose her, she had walked out before the whole town to place her hand in Dylar's, and heard the simultaneous "Ah!" of the whole crowd set the deep silence rustling. Why had he not come one step to meet her? Her eyes were downcast after the flashing glance that met her own when he had called her forth. She had not looked once in his face; and it had seemed to her that, had there been one step more, she could not have taken it, but must have fallen at his feet. True, his hands, both tremulous, had gathered hers most tenderly; but why had he not taken at least one step? Could it have been coldness that kept him fixed to that square stone he stood on? It was a smooth gray stone with little silvery specks in it, and a larger spot at one corner. Dylar's right foot was a little advanced to that spot, a neat foot in a black shoe with a silver buckle, and the edge of his long white robe, open over the shorter tunic, just touched the instep. She had not raised her eyes above that white hem and the border of her own veil.

"Oh, why is he not here for one moment!"

She recollected Italian lovers. There were young men in the provinces who, late on the night before their marriage, went to scatter flowers from the door of their beloved one to the church door; and rude people even who went abroad at early morning would step carefully not to disturb a blossom dropped there for her feet to pass over. And then, the stolen interviews, the whispered words, the sly hand-pressure!

Ah! Dylar would never love in that way. Perhaps he had no ardor of feeling toward her. And yet — and yet —

She smiled, remembering.

There was the sound of a step below, and some one stopped underneath her window. Her heart gave a bound, half joy and half fright, and she ran to lean over the railing. No; it was not Dylar.

"I am the college porter," said a voice below.

"I bring you a note. Drop me a ball of cord, and I will send it up."

She flew to find the cord, dropped it, holding an end, and in a minute held the note in her hand.

"I will come back in fifteen minutes to see if there is any answer," the man said. "The prince, my Lady's betrothed, told me to wait."

After all, it was better so. His presence would have agitated her. Besides, he was obeying the rules of the place.

But the light to read her letter by! For the first time in her life, it seemed, she had no light at hand, and this of all times in her life when most it was needed. Neither was there a match in her chamber, nor match nor candle in the anteroom, nor in the dining-room. "Fool that I was!" she cried desperately, and ran to the balcony again. The porter would be sure to have a taper with him.

She spoke; but there was no reply. The man had gone away.

There was no reply from him; but was this a reply, this little lambent shining at her hand? The glow-worm she had seen was on the rail. As it lightened, a spot of light like sunshine lit the stone.

Tacita in breathless haste brought a large sheet of card-board and set it in the blessed little creature's path; and when she had enticed it, carried the sheet to her table, cut the silken thread that bound her letter, and slipped the page along toward the spot of light that, ceasing for a while, began again.

Turning the paper cautiously, her heart palpitating, her lips parted with quick breaths, she read her letter, word by word, till the whole message was deciphered.

"I cannot sleep nor rest for thinking of you," he wrote. "I have to put a strong force on myself not to go and speak from under your window. I am drawn by chains. I have a thousand words of love to say to you. How can I wait a week to say them! I have been whispering them across the dark to you. How you came to me to-day, my own! I know just how many steps you took, and I shall set a white stone in place of the gray one where you stopped. DYLAR."

She found pencil and paper, and aided by the same fitful lamp wrote her answer.

"My Love, like you I could not sleep nor rest. You have made me happy. I have only a glow-worm to read and write by. Sleep now, and love your TACITA."

The man came, and she gave him her note; then, finding her love's lamp-bearer, she set it carefully on the railing of the balcony.

"Dearer than Sirius, or the moon, good-night!" she said.

The marriage differed but little from the betrothal. It was the only marriage possible in San Salvador, a solemn pledge of mutual fidelity made in the presence of God and of the people. Dylar came to the Arcade for his bride, and led her over the flower-strown path to the Basilica, which they were the first to enter.

It was a white day, all being dressed as on the Monday before, except the bride, who was in rose-color, robe and veil, and the bridegroom, who wore dark blue.

That afternoon they set out for the castle, going through the Pines.

The preparations at the Olives were not less joyous. It was long since a Dylar had brought a bride home to them; and they looked on Tacita, with her white and golden beauty, as an angel.

For a time the bride and bridegroom lived only for each other. They had all their past lives to bring in and consecrate by connecting it with the new. It seemed to them that every incident in those lives had been especially designed to bring them together.

Then, after a fortnight, they returned as they had come, and walked over flowers to their new abode, to finish which half San Salvador had been like a beehive while they were gone.

The two new rooms were noble and picturesque, the difficulties of approach had been cleared away, and the background of the college-buildings gave a palatial air to their modest home. Whatever defects of newness there were were covered artfully, and the whole was made a bower of beauty.

Then began their quiet home-life, and the brief stir of change subsided to the calm of a higher level.

The week after their return Elena was to go out. A dozen little children had been sent out to different houses, and she would gather and take them to their new homes. A day or two later, twenty young men, Ion among them, would go.

CHAPTER XXIV.

It was the day before that fixed for the departure of the students, and all the town was gathered in the Square, now changed to an amphitheatre, and roofed with canvas. Professor Pearlstein was to give the young men a last charge, repeating admonitions which they had already heard, indeed, but which in these circumstances would make a deeper impression.

The speaker began gently: —

"When a father sends his child on a long journey in foreign lands, he first provides for his sustenance, furnishes him with suitable clothing, and tries to secure friends for him in those far-off countries. He tells him all that he knows, or can learn concerning them, warns him against such dangers as he can foresee.

"Having done all this, his anxious love is still unsatisfied. He follows to the threshold of that parting, and beyond, trying to discover some new service that he can render, looks again at the traveler's equipments, repeats once more his admonitions, gives lingeringly his last blessing, his last caress; till, no longer able to postpone the dreaded moment, he loosens his hold upon the loved one, strains his eyes for the last glance, then sits down to weep.

"But even then, when the first irrepressible burst of grief is over, he forgets himself anew, and sends out his imagination in search of the wanderer — in what vigils! with what fears, what prayers for his well-being!

"While the child, amused and distracted by the novelties of this foreign life, forgets sometimes the parent he has left, those sad eyes at home gaze down the empty road by which he disappeared, or weep with longing to see him once more. Would the wanderer's song and laugh displease him if he knew? Oh, no! He would rejoice in that happiness. The only inconsolable anguish that he could feel would be in knowing that the virtue with which he had labored to fortify that child's soul was cast aside and forgotten.

"But I did not mean to make you weep. I wish you to think, resolve, remember, and persevere.

"Once more I warn you of the dangers of that life which you are about to enter. Let not your minds be swept away by the swift currents everywhere rushing they know not whither, all human society rising in great waves on some tidal throe which may land it on a higher plane, or may cast it into the abyss, one leader with a blazing torch striving in the name of Liberty to shut the gate of heaven, and the other, his unconscious accomplice, in the name of Order, setting wide the gates of hell.

"Trust not the visionary who will tell you that science everywhere diffused will bring an age of gold. Trust not the bigot who will say that knowledge is for the few.

"Trust not those orators who, intoxicated by the sound of their own voices, proclaim that from the platform where they stand gesticulating they can see the promised land. Long since the Afghan heard just such a voice, and made his proverb on it: 'The frog, mounted on a clod, said he had seen Kashmir.'

"Wait, and examine. Look at both sides of a question, before you form an opinion.

"See what children we were but yesterday. We thought that we knew the Earth. Complacently we told its age, and all its story. We told of a new world discovered four hundred years ago, of its primeval forests and virgin soil, of its unwritten pages on which we should inscribe the opening chapters of a new Genesis. And, lo! the new world, like the old, is but a palimpsest! Under the virgin soil is found a sculptured stone; through the unlettered seas rise the volcanic peaks of lost Atlantis. The insulted spirit of the past lifts everywhere a warning finger from the dust. It points to the satanic promise: *Ye shall be as gods*. It points us to the tower of Babel. It underlines the haughty Jewish boast: *Against the children of Israel shall not a dog wag his tongue*. Samples every one of arrogant pride followed by catastrophe sudden, utter, and inevitable.

"In the face of such a past, can we make sure of our stability? We cannot. Beware of pride.

Unless the Lord build the house, they labor in vain that build it. Unless the Lord keep the city, he watcheth in vain that keepeth it.

"Hold yourselves aloof from any party that excludes your King. Bind yourselves by no oaths, and have no fellowship with him who has taken an oath.

"If a man sin, and hurt no other knowingly, be silent and save your own souls. If he sin in wronging another, speak for his victim, or bear the guilt of an accomplice. Do not sophisticate. You are your brother's keeper, or his Cain.

"Do not bid a sufferer be calm, nor talk of reason to him while he writhes in anguish. The man of cold blood may be as unreasonable as the man in a passion. There is a reason of flame as well as a reason of snow.

"Remember that freedom means freedom from criticism as well as from force.

"Never allow yourselves to think or speak of the poor, of condemned criminals, or social outcasts as the dangerous classes. Your nativity forbids. Justice and mercy forbid. If there is a class which can truly be called dangerous to heavenly order and all that is noblest in life, it is that great stall-fed, sluggish, self-complacent mass which makes a god of its own ease and tranquillity, shuts its eyes to wrongs that it will not right, and cares not what power may rule as long as its own household is protected. It praises the hero of a thousand years ago, and is itself a skulking coward.

It calls out a regiment if its sleeve is but brushed against, and steps upon a human neck to reach a flower. Seek not their friendships, nor their praises, and follow not their counsels. Be courteous, sincere, and inflexible. Be loyal, and fear not!

> 'Non è il mondan rumor altro che un fiato
> Di vento, che or vien quindi ed or vien quinci,
> E muta nome perchè muta lato.'

"Do right, and trust in God. Remember that Christianity is heroism. *We are not given the spirit of cowardice*, says Saint Paul. An Arabian proverb goes farther. 'There is no religion without courage,' it says.

"This life of ours is woven as the weaver makes his tapestry. He stands behind the frame, seeing the wrong side only of his web, and having but a narrow strip of the pattern before him at a time. And with every strip the threads that it requires are given. It is all knots and ends there where he works; but he steadily follows the pattern. All the roughnesses that come toward him testify to the smoothness of the picture at the other side.

"So we see but a few steps in advance, and the rough side of our duty is ever before us. But weave on, weave faithfully on in the day that is given you. Be sure that when, your labor done, you pass to the other side, if you have been constant, you will find the most glowing and beautiful part of your picture to be just that part where the knots were thickest when you were weaving.

"I wish to tell you a little incident of to-day that clings to my mind. It is but a trifle; but you may find a thought in it.

"As I sat aloft at dawn, thinking of you and of what I would say to you, I saw an ant in the path at my feet carrying a stick much longer than himself. He ran lightly till he came to two small gravel stones, one at either side of his path. The stick struck on both stones and stopped him. He dropped it, and ran from side to side trying to drag it through.

"For a while I watched the little creature's distress; then with a slender twig I carefully lifted the stick over the obstacles, and laid it down on the other side.

"The ant remained for a moment motionless, as if paralyzed with astonishment, then ran away as fast as he could run, leaving the stick where I had placed it; and I saw him no more.

"Can you not understand that I was grieved and disappointed? The labor, the loss, and the fear of that little insect were as great to him as ours are to us. I was so sorry for him that if I had had the power to change my shape, as fairy stories tell, and take it safely back again, I would have run after him as one of his own sort, yet with a tale marvelous to him, would have reassured him of my good-will, promised him a thousand timbers for his dwelling, and a store of food and downy lining for his nest, when I should have resumed my proper form and power.

"Oh! would the ants have caught and crucified me in the shape I took from love, and only to serve them!

"Children, it is at this very point that the world will fight with you its most demoniac battle.

"There have been, and there are, men and women whose lives shine like those pure flames in the long, dim corridors of our cemetery, making a circle of holy light about them, some tranquil and hidden, some in constant combat. But for the majority of the race, all the primal Christian truths have become as worn pebbles on the shores of time. It is not long since there was yet enough of public sanity and faith to compel a decent reverence; but now they utter their blasphemies, not only with toleration, but with applause. They have an infernal foolishness that sounds like wisdom to the ignorant unthinking mind. This spirit puts on the doctor's cap and robe and reasons with you. It twists up a woman's long hair, and breathes out brazen profanities and shameless mockeries.

"Or some being, half saint and half siren, will praise the beauties of our faith as you would praise a picture or a song, and smooth away its more austere commands, so covering all with glozes and with garlands that there would seem to be no other duty but to praise and poetize; and you might believe yourself floating painlessly toward the gates of Paradise when you are close to the gates of hell.

"I will tell you some of the arguments of these people.

"They say that Christ taught nothing new, that his moral lessons had been taught before, and even in heathen lands.

"He did not pretend to teach a new morality. He fulfilled the law already given by making Charity the consort of Justice.

"Is it to be believed that the Father of mankind left his children, all but a favored few, in total darkness during the ages that preceded Christ? 'Teste David cum Sibylla,' sings the 'Dies Iræ.'

"They will tell you that the miraculous circumstances of Christ's birth are but a parody on old heathen myths, that a woman with a Divine Child in her arms was worshiped by the Indus and the Nile, and that many an ancient hero claimed a divine paternity. They will go to the very root of revelation and tell you that Vishnu floated on primal seas even as God moved on the face of the waters; that while the Norse Ymir slept, a man and a woman grew out from under his left arm like Eve from sleeping Adam's side. The fragmentary resemblances are countless.

"Our God be thanked that not the Israelite alone, but even those step-children of the Light had some sense of his coming footsteps! They had caught an echo of the promise, for it was made for all. It was moulded into the clay that made their bodies. It aspired in the spark that kindled their souls.

"I have seen the nest of a swallow all straightly built of parallel woven twigs, except in one corner. In that corner, in a shoal perspective, was an upright end of pale brown stick shaped like an antique altar. Two tiny twigs were laid on top as for a fire, and from them rose a point of bright yellow leaf for a flame. A pencil could not draw the shapes in better proportion, nor color them more perfectly.

"Above the leaf-flame was hung a cross like a letter X, which is a rising or a falling cross. This, floating in the air above the altar, seemed a veiled interpretation of the sacrifice. Larger, inclosing all, was an upright cross, the beam of which formed one side of a triangle, the figure of the Trinity.

"These figures were laid, one over the other, increasing in size from the altar outward, the victim announced, the mode of his sacrifice hinted, and his divinity proclaimed, — all the emblems of Christianity plainly and chronologically set. What breath of the great all-pervading harmony blew these symbols to the beak of a nesting bird!

"From the first records that we possess of human life, a divine legend or a divine expectation looms before the souls of men, vague as to time, sometimes confused in outline, but ever striking some harmonious chord with their own needs and aspirations, and with the visible world about them.

"See those southern mountain-tops half hidden in a fleet of clouds just sailing over! Even we who know those heights from infancy can scarce be certain what is rock and what is mist in all those outlines. A cliff runs up in shadow, and masses of frowning vapors catch and carry its profile almost to the zenith. There is a rounded mountain where the snow never lingered; and a pile of snowy cumuli has settled on its grayness, and sharpened itself to a fairy pinnacle to mock our ice-peaks, and sifted its white drifts into crevices downward, and set its alabaster buttresses to confuse our knowledge of the old familiar height. Yonder where the White Lady has stood during all the years of our lives, pure and stainless against the blue southwest, a dazzling whirl of sun-bleached mists has usurped her place, leaving visible only her pedestal wreathed about with olive-trees.

"But if you watch awhile the slowly moving veil, gathering with care each glimpse of an unchanging outline, you can build up again the solid mountain wall.

"So the heathen, yes! and the Jew also, saw the coming Christ. Anubis, Isis, Osiris, Buddha, Thor, — they had each some inch-long outline, some divine hand-breadth of truth running off into fantastic myth.

"Were they content with their gods, those puzzled but reverent souls? No; for they were ever seeking new ones, or adding some new feature to the old. Their Sphinx, combining in herself the forms of woman and lion, dog, serpent, and bird, seemed set there to ask, What form will the Divine One choose? Are these creatures all the children of one primal mother? Of what mysterious syllogism is the brute creation the mystical conclusion?

"The German Lessing has well said that 'the

first and oldest opinion in matters of speculation is always the most probable, because common sense immediately hit upon it.' And, converging to the same conclusion, an English writer, borrowing, however, from the Greek, has said that 'both Philosophy and Romance take their origin in wonder;' and that 'sometimes Romance, in the freest exercise of its wildest vagaries, conducts its votaries toward the same goal to which Philosophy leads the illuminated student.'

"The early ages of the world were ages of romance.

"In this supreme case, Imagination, with her wings of a butterfly and her wings of an eagle, soared till her strength failed at a height that was half heaven, half earth. To this same point philosophy climbed her slow and cautious way. They found Faith already there, waiting from the beginning of time at the feet of the God-made Man.

"Again, these apostles of skepticism will tell you that the superstitions of the time, and the prophesies concerning Christ, favored his pretensions.

"If Christ had been an impostor, or self-deceived, — the King's Majesty pardon me the supposition! — in either case he would have striven to conform as much as possible to the prejudices of that expectation; and he would have taken advantage of the popular enthusiasm, as impostors and visionaries do. Instead of that, he set up a pure spiritual system and acted on it consistently, *obe-*

dient (the Scripture says) *unto death.* He flattered no one. He boldly reproved the very ones whose support he might naturally have desired. In the height of his fame he predicted his martyrdom.

"Nor was that time more superstitious than the present, nor the followers of Christ more credulous than people of to-day, and not among the ignorant alone. It is, in fact, notable how many proofs they required. I should say that the Apostles were hard to convince, considering the wonders they had seen. How many times had Jesus to say to them, *O ye of little faith!*

"When the women went to the sepulchre, it was not to meet a risen Lord, but to embalm and mourn over a dead one. When Mary Magdalen went to tell the Apostles that Jesus had risen, her words *seemed to them an idle tale, and they believed it not.* But Peter went to see. *He ran,* Saint Luke says. He saw the empty grave, the linen cloths laid by; and he went away *wondering,* not yet believing, though Magdalen had testified to having seen and spoken with Jesus, and had given them a message from him, though he had predicted his own resurrection, and though Lazarus and the ruler's daughter were still among them. Does this look like credulity?

"It is not for the present to reproach the past with superstition, now when every wildest fantasy flourishes unchecked. Some turn their longing eyes back to the old mythologies. Like the early Christian gnostics, they like to flatter themselves by professing an occult worship which the vulgar cannot understand, and building an inner sanctuary of belief where chosen ones may gather, veiled from the multitude. It is scarcely an exaggeration to say that the day may not be far distant when, in lands called Christian, temples and altars may again be erected to Jove, Cybele, Diana, Osiris, and the rest.

"The mind, like the body, may, perhaps, feel from time to time a need to change its position. But the body, in all its movements, seeks instinctively to keep its equilibrium. The equilibrium of the soul is in its position toward its Creator.

"The paganism of to-day has this evil which the earlier had not: it is a step in a descending scale. In those other days mankind seemed to be rising from the abyss of some immemorial disaster, of which all nations have some fragmentary tradition. In Christ the human race reached its climax. He was the height of an epoch which now, perhaps, declines to a new cataclysm.

"Again, the skeptic tells you that there were and are no miracles. Presumptuous tongue that utters such denial! How do they know that there are no miracles?

"But what is a miracle? Is it necessary to set aside a law of nature in order to perform a miracle? Was not he who made the law wise enough to so frame it that without infringement he could perform wonders? The miracle of one age is the science of the next. Men do to-day without exciting wonder what a few centuries ago would have consigned them to the stake as magicians.

"The miracles of Christ were the acts of one having a perfect knowledge of the laws of the universe, and are a stronger proof of his divinity than any invasion of those laws could be. It was miraculous that a seeming man should have such knowledge.

"Another criticism of religious teachers in both the old and the new law is their ignorance of physical science, evident by commission as well as by omission. Whether they knew or not, common sense alone should teach us that if any one announcing a new religious truth should disturb the preconceptions of his hearers regarding physical truths he would in so much distract their attention from that which he wished to teach them; and their credulity, under this double attack, might fail to accept anything.

"Juvenal's dictum, 'bread and games,' for the government of a people, is true of all mankind in a higher sense. Physical science is man's *circenses.* It exercises his intellect, amuses him and his kind, and every new discovery should excite in him a higher admiration of the Creator. It was not necessary that the Son of God should become man, or rise from the dead in order to teach the movements of the starry spheres, or the secret workings of terrestrial powers. *Circenses!*

"What matters it to the interests of man's immortal soul if the earth is a stationary platform, or a globe rolling through space with a double, perhaps a triple motion! What cares the dying man for the powers of steam, or electricity, or the laws of the ways of the wind! *Circenses! Circenses!*

"Christ came to bring the bread of life, the heavenly *Panem*, without which there is no life nor growth for the spirit.

"My children, you are counseled to patience and gentleness. But listen not in silence when any one reviles your King. Say little to them of the God, lest they blaspheme the more; but say, *Behold the man!* It is not pious people alone who have lauded him, nor theologians only who have borne testimony to him.

"Napoleon I., a warrior, an eagle among men, said of Jesus Christ: 'I know man, and I tell you that Christ was not a man. Everything about Christ astonishes me. His spirit overwhelms and confounds me. There is no comparison between him and any other being. Alexander, Cæsar, Charlemagne, and I have founded empires; but on what rests the creation of our genius? On force. Jesus alone founded his empire on love.'

"You will find no peer of Napoleon I. among those who can see no greatness in Jesus Christ.

"Carlyle says of Christ that he was 'the highest soul that ever was on earth.'

"Such names will more impress the mocker than will the name of saint or apostle.

"Bid them look at his humility when he was personally criticised, and at his sublime assumption when proclaiming his mission. *I am the Light of the world. I am the resurrection and the life. All power is given unto me in heaven and on earth.*

"Did any other teacher of men ever utter such words? See him with the scourge in his hand! See him with the lily in his hand!

"O happy blossom! to be so looked at, touched and spoken of. Did it fade away as other blossoms do? Does its seed yet live upon the earth? Does the Syrian sunshine of to-day still paint the petals of its almost nineteen hundredth generation?

"How dare these preachers of destruction try to rob the human race of such a teacher? What have they to give in exchange for him? Who among them all has a message that can gild the clouds of life, and make of pain and of obscurity a promise and a crown? Never in our era as now has there been such temporal need of the softening influences of Christianity. The poor and the oppressed of all the world, maddened by suffering and insult, outraged by hypocrisy and deceit, are rising everywhere with the desperate motto almost on their lips, *Let us eat and drink, for to-morrow we die.* A Samson mocked at by fools and fiends, their arms grope blindly out, searching for the pillars of a corrupted state.

"And this is the moment chosen to dethrone the Peacemaker of the universe! Verily, whom the gods would destroy they first make mad!

"Will teachers like these incite men to heroic deeds? They destroy honor and heroism from off the face of the earth! They forge their chains and lay their traps for anarchy; yet there is no preacher of anarchy so dangerous, even for this life, as he who seeks to dethrone in the hearts of men their martyred Lover, Jesus of Nazareth!"

The old man paused, and, with his eyes fixed far away over the heads of the audience to where the sky and mountains met, lifted his arms in silent invocation. Then, drooping, he came feebly down from the pulpit.

The boys for whom his address had been especially meant pressed forward to receive him, and conduct him to a seat.

Then the chimes began softly, and they all sang their last hymn together:

"Let veiling shadows, O Almighty One,
Hide from thy sight the dust wherein we lie!
Look, we beseech thee, on thine only Son:
No other name but Jesus lift we on high!

"Fallen and alien, only him we boast
Strong to defend from Satan's bonds of shame:
Jesus our sword and buckler, Jesus our host, —
No other name, Creator, no other name!

"No other name, O Holy One and Just,
Call we to stand between us and thy blame:
Jesus our ransom, our advocate and trust, —
No other name, Dread Justice, no other name!

"No other name, O God of gods, can rise
Pure and accepted on thine altar's flame:

Jesus our perfumed incense and our sacrifice, —
  No other name, Most Holy, no other name!

"No other soul-light while on earth we grope,
  Only through him eternal light we claim:
Jesus our heavenly brother, Jesus our hope, —
  No other name, Our Father, no other name!"

CHAPTER XXV.

THEY were gone; and San Salvador resumed its usual life, too happy to have a history. A messenger went out and a messenger came in once a month, and Dylar held in his hand the threads of all their delicate far-stretching web.

Iona before going had obtained his approval of some of her plans, which were in fact his own, and the first messenger from her went directly to the Olives, where he bought a large tract of land.

"Do not seek now to preserve a compact territory," she said. "You may find yourself hemmed in. Buy some of the rising land southward along the river, and let the next purchase connect it with the Olives. Let that connection be made as soon as possible."

"Iona has force and foresight," Dylar said. "It is well. I sympathize with her impatience. But I know my duty to be more one of conservation than of enterprise."

After leaving his wife for a week, which he spent at the castle, "I have bought land all along the river for two miles," he told her; "and our friend has bought a tract crossing mine, but not joining it. It is sand and stones; but planted first with canes, can be coaxed to something better. Water is going to be as important a question with us as it was with the Israelites. I thought of them as I walked over my parched domain, and it occurred to me as never before, that a spring of water is one of the most beautiful things on earth, to the mind as well as the eyes."

"I am glad that you have gratified Iona's first expressed wish," his wife said. "Naturally, the first wind of the world in her face fanned the idea to a flame. She is now occupying herself with other thoughts."

Iona was occupied with other thoughts.

Let us take two or three glimpses of her through a clairvoyant's mind.

It is a wretched-looking street in an old city. A lady and a policeman stand on the sidewalk at an open door, inside which a stair goes up darkly.

Said the man: —

"You had better let me go up with you, lady. She 's always furious when she is just out of jail. We find it best to let her alone for a while."

"I would rather go up alone," the lady said. "Is the stair safe?"

"There 's no one else will touch you," said the policeman. "It is the room at the head of the last stair. I will stay round till you come down. But you must be careful. She does n't like visitors, especially missionaries."

The lady went upstairs. There were three dirty, discolored flights. She tapped once and again at the door of the attic chamber; but there was no response. She opened the door.

There was a miserable room where everything seemed to be dirt-colored. In one corner was a bed on the floor. There was not a thread of white about it. From some rolled-up garments that answered for a pillow looked out a wild face. The dark hair was tangled, the face hollow, dark circles surrounded the eyes. "What do you want?" came roughly from the creature as the door softly opened.

"Let me come in, please!" said a quiet voice. "I have knocked twice."

"What do you want?" the voice repeated yet more roughly.

The lady came in and closed the door behind her. She stood a moment, hesitating. Then, hesitating still, approached the bed, step by step, saluted again fiercely by a repetition of the question, "What do you want?" the woman rising on one elbow as she spoke.

The visitor reached the side of the pallet. She was trembling, but not with fear. She fell on her knees, uttering a long tremulous "Oh!" and leaning forward, clasped the squalid creature in her arms, and kissed her on the cheek.

The woman tried to push her away. "How dare you!" she exclaimed, gasping with astonishment. "Do you know what I am? How dare you touch me? I am just out of jail!"

"You shall not go there again, poor soul!" the lady said, still embracing her. "Tell me how it came about. Was not your mother kind to you when you were a child?"

The woman looked dazed. "My mother!" she said. "She used to beat me. She liked my brother best."

"Ah!" said Iona.

Another scene. It is a fine boudoir in a city in the New World. A coquettishly dressed young woman reclines on a couch. Before her, seated in a low chair and leaning toward her, gazing at her, fascinated, is a young man scarcely more than half her age. At the foot of the couch is a tall brasier of wrought brass from which rises a thread of incense-smoke. Heavy curtains half swathe two long windows opening on to a veranda that extends to the long windows of an adjoining drawing-room. In one of these windows, nearly hidden by the curtain, sits another lady with a bonnet on. She looks intently out into the street, as if watching some one, or waiting for some one. The curtain gathered before her head and shoulders, leaves uncovered a fold of a skirt of dark gray, and a silver chatelaine-bag.

"I hope that you will conclude to choose journalism," said the lady on the lounge, continuing a conversation. "It so often leads to authorship. And I have set my heart on your being a famous poet."

"I, madam!" exclaimed the young man, blushing. "I never attempted to write poetry. It is true that when with you I become aware of some mysterious music in the universe which I know not how to express."

The lady smiled and made a quick, warning signal to remind him of the other occupant of the boudoir.

"I am, then, stirring your ambition," she said. "I have done more. I have spoken of you to a friend of mine who is connected with a popular magazine. That would allow you leisure to cultivate your beautiful imagination."

"How kind you are!" her visitor exclaimed. "But my principal depends on me; and I think that I can be useful to him."

The lady made a pettish movement.

"He can get others to do his humdrum work. I heard him speak once, and did not like him. They call him 'broad.' Oh, yes! he is very broad. He reminds me of one of my school-lessons in natural philosophy. The book said that a single grain of gold may be hammered out to cover — I have forgotten how many hundreds of square inches. Not that I mean to call your principal a man of gold, though. Yes, he is broad, very broad. But he is, oh, so very thin!"

The young man looked grave. "I am pained that you do not esteem him. Perhaps you do not quite understand his character."

"Now, you," said the lady, fixing her eyes on his, "you seem to me to have great depth of feeling and profound convictions."

There was an abrupt rustling sound at the window. The lady there had risen and stepped out into the veranda. They could hear her go to the drawing-room window and enter.

"She is so much at her ease!" said the lady of the lounge. "She was recommended to me by a friend as a companion with whom I could keep up my French. We speak no other language to each other. But she does not act in the least like a dependent. I must really get rid of her."

A servant opened the door to say that the carriage the gentleman expected had come.

"Must you go?" the lady exclaimed reproachfully.

"I promised to go the moment the carriage should come. I don't know what it is for; but it is some business of importance. I am sorry to go. When may I come again?"

"To-morrow." She held out her hand.

He took it in his, hesitated, bent to kiss the delicate fingers, blushed, and turned away.

She looked smilingly after him, bent her head as he turned and bowed lowly at the door, and when it closed, laughed softly to herself. "Beautiful boy!" she murmured. "It is too amusing. He is as fresh as a rose in its first dawn and as fiery as Pegasus."

The young man entered hastily the close carriage at the step before perceiving that a lady sat there. She was thickly veiled.

"I beg your pardon!" he began.

Without taking any notice of him, she leaned quickly, shut the door with a snap and pulled the curtain down, and left a beautiful ringless, gloveless hand resting advanced on her knee. He looked at the hand, and his lips parted breathlessly. He tried in vain to see the face through that thick veil.

The lady pushed the mantle away from her shoulders and arms, so that her form was revealed.

The young man made a start forward, then recoiled; for, hanging down the gray folds of the lady's skirt was the silver chatelaine-bag he had seen in the boudoir. What did her companion want of him?

The lady flung her veil aside.

"Oh, Iona!" he cried, and fell into his sister's embrace.

After a moment she put him back, looking at him reproachfully.

"Oh, Ion, so soon in trouble! I heard of you in the hands of a Delilah, and I left everything. I obtained the place which would enable me to know all — her guile and your infatuation. She amuses herself with you. She has said to me that you are in love with her, and do not know it. Her husband is angry, and people talk. So soon! So soon! Oh, Ion!"

"She said it!" he stammered, becoming pale.

"She said it to me laughing. She described you gazing at her. She laughs at your innocence."

The boy shuddered. "I will never see her again!"

Again the clairvoyant.

It is a bleak November day in a city of the

North. Pedestrians hurry along, drawing their wrappings about them. Standing close to the walls of a church in one of the busiest streets, an old man tries to shelter himself from the wind. He is thin and pale and poorly clad, but he has the air of a gentleman, though an humble one. There is delicacy and amiability in his face; his fine thin hair, clouded with white, is smoothly combed, and his cotton collar is white. On his left arm hangs a small covered basket, and his right hand holds a pink wax rose slightly extended to the passers-by, with a patient half smile ready for any possible purchaser.

For a week he had stood there every day, cold, weary and tremulous with suspense, and no one had even given him a second glance. But that he did not know, for he was too timid to look any one in the face.

The afternoon waned. People were going to their homes; but the old man still stood there holding out the pink wax rose. Perhaps the most pitiful thing about him was that what he offered was so worthless, and he did not know it. Some, glancing as they passed, had, in fact, laughed at his flower and him.

At length a lady, walking down the other side of the street, caught a glimpse of him. She stopped and looked back, then crossed over and passed him slowly by, giving a sidelong, searching look into his face. Having passed, she turned and came back again.

"Have you flowers in the basket also, sir?" she courteously asked.

He started, and blushed with surprise and agitation.

"Yes," he said, and opened the little basket with cold and shaking fingers, displaying his pitiful store.

"What is your price for them all?" the lady asked.

He hesitated, still trembling. "If you would kindly tell me what you think they are worth," he said. "I do not know. My daughter made them when she went to school."

"Does she make them now?" the lady asked, taking both rose and basket from his hands.

A look of woe replaced his troubled smile. "She is dead!" he said with a faint moan.

"Have you other children?" was the next question.

"No. My daughter left a little girl who lives with us, my wife and me."

"Will you be satisfied with this?" the lady asked, and gave a larger sum than the old man had dreamed of asking. "If you think they are worth more, please tell me so."

"I didn't expect so much," he said. "It was my child's hands that gave them their value to me."

Tears ran down his cheeks. He tried to restrain them, and to hide that he must wipe them with his sleeve.

The lady slipped a folded handkerchief into his hand. "Farewell, and take comfort," she said hastily. "God will provide."

She turned to a man who had followed, and paused near her.

"Find out who he is, what he is, and where he lives, and tell me as soon as possible," she said in a low voice.

The same evening, in a suburb of the city: a little unpainted cottage, black with age, set on a raw clay bank. A railroad has undermined the bank and carried away the turf.

A faint light showed through one window. In a room with a bed in one corner an elderly woman was making tea at a small open fire of sticks. In the adjoining kitchen Boreas reigned supreme. All the warmth that they could have was gathered in this room, where the child also would sleep on an old lounge.

She sat in the corner of the chimney now, wistfully watching the preparations for supper.

In the other corner sat her grandfather. He had taken a blanket from the bed and wrapped it round him. He was shivering.

"It was hard to part with the flowers," the man was saying. "They were all that we have left of her! But to a person like that, — a lady, a Christian, an angel! — it seemed like giving them to a friend who will keep them more safely than we can." He choked, and wiped his eyes.

"Well," said the wife drearily; "we must economize the money she gave you for them. We have nothing else to sell."

They were silent, trying not to think, and daring not to speak. They had once been in comfortable circumstances; and now beggary stared them in the face, and the horror of the almshouse loomed before them, not for themselves alone, but for the child. If they found a home for her, she might not be happy there; and they would see her no more.

Suddenly the old man burst out crying. "I can't stand it!" he sobbed. "I can't stand it! I almost wish I had n't seen the lady. I was growing hardened. I was forgetting that any one had ever addressed me as a gentleman. It was becoming an ugly dream to me, all this downfall! And she has waked me up!" He sobbed aloud.

"Don't! Don't!" said the woman. "And there is some one knocking. Nellie, take the candle, and go to the door."

The old man got up, throwing the blanket from his shoulders; and the two stood in darkness, holding their breath.

There was a murmur of voices at the door, and the candle came shining into the room again, and steps were heard, both light, as if two children were about to enter.

Then a lady appeared on the threshold, looking in eagerly with bright eyes.

"Ah, 't is you, sir!" she said. "I am sure that you expected me. I am so glad to have found you! Your troubles are all over!"

One more glimpse through space.

A train of cars is going through the Alps, from Lugano southward. Four persons occupy one of the easy first-class compartments. There are two talkative ladies in the back seat who seem quite willing to dazzle the gentleman sitting opposite them. He has an interesting face, an athletic frame, and gray eyes that are at once enthusiastic and laughing. When serious, the face is very serious, and the attitude changes a little, assuming more dignity. He is evidently enchanted with the scene, for he smiles faintly when lifting his eyes to the snowy heights with their cascades, or leaning close to the window to see the green waters below dashed into foam among the rocks.

Once he glanced at the ladies before him as if for sympathy, but perceiving none, restrained some expression of admiration which he had seemed about to utter.

More than once he glanced at a lady who sat in the farthest corner of the compartment, looking out in the opposite direction. She had a somewhat dusky oval face, dark eyes with long lashes, and black hair heavy about the forehead. She looked like a grand lady, though she was traveling alone. She wore a simple costume of a dark dull purple and a full scarf of yellow-tinted lace loosely tied around her neck.

She took no notice of her traveling companions. The wild grandeur of the scene was reflected in her uplifted eyes, and woke an occasional sparkle in them; but she seemed not strange to the mountains.

Once, when the rock wall shut close to her side of the carriage, she turned toward the other side, just skimming the three strangers with a glance. At that moment their progress unrolled an exquisite mountain picture, and the gentleman turning toward her quickly, they exchanged an involuntary smile.

"I never was so enamored of the Alps as some people are," said one of the other ladies to her companion. She had caught this sign of sympathy. "They are so theatrical."

Her friend laughed. "You remind me," she replied, "of the man who said that there was a good deal of human nature in God."

The stranger lady started.

"Madam!" she exclaimed.

The one who had spoken shrugged her shoulders.

The gentleman changed his seat for one opposite the stranger.

"Madam," he said, removing his hat, "if you will not allow me the liberty of expressing to you the delight I have in these mountains, I shall be forced to soliloquize. I find it impossible to contain myself."

"Speak freely, sir!" she said with a pleasant look, but some stateliness. "If I were not a daughter of the mountains, I think this scene would force me to speak, if I had to soliloquize."

"I have never been here before," the gentleman said. "I had not known that Mother Earth could be so beautiful, so eloquent. Does she not speak? Does she not sing? Who will interpret to us her language, her messages?"

"Once upon a time," the lady said, "a saintly ruler showed his people a grain of gold that had been dug out of a wild rough place in the earth; and he told them that where he found it the earth had given him a message for them. It was this:

"'Dig for your gold, my children! says Earth, your Mother. Deep in your hearts it lies hidden.'"

The gentleman looked out of the window in silence for awhile. Then he opened a hand-bag that lay on the seat by his side, and wrote a few words in a note-book there. The book was a little red morocco one, with the name Ludwig von Ritter in gilt letters on the cover.

They spoke of the scenery as they went on, and presently approached a station.

"I shall in future take my recreation in traveling," the gentleman said. "I have heretofore taken it in the social pleasures of Paris or Vienna. One spends time very gayly in either of those capitals."

The lady was silent a moment, then murmured as if to herself:

"*E poi?*"

He looked at her with a smile. "Why, then," he said, "it is true that one sometimes has a headache, and is willing to resume one's duties."

The train drew up. The lady called a porter, and, with a courteous but distant salutation to the gentleman, departed.

CHAPTER XXVI.

WHEN spring came round again, Tacita was a mother, having given birth to the tenth Dylar.

"And now we say a *Pater Noster*," she said. "Is there more than a decade without change?"

Becoming a mother, it seemed as if she had ceased to be anything else. The most that the people saw of her was when she sat under the awning of her little terrace with some work in her hand and her foot on the rocker of the cradle, her eyes scarce ever straying beyond the one or the other, and thinking, thinking.

Dylar had removed her decidedly from all outside duties. It was the custom in San Salvador for the mother to leave all for her child; and more depended on this sunny-faced infant than on any other. It was enough for her to train the child, to note every manifestation of character, to watch with dilating eyes every sign of intelligence, to cry out with delight at every mark of sweetness, or tremble at what might be a fault.

He was sometimes astonished at her far-sightedness, but never at her strength. He had seen the steely fibre in her gentle nature even when, a child, she had mistaken him for a beggar and called him "brother."

That strength manifested itself now in the firmness with which she faced the necessity of soon giving the child into the hands of others for the greater part of his education. Dylar had not the courage to remind her of this necessity in the first rapture and tremor of her motherhood. There were times when he even asked himself if it might not be evaded.

It was Tacita who spoke first, one evening, as she sat with the child in her arms.

"I have fought a battle, and conquered," she said, smiling. "I looked forward to the time when my son must go to school, and I was jealous. To miss him all day, and know that others are listening while he lisps his first little lessons! I counted the weeks and days. I searched for some way of escape. His birthday is in April, and in April it is too early in the year to have a grief.

"Then — would you believe it, dearest? — I meditated a dishonesty! The school is dismissed, I said, for the harvest, and does not open again till the last week of October. It would be a pity for him to begin study and his little industries, his infant carpenter-work and his small gardening, and then forget, and have to begin all over again. He had better not go till after harvest-time. I had my excuses all planned, when I discovered the little wriggling serpent in my mind. Oh, Dylar! What if I should have given the boy a taint of that blackness which I did not know was in me! I am not worthy to train him!"

She did not raise her eyes; but her husband knelt and surrounded both mother and child with his arms.

"You say that you have conquered, Tacita. I had the same battle to fight and had not conquered. Dear wife, how a spot shows on your whiteness! What did you resolve upon?"

"This," she said. "On the very morning of his birthday, instead of making holiday at home, we will take him by the hand and lead him to the school, and his *festa* shall be to meet for the first time all the dear brothers with whom he is to go through life, whom he is to help and be helped by when his father and mother shall be here no longer."

They embraced, and Tacita wiped two bright tears from her husband's eyelashes. "I am impatient for Iona to come and see the boy," she said more lightly. "Nearly all her letter was of him, and she comes only to see him. She thinks that his hair will grow darker. I want it to be like yours by and by; but this gold floss looks well on a baby. You must read her letter. She wishes me to have a little oil portrait of him taken that she can carry away with her. The messenger who came yesterday is an artist, she writes, and makes lovely pictures of infants. She chose him for that reason."

Iona appeared to them suddenly on one of those June days. She came laden with gifts, letters and photographs, and had so many messages to deliver, and so much to tell, that for several hours of every day for a week she sat in the dance-room at the Star-house, to talk with any one who might wish to come to her. The rest of her time was spent at the school, or hanging over the infant Dylar.

Those who had never been outside could not tire of hearing her talk, and looking at the photographs and prints she had brought. These pictures had been carefully chosen. The sunny beach was contrasted with the storm-tossed sea; the stately ship, all sails and colors, with the lonely wreck and its despairing signal; the beauty of luxury with the deformity of poverty; the dark street and unclean den with the palace and garden.

She had faces made terrible by crime, despair, sickness, shame and sorrow. These to a people who made health and strength a virtue were her most effective antidote against any allurements of that larger life that held such perils.

"It is worse than I thought, my friends," she said to Tacita and Dylar. "Perhaps the world never was any better; but it is worse than I thought. It is not so much the wickedness of the smaller number, but the carelessness of the majority. Nothing but a calamity stirs them up. Nothing but a danger to themselves sets them thinking of others. The prosperous seem really to believe that prosperity is a virtue and misfortune a vice. Oh, if they only knew the delight of helping the needy, and helping in the right way, not thinking that by a gift you can buy any person's liberty, or that gratitude for any assistance whatever should bear the strain of any assumption the helper may be guilty of, but giving outright, helping outright, and forgetting all about it. There is no pleasure like it. Much is said of ingratitude: far more should be said of the coarseness of fibre in those who impose a sort of slavery on the recipients of their favors.

"But, much as I wonder at the living, I wonder yet more at the dying, or those who are looking forward to their own death. There are men and women who leave fortunes to the already rich, or to institutions which are not in need, or to found or endow libraries which bear their names, while all about them reigns an earthly hell of poverty to which they never give a thought.

"Now and then one hears of something lovely. I remember a man in America who, dying, left money to give a house, an acre of land, and a pension sufficient to live on modestly, to a number of homeless women, single or widows. The only notice I ever saw of that tender and sympathizing remembrance of the homeless called it 'eccentric.' Most people who give wish to herd the unfortunate together, making a solid and permanent exposition of their benevolence which they can describe in the newspapers."

"What are women doing?" Tacita asked. "Some things I saw gave me a troubled feeling. It was so different from our women here, so noble, harmonious and restful as they are!"

"It is, perhaps, inevitable," Iona said. "I do not like to find fault with my sisters when they strive to be something better than dolls. Every transition state is disagreeable. I hope that, having made the circle, they may come back to a higher plane of the same hemisphere they have occupied in the past. At present many are ruining what they propose to regenerate. Boasting that they will bring back the lost Paradise, they go no farther than Cain, the serpent, and partial nakedness. Woman as a law-maker is meddlesome and tyrannical. She goes too much into detail. There is a pertness and shrillness in their way of bringing in the millennium which irritates my nerves. They won't let you alone. They nag at you. With some, you cannot speak in their presence without repenting of having opened your mouth. You deplore the evils of society, and they call you a pessimist; you praise the beautiful, the sublime, and discern a rainbow somewhere, and they dub you optimist; you venture to touch on some half possibility of intimations reaching the living from the dead, and they pin 'Spiritist' on your shawl; you surmise that we cannot be sure that we are to live only one life upon the earth, and they discover that you are are a Theosophist, and make remarks about your Karma. They have a mania brought from their jam-pots for labeling things. It is a relief to turn from them and talk with a sensible man whose ideas are more in the *affresco* style, and do not scratch.

"And then, on some happy day you meet a woman, *the* woman, noble, judicial, kind, courageous, modest and sympathizing, and you fall at her feet."

"I think that something ideal may result from this uprising of women," said Dylar. "It is crude now, as you say. But when they shall have shown what they can do, they will voluntarily return, the mothers among them, to their quiet homes, and say to man, 'As we were before, we could not help making many of you worthless. Now we are going to make a race of noble men. We will rule the state through the cradle."

"Like our Tacita," said Iona with a smile. "Elena always said that she was fit to rule a state."

"Dear Elena!" said Dylar's wife. "I am so impatient to see her. It will be delightful to have you both here together, if but for a day."

For Elena was on her way to San Salvador, and near; and they meant to keep her. She had had enough of travel and unassisted labor; and she was needed at home.

"Do you see how our little palm-trees grow?" Tacita asked. "We are going to have them set in the green of the Basilica, after all. They will be ready in the autumn."

Iona looked at the young trees thoughtfully.

"I would like to earn a leaf," she said.

CHAPTER XXVII.

While they were speaking, three visitors whom they did not expect were approaching San Salvador.

A German, a Frenchman, and an Italian, who had known each other many years, meeting occasionally in the society of different European capitals, had met in Paris that spring, and weary of a round of pleasures which led to nothing but weariness, had started off on a long rambling journey.

They made no plans except to go to places they had heard but little of, and to be ready to stop at a moment's notice.

It was the German who had discovered that their pleasures led to weariness alone; but his friends readily agreed with him.

"I am inclined to think," said the Italian, "that the only refuge of civilization is in barbarism."

"Or in a truer civilization," said the German.

"Or in a more robust physical health," said the Frenchman. "So many of our moral impressions proceed from the stomach, or the nerves."

Though the German had given expression to the unrest of his companions, he was indebted, and perfectly aware that he was indebted to another for his own awakening. It was but a word uttered by a stranger whom he had met in travelling through the Alps; yet the word had often recurred to his mind. How many times when contemplating some act, not dishonorable, indeed, yet worldly, as he had studied and doubted, a lowly murmured word had stolen up in his memory: "*E poi?*"

In preparing for some reception or fête like a hundred others, in returning from some dissipation, in looking forward in his career and planning out his future life, with what a solemn impressiveness the quiet interrogation had been heard in the first pause of excitement: "*E poi?*"

Their holiday was almost ended for the three friends, and they were now on their homeward way, the line of their travels forming a long loop, now a little past the turn. The Italian had a young wife who might be pouting at his absence; the Frenchman was a banker, and his partners were getting impatient; the German was an official on leave, and his term was nearly out.

Yet when their train drew up for a few minutes at the lonely station of the Olives, and the Frenchman, usually the leader in all their enterprises, exclaimed, "Once more, my friends! I am sure that no one ever stopped here before," the other two hailed the proposal, and snatching their valises, they stepped from the carriage just as the train was about to start.

The Italian, one of whose nicknames was Mezzofanti, or Tuttofanti, was always spokesman when they were likely to encounter a *patois;* but somewhat to their surprise, this simple-seeming station-master spoke both French and English passably.

There was an orange-farm twenty miles northward, he said, but no means of reaching it at that time. Fifteen miles southward was a castle, and a hamlet called the Olives. The man with the donkey-cart just leaving the station was going there.

A castle! It sounded well.

Mezzofanti called the man and entered into negotiations with him; and he, after looking the travelers over with a somewhat critical expression, consented to take them to the Olives on condition that they would take turns walking each a part of the way. He himself would walk half the distance. His donkey would not be able to carry them all.

He further told them that they could not stop at the castle, the master being absent; but they could stop at his house, and could have donkeys to return to the station the next day. They would want a number of donkeys there, as they were expecting supplies. He could give them three good ones, so that they could ride all the way.

There was a certain calm dignity about this man, though his dress was that of a laborer, and his French imperfect, which won their confidence; and they accepted his offer. He had learned French, he said, from his mother, who came to the Olives from France before he was born. He was called Pierre at home. It was the name his mother gave him.

The first part of their road was over an arid

plain, dull thin grass and a few parched shrubs spotting the sandy soil; but in the distance was a mass of rich dark-green foliage with keen mountains, black and white, rising into the splendid blue above them.

The German remembered one who had said: "I am a daughter of the mountains." He never saw one of those masses of rock and snow rising into the air without wondering if it might not be there she drew her first breath.

The man, Pierre, did not know the names of the mountains. Some of them had their own names. That highest peak at the left was called the White Lady, and was beyond the castle. The castle was very ancient, and one part in ruins. There were many stories about it. His mother knew them. For him, he was content with the present. The past interested him but little. The castle was set on a spur of the mountains, and quite close to them. The inner wall of the court was a cliff. Their road would lead them ten miles straight to the mountains; then they turned southward, and after five miles would reach the Olives, which was south of the heights and just round a turn. At the first turn was a fountain where they could water the donkey, and rest a little while, if they liked. There was an old ruined house there where they usually stopped, going to and from the station.

"Did the prince live much at the castle?" one of the gentlemen asked.

"No; he came occasionally. He lived abroad,

now here, now there. He had spent a fortnight the year before at Castle Dylar with his bride."

"Oh, there is a bride!" said the Frenchman. "What is she like?"

The man had spoken in a serious and matter-of-fact way; but at the question a smile flitted over his face.

"She is tall and slender, and white and golden-haired," he said. "She is very silent; but when she smiles, you think that she has spoken."

The Italian changed color. "Do you know her name — her maiden name?" he asked.

"We call her Lady, or Princess," the man said. "I know no other name."

"Where is she from?"

"Oh, far away!" he replied with a vague gesture.

The Italian asked no more; but his face betrayed excitement.

Their road had begun to rise and to be overshadowed by trees. After a while they reached the ruined house built up against the rock, and they alighted to rest, or look about them.

The German exclaimed: "Did you ever see such a green atmosphere! I do not think that you will find such a pine-steeped dimness even in your Italy, Loredan."

Beside the house a small stream of water from the heights dropped into a trough. Dropping, it twisted itself into a rope. Overflowing the trough, it rippled along beside the road they were to follow.

Pierre drank, washed his face and hands, and watered his donkey. The three travelers went to look at the house. Everything betokened desertion and ruin. The door and shutter hung half off their hinges, and only an upper shutter was closed. A stone stair went up from the one room below; but a heap of brushwood on it barred the passage.

They pursued their way; and as they went, the scene softened. A narrow space of rising grassy land, planted with olive-trees, interposed between them and the rocks, which only here and there thrust out a rude sentinel; and their road, having risen gradually to the house in the pines, began to descend as gradually. The afternoon sun had been excluded; but now it shone across their way. Olive-trees quite replaced the pines, and allowed glimpses of an illuminated landscape to be seen between their crisped-up leaves. They rounded a curve and entered the village. At their right, under thick olives that hid all above them, grassy terraces rose to the castle; at their left were the farms with great white houses sunk in luxuriant vegetation.

The travelers were enchanted. It was a picture! It was a paradise!

Pierre conducted them to his house, and the whole family came out to welcome them with a rustic frankness and an urban courtesy. There was the mother of their host, a woman of eighty, his wife, two tall boys, a girl and a baby. From the roof terrace another girl parted the long palm-leaves to peep down at them.

Entering the wide door was like entering a church. The only partition of the whole ground-floor was made by square pillars of whitewashed masonry which supported the floor above on a succession of arches. But the pillars were so large that they gave an effect of different rooms. Over some of the arches curtains were looped to be used when greater privacy was desired.

One corner next the door seemed designed for a parlor. Far to the right in another direction could be discerned a hand-loom and spinning-wheel, and a stone stair. Far to the left was a kitchen where something was being cooked at an open fire, and nearer, between the white arches, a table set for supper.

Pierre led his visitors up the nave of this strange house, and up the stair to their chambers. They were whitewashed rooms with green doors and small casement windows, over which hung full white linen curtains. Green wooden shutters were opened outside. There were no carpets, only straw-mats; yet there was no sign of poverty. The simplicity was artistic.

One of the boys went up with them to the castle. The sun was low, and sent long lines of orange light across the greensward under the trees. Three flights of stone steps led them to the lower hall, where they waited till their guide obtained for them the readily accorded permission to see the castle.

"There is very little to see," the housekeeper

said. "But what there is I will show you with pleasure."

They questioned her as they went from room to room, and by secret passages to the upper terrace. Was there any pass through the mountains? Her replies made them wonder that so intelligent a woman should feel so little interest in her immediate neighborhood.

She knew of no pass except one far to the northward; but as the mountains were a group and not a chain, it did not matter. Climbing in the vicinity of the castle had proved so dangerous that the prince had forbidden it.

The Italian spoke of the prince and princess, but learned no more than he already knew, though the housekeeper showed no unwillingness to enlighten him. She was enthusiastic in her admiration for the princess, but did not hear him ask what the lady's maiden name was, — did not or would not.

Before going away, the three gentlemen laid their cards on the drawing-room table; and when they were gone, the housekeeper looked at them. She read: —

Don Claudio Loredan, Venice.

Vicomte François de Courcelles, Paris.

Herr Ludwig von Ritter, Berlin.

"These must be sent in early to-morrow morning," she said. "A gentleman from Venice! Perhaps he may have known the princess."

After supper the travelers went out to smoke their cigarettes under the palm-tree, and the old woman, knitting-work in hand, followed them. She evidently expected their request that she would tell them something of the history of the castle, and complied with it with the eagerness of a professional story-teller.

"The origin of Castle Dylar is wrapped in mystery. It is believed that an army of builders once went from land to land building churches, castles, and monuments of various sorts. They built fortresses, and walls for cities, too, and had means unknown to us of moving great stones and fitting them cunningly together. It is believed that Castle Dylar was built by them.

"As for its owner, we will say no evil of the dead. His few poor tenants lived in huts, and knew not how to cultivate the land. They raised a little, which they and their beasts shared; and when their provisions failed, they killed and ate the beasts, being the stronger and more intelligent. When the owner — I know not his name — when he came here from time to time, often with a number of companions, they fared better. But, from father to son, the master came less and less, till one was left who came not at all, but sold the castle and land to a Dylar.

"Oh, then were the people cared for! Then were they lifted out of their misery! Then did the land bloom! The first tree planted by Dylar was an olive-tree. 'I dedicate the land to peace and light,' he said; and, gentlemen, peace and light have dwelt in it to this day. The stupid children of the tenantry were taught. Men came and built these houses to last a thousand years, and then another thousand. They dug a hole to let the river through the mountains. They cultivated land. Men did great works, and went away when they were paid; but other men and women came in, one by one and two by two, and dwelt here. They were children of sorrow chosen out of the world to come here and live in peace. We have all that we want, and we know not drouth. The sun and the snow-peaks fill our cups to overflowing. When the land grows dry, our men set donkeys to turning the great wheel you see yonder, with a bucket at every spoke; and they fill a tank that sends out little rivulets running over all the land. They go to every plant and tree, like mothers giving drink to their children. We know not drouth; and Christ is our King.

"There have been nine Dylars with the present one. Each Dylar uses his number to his name, or sometimes alone. If a written order had the figure nine alone, or nine straight lines signed to it, that order would be obeyed. We put it on all things for them, too. When our prince was here last year with his bride, we sent everything up in nines, nine jars of olives, nine boxes of oil; and the child who could find a bunch of nine cherries, or a sprig of nine strawberries to send up to the princess' table was a happy child. We sent her a box of olive-wood to put her laces in. It was fluted in groups of nine all round, and had nine lilies on the cover, and a border made of the figure interlaced and flowering out. And in the centre of the cover were the initials J. C., with a crown above them; for Christ is King of us all. I found on the jasmine-tree on our terrace a flower with nine petals, which was a wonder; for they have usually only five or six, sometimes only four. The princess pressed the flower to keep, and said it was the prince's flower.

"The Dylar made it a virtue for their people to be healthy and clean and cheerful. They gave them games and pleasures as well as labor. And whenever they find a young man, or a girl who has a gift for some airy kind of work that needs a nicer study, they send them out to learn. They seldom come back to stay; but they come, sooner or later, to see their old home before they die.

"For us, we do many things. We spin thread of linen and silk, we weave and embroider and make laces. We make wine and preserve olives and make oil. We knit hose that a queen has worn, and would have more. For we have a silk farm, and a silk that reels off like sunshine. And Christ is our King."

"Who governs you?" asked the vicomte. "Of course your prince, and the housekeeper told us, three of your oldest men. But is there nothing else?"

"Oh, now and again, some people come from far away, and ask some questions, and get some taxes, they call them. They have need of money, those who send. I know not. They come and they go. We welcome them, and we bid them godspeed."

"But if two of you should disagree?"

"Then each tells his story to the Three, and they decide. And if they cannot decide, they write to Dylar, whose messenger comes."

"But if some one accuse you, have you no one to see that no damaging truth, or no lie, is proven against you? Have you no one to speak for you?"

"Why should another tell my story for me? And is it not the truth which all wish to have proven? Are we children? or bees? See, now: if I prove a lie to-day, and gain a pound of silk by it, or a gallon of oil like honey distilled, then the spirits of peace in the air about me are disgusted with the evil scent of my vice, and they fly away, and evil spirits, who love an evil deed, come near; and of three pounds of silk they weave a chain that binds my thoughts all down to that sin I have committed, or of three gallons of bad oil they kindle a lamp in my heart that burns: and the only way to have peace is to go to him I have robbed, and say: 'I lied; and here are three pounds of silk for the one:' or, 'I lied; and here are three gallons of pure oil for one.' Moreover, the King, when I do evil, is no longer my king; but the Dark One rules over me. What have I gained, though the silk or the oil were like Basil's gold?"

"Who is Basil?" asked the German, smiling. "And what was Basil's gold?"

"Basil was a Dylar, one of the first. It is said

that he was as wise as Solomon, and could understand the language of all growing things; that he knew what the curl of a leaf meant, or the sob of the wind. He came and went. There are wild stories, that he was borne over chasms. I know not. But he gave his people a message from the earth that he read in a grain of virgin gold."

The German was shaken by a strong tremor. "The message! The message!" he exclaimed.

The old woman smiled at his eagerness. "Listen!" she said. "'Dig for your gold, my children, says Earth, your Mother. Deep in your hearts it lies hidden.'"

"Is there any other settlement near of the Dylar?" the German asked impetuously.

"None, sir."

"One has gone forth into the world from this place, a woman, tall, dark-eyed, with black hair heavy about the brows, and a soft voice. She is a lady. Who is she? Where is she?"

"I know no such. There is one abroad who sings. She is famous, and she returns no more. I do not know where she is, nor what name she sings by. There are others who are married. There are two young girls who study. I know no such lady. It might be one of Dylar's messengers; but she is away."

"Could I learn at the castle?"

"Ah, no! we do not keep their track. They come and they go. There was one who came last year. She was something like your lady. She stayed a week; and she reaped a field of wheat. She is strong to work in the fields."

The German sighed, and said no more.

"The present Dylar is young, is he not?" asked the Italian.

"Oh, yes; but little over thirty. But he is very serious. His father was gay till he lost his wife. Then he never smiled again. But when our Dylar came here with his bride last year he was different. His eyes followed her everywhere."

"What did he call her?" asked the Italian.

"He called her Love; nought else. We called her princess. How fair she was! If you should tell her a story, when you had ended, it would seem to you that she had been the one who talked, and not you. She has changes of expression, and little movements, so that she seems to have spoken when she has not uttered a word. At the castle they saved all the hairs that were in her combs and brushes, and I have a little lock of them that coils round so soft and shining!"

When they went in, the Italian lingered behind his companions, and detained the old woman. "Show me the lock of hair you told us of," he said.

She brought it with pleasure, and carefully unfolding a paper by the light of a lamp hung against one of the pillars just inside the door, showed a glossy golden ring, and lifting it, let it drop in a long coil.

"I will give you a gold piece for one hair!" said Don Claudio.

"I do not want the gold," she said; "but you shall have the hair." She drew out two or three of the shining threads and gave them to him; and he laid them inside a clasped fold of his pocket-book.

CHAPTER XXVIII.

PIERRE was to go to the station the next morning to meet Elena; and in consultation with his advisers it was decided that he should set out early and alone. He could then warn her of the presence of these strangers. A considerable quantity of provisions would come by the same train; but as a part of them were to be left at the Pines, they would be brought later in the day.

The strangers could therefore go at any hour they might choose, needing no guide, and leave the donkeys at the station.

The gentlemen set out as soon as they had eaten their breakfast, and half way to the Pines met Pierre coming back on foot.

He had been taken sick on the way, he said, and a friend whom he had fortunately encountered would go to the station for him. It was a sickness he sometimes had, and it would last him several days. He declined their offer to return with him; and they took leave of each other, and went on their separate ways. But Pierre had not gone many steps farther before doubts began to assail him.

"I might have waited there till these men had gone by," he thought.

He turned the situation over in his mind.

Alexander and his wife were the guardians of the week. There was no woman in San Salvador better able to take care of the house than Alexander's wife. She knew every signal, was prompt and courageous. Above all, she would do exactly as she was ordered to do if the skies should fall on her for it. And both he and her husband had charged her not to leave her signal-post a minute, and to give instant notice to San Salvador of anything that might happen.

"I wish I had asked if the door was unbarred," he thought uneasily. It occurred to him that the men inside would have left San Salvador early in the morning, before it was known that these strangers were at the Olives. Alexander and his wife had not known it till he told them that morning. When he passed the evening before, stopping purposely that they might observe well his companions, they had been occupied in receiving orders from San Salvador, and had not known that he was not alone.

He grew more uneasy every moment.

"Of course they would n't unbar the door till it was needed," he muttered. "And of course Alexander spoke to them before he started. But I might have waited."

In fact, Alexander had called to the men; but they were out of sight and hearing. They had retired to a more convenient place to wait, knowing that they would not be needed for several hours.

"I wish that I had waited!" Pierre repeated over and over. "I could have waited."

He recollected stories of men who had been faithful even to death to interests committed to their charge; and when had greater interests been at stake than this of the secret of San Salvador!

Texts of gold wrote themselves in the air all about him, and on the dark earth under his feet.

"*He that endureth to the end shall be saved.*"

"*Well done, good and faithful servant.*"

"*Watch and pray.*"

The guardianship of the house in the Pines was in the hands of a hundred men, each of whom served a week at a time, with any one whom he might choose as a companion. Dylar himself took his turn. The rules were strict. Pierre remembered them when it was too late.

When the three travelers reached the house, therefore, there was a woman alone on guard, with strict orders to signal everything, but on no account to allow herself to be seen nor heard; and the hidden door was unbarred, and the torrent that shut the road to San Salvador was turned away.

They alighted and tied their donkeys to a post, where they could drink or browse at will.

"My opinion," said the viscomte, "is that this old building was not always so innocent as it probably is now. It was perhaps a hiding-place for plunder or prisoners, used by the wicked old family which preceded the Dylars at the castle."

They hung their basket of luncheon to a pine-branch, set their bottle of wine in the running water, and looked about them. To men accustomed to the luxuries of civilization, and for a time, at least, weary of them, there was something delightful in this superb solitude of rock and tree, this silence stirred only by the sweetest and most delicate sounds of nature. It seemed but a day since a pushing crowd had surrounded them, the paving-stones of a city had been beneath their feet, and the Gleipnir cord of social etiquette had bound them; and to-morrow again all that world would possess them, and this scene become as a fairy dream in their memories.

They wandered about a while under the trees, explored a few rods of the northward road, and came back to eat their luncheon, sitting on the moss and pine-needles.

The Frenchman looked up at the beetling rock that overtopped the house before them. "I have a vision," he said. "I am clairvoyant. I see through the rock yonder into a long succession of low caves where you must walk stooping. At the entrance of these caves sits '*une blanche aux yeux noirs*,' and all the floor is strewn with ingots of pure gold. As you look along the windings for miles, that gold lights the place up like a fire."

"I also am clairvoyant," said the Italian. "I see beyond those mountains a happy country where ambition never thwarts true love, and partings are unknown. It is the promised land of the heart."

"I see farther yet," said the German. "Beneath that cliff is your El Dorado. Beside it is your Love's paradise. But farther yet, hemmed in by precipices, is a great black castle of which Castle Dylar is but an offshoot. There dwells a princess held in bonds by a fierce giant. He wishes to marry her, would give her all the gold you see, and make her queen over your paradise; and she will not. If I could pass this wall, if I could thread the labyrinth of gorges leading to that castle, I should find her there, dark and splendid and stately. She is as free and fierce as an Arab. She is as tender as a dove. She looks like a goddess. Her name is — is — Io."

They ate their luncheon in the green fragrant shadows. The viscomte went into the house while the other two smoked their cigarettes, dreaming with half-closed eyes, till they were startled by an excited call from the house: "Come here! Come!"

They hastened to obey.

"I have found a secret door!" said the Frenchman's voice from under the stair. "It is surely a door! The wall moves. See! it retreats an inch or two without displacing a stone. Let us get sticks and pry it open. We are on the eve of a discovery!"

CHAPTER XXIX.

MEANTIME, San Salvador, unconscious of danger, was all joyful expectation. The coming home of Elena was always a holiday for them.

True, Iona was to go out again the next day; but Iona had never taken the hold on their familiar life that Elena had always maintained. Besides, they had this pleasure connected with her going, that she would take messages to their friends. Many were busy preparing letters and little gifts.

Dylar was busiest of all. He had gone up to his cottage, which might still be called his study, to prepare letters of direction, and plans which would be supplemented by Iona's word.

In the little terrace of their house sat Tacita and Iona with the child.

"Spare yourself a little for our sakes," the princess was saying.

"Never fear, my princess!" said Iona with a smile. "I have a presentiment that I shall come back here at last to die. It is the only thing that I ask for myself. If I should not be so happy, I know that you will bring my body back. It is pleasant to think of lying asleep in our great quiet dormitory when one can work no longer."

"The whole earth should not hide you from us, nor keep you back!" was the fervent reply.

"Inaction, or even moderate action, is impossible with the vision that I have of the world," Iona went on. "You think that you know it. Ah, you do not know a thousandth part! You were safe in your family, guarded and protected. What if you had been poor and friendless? I tell you that to such human society is sometimes a society of wolves and tigers. Nor is an active and conscious malignity necessary. Narrow sympathies, self-complacent egotism and conventional slavery suffice. Why, who shall say that a tiger may not rend a man, or a child, with an approving conscience, if conscience he have!

"Life has become like a cane-brake duel, where two men enter, each from an opposite side, creeping and searching for each other with the dagger-hand drawn back, and the blade up-pointed for the *stoccata*. Ah! Let us not think of it. For the work needed to-day, the soul must not stop to think, but must march straight on in the name of God. I will think of my coming back and of my rest at last. It is sweet. Carry me up at sunrise, and give me a rose in my hand. I would that I could have a palm. But a rose is the flower of love; and whether it has seemed so, or not, I have loved so much! I have loved so much!"

She bent, and softly kissed the sleeping infant; and rising to go away, glanced back toward the unseen cemetery.

As she looked, a swift change passed over her face, a keen present interest took the place of her forward-looking. Her raised brows fell and were drawn together. She was facing the signal station connected with the Pines, and it changed as she looked. Already they knew by signals from the castle that three strangers had passed the night at the Olives, that a messenger was coming in to give them details, that Pierre was on his way to the station to meet Elena, and that the strangers had also gone. From the Pines they knew that all was prepared for Elena's entrance.

"What does this mean?" said Iona. "Can it be that Alexander's wife is alone at the Pines! Tacita, will you call Dylar?"

Tacita went to the gallery from which she could see her husband's cottage, and him sitting at a table covered with papers inside the open door, and she blew a trilling note on a silver whistle she carried in her girdle.

He looked up quickly, and came out. It was the first time she had ever called him down.

She waved her hand toward the signal-station, and he understood, and turned that way. Another signal had been added.

"Yes," said Iona. "Pierre has returned home, and Alexander gone to the station, against the rules. Pierre has sometimes severe attacks of sickness, and he feels them coming on. But why did not they call one of the men from inside, and send him to the station?"

She was talking to herself. Tacita glanced up the hill, and saw Dylar standing on his terrace watching intently the signals. They changed again. The strangers were at the Pines, and the men from San Salvador were not there.

Without a word, Iona hastened down and went to the Arcade. Half way across the town she turned to look again. The whole situation was signaled now. The torrent was off, the door unbarred, the men out of sight and hearing, and three strangers were at the Pines.

"Impossible!" she exclaimed, and began to run.

When Dylar reached his house and read the signals, which had been hidden from him as he came down, he looked across and saw Iona coming out on to the mountain-path above the Arcade. This road ran for half a mile along the rock in sight of the town. Then it turned backward and out of sight, joining the road from the Pines, and that lower one by which Tacita had come to San Salvador. Near this junction of the roads was the water-gate by which the torrent was turned.

"Impossible!" Dylar also had exclaimed on reading the signals. To escape for almost three hundred years, and fall to-day! So many accidents and incidents, so many items of neglect coinciding to form a crime and a supreme calamity, were incredible! It was impossible that accident could do so much. A vision of treachery rose before his mind.

He ran down to the town where people were gathering on the house-tops and in the streets. He called for two of the swiftest runners and climbers to follow Iona to the water-gate; and they sprang out like greyhounds. It was useless for him to go. There was nothing to be done but turn the torrent on again. He stood silent and white, watching with a stern face the signals, and glancing across the town to the mountain-path along which moved Iona's flying feet.

The people gathered about him; but no one spoke. A vague alarm, mingled with, or alternating with incredulity, showed in every face.

The gate was turned by a beam acting as windlass, and two men were always sent to turn it on at the Pines. It was less difficult than to turn it off; for when the beam was once started, and the water got a wedge in, it carried the gate round of itself.

Iona remembered this as she fled along. She had not seen the men who were sent to follow her. They had taken the inner road, which was a little shorter.

From all the road she followed and from the water-gate, the signals were visible; and running breathlessly, she yet kept them in view.

They changed.

The strangers were searching the house!

They changed. The door was discovered!

Even at that distance it seemed to Iona that she heard a sharp outcry rise from the town as that signal slid out, the first time that it had ever been run out in San Salvador.

Their secret was gone!

But her hope was not gone. In ten minutes she would be at the gate; and it must turn for her. To have discovered the door was not infallibly to open it; or, opening it, there must be some delay.

Moreover, the cave was prepared to detain the strangers a few minutes, at least.

And then an awful question presented itself to her mind. Should she turn the gate if the strangers were on the bridge? What were the lives of three intruders to the existence of San Salvador! An insinuating whisper made itself heard in her heart: "Run and turn the gate. You need not look at the signal!"

It was the voice of the world, the voice of the serpent.

"*A l'aide, mon Dieu!*" she panted. "I will do no evil. If we fall, we fall!"

Was it the heavenly voice once heard, or but an echo of it in her memory, which now seemed repeating those words of miracle: *Come unto me* — the *well done* that had accepted and rewarded her plea for help! Her fleet feet skimmed the mountain-path, her panting lungs drew in the mountain air; but her mind saw once more the golden dusk of the Basilica, the rich molten coloring of the walls, the words of God sparkling out here and there in letters of gold, the Throne and the tiara; and her soul felt the coming of that Presence which had filled the sacred cloister. Half unconscious of her body, she seemed to be borne along by wings set in her fluttering temples.

Then the path turned, and the water-gate was before her. One swift glance over her shoulder told that the door was not yet open.

Iona ran to the beam, and leaning on it, pushed with all her strength. It did not stir. As she leaned, she saw the signal-station on the opposite mountains. It had not changed. The door was discovered; efforts had been made to open it; but it was not open.

With a frantic effort she pushed. The beam trembled, but did not move.

"*A l'aide, mon Roi!*" she whispered, and threw her whole being against the beam, while her ears rang, and her temples ached with the strain.

It started, moved; the water caught the gate. Iona was carried along, her glazing eyes fixed on the signal.

The course of the beam ended against a mossy bank. When it stopped, Iona's failing form rested as if kneeling on the moss, her arms on the beam, her cheek resting on the moss above it. And over her lips, and over the wood, the moss, and the rock flowed a stream of bright red blood.

Her head drooped slowly, and she fell asleep!

So intense had been that flash and strain of soul out through the flesh, it might be said that the cry she had uttered was not more on earth than in heaven, as she sank and rose upon its threshold, having earned her palm!

CHAPTER XXX.

THE whole town, gathered below, waited in an awful silence. The shock of this danger had come upon them like a day of judgment.

Dylar stood apart, gazing alternately at the signals and at Iona's form, the blue flutter of her garments like a puff of smoke on the mountain-side.

No one ventured to approach him.

There was a struggle in his mind. What should he do with these men? A fierce rage was boiling in his heart toward them. It was of their own seeking — the meddlers!

A hand was laid on his arm. Professor Pearlstein stood beside him. They were in the Square near the pulpit, on the front of which were letters of gold. His hand still pressing Dylar's arm, the old man stretched his staff out and drew it along the words: *Thou shalt not kill.*

Dylar turned away, and began to walk to and fro. He became aware of his people all about him, and of Tacita, her child in her arms, crouched on a mat at his feet. She gave the infant to a woman near her, and went to link her arm in his.

"My Love," she said, "the torrent is turned. It was turned before the door was open."

He stopped to look at the signals. He had not

looked for half an hour. The door was open; but the road had first been closed.

A murmur of prayer rose trembling. The shock had been too great. The strain was yet too great.

And then again the signals changed. All danger was over. The strangers were gone on their way.

And yet the people waited, only whispering their thanksgiving.

Soon came the signal that all was well, and Elena at the Pines ready to enter.

Then the bells were rung and they sang "Te Deum."

But no one went indoors. Not till Elena had come, till all was explained, could they think of anything else.

The messenger from the castle arrived with his story, and the cards of their visitors.

"Don Claudio Loredan!" exclaimed Tacita, looking at her husband.

CHAPTER XXXI.

"Is it our business if there should be something concealed?" the German asked when called upon to help pry the masked door open. "The house is not ours."

His companions, full of excitement, broke out upon him. Where was his enterprise, his romance, his courage! It was a deserted house. Perhaps its owners knew nothing of this door.

Their excitement was contagious; and he went with them in search of a lever. They found saplings that bent and dry sticks that broke. But their determination increased with the obstacles; and at last the right touch was given, the door was on the hinge and rolled slowly back, disclosing a dim descent between walls, with a light shining across from below.

All three recoiled a moment at their own success. "We enter at our risk," said the German. "We have no right here."

The other two went down cautiously, and after a moment called to him, and he followed. They had pried open an old chest from which the lock dropped almost at a touch, and were eagerly pulling out the twigs and dry leaves with which it was filled. All had the same thought. Surely such pains would be taken only to conceal a treasure. And it must have been there a very long time.

One of them went up to keep watch while the other two worked, changing hands; for the chest was large, and the débris could be removed only in sifting handfuls.

When the bottom was reached, a chorus of somewhat bitter laughter rose; for there was nothing there but a few rough stones. It had evidently been prepared as a mockery, probably long years before.

They prepared to go on their way. But first they went to the mouth of the cave, and outside on the narrow ledge. There was no passage. Only chasms, precipices, and a dashing torrent that sprinkled them as it fell, met their eyes.

They went up, leaving the door open, mounted their donkeys, and started for the station.

At a little distance down through the pines they met a man and woman coming up. The woman's face was covered with a veil, the man only nodded in passing them.

"Don Claudio Loredan!" said Elena to herself when they had passed. "What in the name of heaven brings him here!"

At the turn of the path the three travelers paused to look back at the old house with its background of mountains.

"Farewell, El Dorado!" said the Viscomte de Courcelles.

"Farewell, my Promised Land!" said Don Claudio Loredan.

The German paused a moment when the others went on, looking back dreamily. "Farewell, Io!" he said.

"It is strange," he said, rejoining his companions, "that sometimes on leaving a place or person one scarcely knows the name of, there comes a feeling of sadness, almost of irreparable loss."

"I suppose," said the Frenchman, "that the veiled lady we have just met is one of the exiles from the Olives. I wonder if they expect her at home."

She was expected. She was looked for joyously and longingly. The people of San Salvador remained watching all the afternoon. The men sent up to follow Iona had not returned. Doubtless all three were waiting to accompany Elena. They watched the turn of the mountain path, sure that they would take the outer one next the town. Spy-glasses were ready to catch the first glimpse of their coming.

"They are coming! They are coming!"

The flutter of a garment was visible around the rock.

Tacita looked through a glass that rested on a man's shoulder. Her other hand was in her husband's arm.

"It is Elena!" she said, "She comes first, and is on foot. She holds her handkerchief hanging straight down at her side. Now she stops and lifts both her arms, then drops them again. It must mean grief for the peril we have been in. The men follow with the donkeys. They seem to carry heavy baggage, or something— What are they doing? There is no one else. What do they carry? O Dylar, where is Iona?"

She gave him the glass, her face losing its light, and growing pale and frightened. The little company on the heights was now plainly seen.

Dylar took the glass, looked through it, and took it away from his eyes. His face was livid.

"My God!" he said. "Where is Iona!"

THE AMERICAN CATHOLIC TRADITION

An Arno Press Collection

Callahan, Nelson J., editor. **The Diary of Richard L. Burtsell, Priest of New York.** 1978

Curran, Robert Emmett. **Michael Augustine Corrigan and the Shaping of Conservative Catholicism in America, 1878-1902.** 1978

Ewens, Mary. **The Role of the Nun in Nineteenth-Century America** (Doctoral Thesis, The University of Minnesota, 1971). 1978

McNeal, Patricia F. **The American Catholic Peace Movement 1928-1972** (Doctoral Dissertation, Temple University, 1974). 1978

Meiring, Bernard Julius. **Educational Aspects of the Legislation of the Councils of Baltimore, 1829-1884** (Doctoral Dissertation, University of California, Berkeley, 1963). 1978

Murnion, Philip J., **The Catholic Priest and the Changing Structure of Pastoral Ministry, New York, 1920-1970** (Doctoral Dissertation, Columbia University, 1972). 1978

White, James A., **The Era of Good Intentions: A Survey of American Catholics' Writing Between the Years 1880-1915** (Doctoral Thesis, University of Notre Dame, 1957). 1978

Dyrud, Keith P., Michael Novak and Rudolph J. Vecoli, editors. **The Other Catholics.** 1978

Gleason, Philip, editor. **Documentary Reports on Early American Catholicism.** 1978

Bugg, Lelia Hardin, editor. **The People of Our Parish.** 1900

Cadden, John Paul. **The Historiography of the American Catholic Church: 1785-1943.** 1944

Caruso, Joseph. **The Priest.** 1956

Congress of Colored Catholics of the United States. **Three Catholic Afro-American Congresses.** [1893]

Day, Dorothy. **From Union Square to Rome.** 1940

Deshon, George. **Guide for Catholic Young Women.** 1897

Dorsey, Anna H[anson]. **The Flemmings.** [1869]

Egan, Maurice Francis. **The Disappearance of John Longworthy.** 1890

Ellard, Gerald. **Christian Life and Worship.** 1948

England, John. **The Works of the Right Rev. John England, First Bishop of Charleston.** 1849. 5 vols.

Fichter, Joseph H. **Dynamics of a City Church.** 1951

Furfey, Paul Hanly. **Fire on the Earth.** 1936

Garraghan, Gilbert J. **The Jesuits of the Middle United States.** 1938. 3 vols.

Gibbons, James. **The Faith of Our Fathers.** 1877

Hecker, I[saac] T[homas]. **Questions of the Soul.** 1855

Houtart, François. **Aspects Sociologiques Du Catholicisme Américain.** 1957

[Hughes, William H.] **Souvenir Volume. Three Great Events in the History of the Catholic Church in the United States.** 1889

[Huntington, Jedediah Vincent]. **Alban: A Tale of the New World.** 1851

Kelley, Francis C., editor. The First American Catholic Missionary Congress. 1909

Labbé, Dolores Egger. **Jim Crow Comes to Church.** 1971

LaFarge, John. **Interracial Justice.** 1937

Malone, Sylvester L. **Dr. Edward McGlynn.** 1918

The Mission-Book of the Congregation of the Most Holy Redeemer. 1862

O'Hara, Edwin V. **The Church and the Country Community.** 1927

Pise, Charles Constantine. **Father Rowland.** 1829

Ryan, Alvan S., editor. **The Brownson Reader.** 1955

Ryan, John A., **Distributive Justice.** 1916

Sadlier, [Mary Anne]. **Confessions of an Apostate.** 1903

Sermons Preached at the Church of St. Paul the Apostle, New York, During the Year 1863. 1864

Shea, John Gilmary. **A History of the Catholic Church Within the Limits of the United States.** 1886/1888/1890/1892. 4 Vols.

Shuster, George N. **The Catholic Spirit in America.** 1928

Spalding, J[ohn] L[ancaster]. **The Religious Mission of the Irish People and Catholic Colonization.** 1880

Sullivan, Richard. **Summer After Summer.** 1942

[Sullivan, William L.] **The Priest.** 1911

Thorp, Willard. **Catholic Novelists in Defense of Their Faith, 1829-1865.** 1968

Tincker, Mary Agnes. **San Salvador.** 1892

Weninger, Franz Xaver. **Die Heilige Mission** *and* **Praktische Winke Für Missionare.** 1885. 2 Vols. in 1

Wissel, Joseph. **The Redemptorist on the American Missions.** 1920. 3 Vols. in 2

The World's Columbian Catholic Congresses and Educational Exhibit. 1893

Zahm, J[ohn] A[ugustine]. **Evolution and Dogma.** 1896